NOTICE

k webster

DEDICATION

To the intense man who noticed me, claimed me,
and never let go.
I love you, Matt.

My past has not defined me, destroyed me,
deterred me; it has only strengthened me.
—*Steve Maraboli.*

Warning:

Notice is an edgy, dark, and unusual romance. Extreme sexual themes and violence in certain scenes, which could trigger emotional distress, are found in this story. If you are sensitive to dark themes, then this story is not for you. If you aren't into super obsessive stalkers, then this story is not for you.

PROLOGUE

Hawk
February 24th, 1990

Eyes on the target.

Always.

I don't have to watch my back because Bull has it.

Always.

Sniper and spotter.

Two best friends since the seventh grade.

"Target is heavily secured. On my command," Gunny says in my earpiece.

I blink but don't move from my position. I'm ready to put the 7.26 by 51 mm bullet in the skull of the Crown Prince's most trusted advisor, Ahmed Hakim. A man whose ties with Saddam Hussein are so thick you'd need a chainsaw to cut through them. My target is enemy number two under Hussein. A traitor to the Crown Prince of Saudi Arabia. On the United States' and my own personal radar.

But the fucker is always hiding behind a wall of men. Armed and dangerous men. Five times over the past week, I've had eyes on the coward but have been told to stand down. The shot has to hit and eliminate the desired target. Injuring him would be considered a failure. Hakim has to die.

"That motherfucker hides behind the big guy every time. If we had the time, we could take out both. No sweat off my goddamn brow," Bull murmurs. He chews on his gum but wisely remains quiet. The constant sound of his chewing is what helps keep me grounded. I can focus because of its consistent smack—a little trick we learned at the academy we both attended in high school. A year after graduation, and we still work better as a team than apart.

Smack. Smack. Smack.

I'm in position and have been for the past four and a half hours, long before people arrived for the ceremony where the Crown Prince is speaking. I've already established a good shooting position. Flat on my belly with my rifle pointed downrange at my target, I'm sighted in and ready to fire.

Smack. Smack. Smack.

A cool breeze skitters across the back of my neck. Sweat is trickling down the side of my temple, but I don't dare move. Instead, I'm calculating the wind not just up here from my position on the top of an abandoned building, but also where my target is. The wind causes the black hair of a teen girl sitting on one of the chairs to slip from her hijab and blow in the wind. She's not just any girl—she's the sixteen-year-old daughter of the Crown Prince. Despite Hakim being a pussy who hides behind the security, his eyes never leave the Crown Prince's daughter. Adara. Pretty, young, vulnerable. Hakim clearly cares for her, and that's saying something for the selfish prick.

Click.

I make an adjustment to the windage turret.

"Elevation?" Bull questions as if I'd forget. I never forget.

I double check the elevation turret, but it's where it needs to be. Bull doesn't require an answer. He knows how we work. When I'm in position, I don't speak. I don't move. I hardly fucking breathe. Any movement could affect my shot. I'm the best goddamned sniper the Marine Corp has for a reason.

Smack. Smack. Smack.

The wind dies down, and I ignore the ache in my thighs. I have to piss but I'd just as soon take a leak in my pants before I moved. From my position on my belly with my legs spread apart to absorb the recoil of my shot, I always become uncomfortable.

And yet, I still don't move.

Smack. Smack. Smack.

My thighs tingle and my shoulders ache, but I tune it out.

Focus.

Smack. Smack. Smack.

"Ceremony begins at thirteen hundred hours," Gunny reminds us all. "Nobody blinks until I say they can." The dig is at me. Gunny hates that I came straight from the academy and earned myself a Lance Corporal position despite being eighteen. I've since been promoted to an E-5 Sergeant at the young age of nineteen. I'm disciplined, hard-working, and an extremely skilled sniper thanks to Dad's insistence I attend military school at Hargrave Military Academy since I was thirteen. Gunny can kiss my ass.

My hold is firm on the pistol grip but my thumb is loose. Another drop of sweat rolls down my forehead and my heart does a patter as it nears my eyebrow.

"Bull." My word is yet a whisper, but he hears.

Carefully, my best friend takes his finger and wipes the sweat away, so it doesn't slide into my eye. He does it gently and makes sure not to touch my scope. Then, he's back to staring at our target through his binoculars.

I blink several times and run my mind through every position of my body. I make sure my rifle isn't canted. My cheek is rested against the butt stock and my eye stares down the scope to Hakim.

Gunny grunts through the speaker. "Stand down, boys. We're not going to get the shot. Hakim knows he's being targeted."

Irritation flits through me.

He always gives up when I know I can take the shot.

I can kill Hakim.

Gunny just needs to let me do it my way.

My way goes against the morals and ethics of most normal men. I'm not normal. I haven't been normal since I put a bullet through a quail when I was nine years old. As soon as the shot finished echoing through the woods and I had her body tossed in my bag, I'd heard a squawk.

I had killed a mother.

One tiny offspring hollered for food in a nearby nest. I knew. Deep down I knew I'd shot that baby's mother. Something inside of me—despite my father's cold upbringing—warmed and softened. I broke for that baby bird.

But I could fix it.

I could care for that bird.

I'd gathered the tiny thing into my small fist and stroked its head with my thumb on my gloved hand. It squawked and squawked. And for the first time in ages, I grinned.

"You hear me, Corporal?" Gunny barks.

I blink away my past and focus on my present.

My target.

My goal.

What's right in front of me.

"I can make the shot. Give me a chance," I murmur, my heart thumping steadily in my chest.

He utters out a string of curse words before conceding. "I'm giving you four minutes, Corporal."

My eyes are on Hakim, my target, but when he glances over at Adara, my heart rate quickens when she beams at him. Her smile is shy but wide. For him. A smile only a woman gives to her lover. Sixteen and fifty-seven. That math sucks.

You dirty dog, Hakim.

That smile proves my research was correct. While Gunny and the team were collecting intel on Hakim, I was doing my own recon. In our short amount of time, I learned a lot about little Adara. I'd suspected she and Hakim had some sort of romantic interest going on.

Click.

Adjust.

My sights have moved slightly to accommodate my target. A target that is clear. Easy.

Focus.

Smack. Smack. Smack.

"Stand down, Corp—"

Despite the suppressor on my rifle, the crack echoes

off the buildings around me the moment I pull the trigger.

Don't breathe.

Bull doesn't dare engage, even though I've gone against direct orders.

I blink once and watch the girl crumple to her knees clutching her chest. Wait? *Chest?* Shoulder. She should be clutching her shoulder. Turning off my mind, I focus on her lover. Hakim. He roars as he breaks free from the cover of his men to be near Adara. The moment I see his fat head, I take my shot.

Crack.

"Fuuuuuck," Bull hisses from beside me. Gunny is screaming in my earpiece but he's being ignored for the time being.

Hakim falls on top of the girl's unmoving body with a deadly head wound, causing blood to rush from his skull. Target eliminated.

"You fucking killed the girl," Bull gripes, but he's already gathering our shit so we can bolt. I'm still in position to make sure Hakim doesn't move despite the gaping hole in his head.

"Hawk!"

I blink away my daze and lift my stiffened body from my position.

Fuck.

RPG.

I see it a second before it whizzes past me.

The explosion is deafening.

The pain is excruciating.

My short life ends before it even began.

ONE

Violet
Present Day

*T*ap. Tap. Tap. Tap. Tap.

"You look busy, Letty," Mr. Collins interrupts in a gruff tone. "I'll just pop in and see if Grayson wants to grab lunch."

Violet.

My perfectly manicured fingers, which were typing away on the keyboard, pause as I lift my gaze to the old man. His beady eyes flit over my silky white blouse to where my full breasts are barely encased in the buttoned-up shirt, slightly jiggling with movement. I purposefully still my body and bring my fingertips to my slender neck to touch the string of pearls my mother gave me long ago to distract him. The action hides my breasts from the leering old man, and he drags his gaze back to my face.

I stiffen but force a polite smile to my lips. "Actually, he's in a very important meeting," I lie to him as I stand. "I'll have him get back to you later, sir."

He seems mildly irritated, but I flash him a winning

smile that's more convincing than the first one. "You're his favorite client, you know," I tell him in a conspiratorial whisper. "I know he'd much rather be downing sushi and sake with you than having to hash out the purchase of that Japanese hotel from Mr. Adachi. Those two have spent so much time discussing it. I'll be glad when they decide on a price, so that Mr. Maxwell can handle his less complicated business." I make a simple motion of my hand to gesture at him.

His white brows furrow together and he rounds his shoulders, as if the motions will make him taller. More formidable. Powerful. But at five foot ten, I tower over the much-shorter man, especially in my spiked heels that easily put me over six feet. With a huff, he shoots an unnerved glare at Grayson Maxwell's door. "Tell him we can go out for celebratory drinks later in the week. I'll accept his offer on my resort. Make sure he gets the message right away."

He storms off, and my false smile morphs into a genuine and triumphant one. With my chin lifted in the air, I strut over to the coffee machine in the kitchen. Mr. Maxwell likes his coffee a certain way. Two spoonsful of sugar and one scoop of creamer. And I don't forget the sprinkle of cinnamon. I even squat slightly so I can eyeball how much sugar is rounded on the spoon before dumping it into the steaming liquid and then stirring.

The run-in with Mr. Collins only solidifies what I already know. I'm damn good at my job. After six years, I'm the best employee Maxwell Subsidiaries has. Not long ago I was just a fraction of my current self. A sliver of what could be. Back when Vaughn pulled my strings. Long before I cut loose from him and danced in my own show called life.

The earlier smile fades at the thought of my ex-boy-friend, Vaughn. A dangerous man. Toxic and vile. I'd fallen hard for a man who tainted me in every way possible. It takes hindsight to realize how deep in his dirty world I'd sunk.

I'm jolted from terrorizing memories of Vaughn when I hear male voices behind me.

"This is the break room," Clint from HR says. "We hardly ever come in here. Our assistants make our coffee. You'll be assigned an assistant as well."

I jerk my head to see the new associate, a handsome male, taking in my appearance with a slight hunger in his eyes.

"Ah, yes, Mr. Truman," Clint tells him with a chuckle. "This is the owner's assistant, Letty."

Violet.

"Will she be my assistant as well?" Mr. Truman questions, hope flickering in his weasel eyes.

I suppress a shudder and force a smile as I clutch the steaming mug of coffee. If he keeps staring at me like he's undressing me with his eyes, I might have to accidentally dump this hot cup down the front of his slacks.

"No, she belongs to Mr. Maxwell."

My heart ceases to beat at Clint's choice of words. *You belong to me.* Vaughn's favorite saying still haunts me seven years later. This time, the shudder ripples down my spine and the coffee sloshes in the mug, stinging my hand when it splashes over.

Turning away from the pompous pricks, who are now laughing at my clumsiness, I snag a paper towel and clean the coffee spill from my flesh. It takes everything in me to keep my lips pressed in a firm line to avoid saying anything. Under my breath, though, I mutter, "I belong to no one."

When I reach Mr. Maxwell's door, I visibly straighten my back and affix the same warm smile I'd used earlier for Mr. Collins before stepping into my boss's office. Just like always, his scent hits me first. Strong. Rugged. Spicy. I'd be lying if I said I didn't enjoy inhaling his unique smell.

I swallow down my silliness and focus on not spilling any more hot liquid on my hand. Walking in stilettos while carrying coffee sometimes proves to be a challenge. Thankfully, it's one I've mostly mastered.

The office is masculine and overlooks the city. Grayson Maxwell sits in his desk chair with his back turned to the door. I can see the top of his messy espresso-colored hair but every other part of him is hidden by his chair.

"Mr. Maxwell," I say, a nervous wobble to my voice. I'm not sure why I get tongue-tied around this man. After six years, you'd think I'd be immune to how handsome he is and not act like a teenage girl every time. "I brought you some coffee."

I'm just approaching his desk when he says in a warm tone, "Thank you."

My surprise catches me off guard, and I struggle with what to say. However, a genuine smile graces my lips, and I feel my cheeks heat. "You're welcome, sir. I mean out of all the years I've worked here, I don't think you've ever thanked me." I let out a small, nervous laugh.

"You're an asset," he says, his voice firm.

This time, it's my neck that's on fire. I fidget with my pearls as I set the coffee down on his desk.

"That's so nice of you to say, sir. While I have your

attention," I start, my voice wobbling slightly. "Mr. Collins—"

"Mr. Collins," he says with a chuckle. "You have nothing to worry about."

I begin to speak when he swivels around in his chair, his phone pressed to his ear. Mr. Maxwell exudes power and strength. The solid muscles in his shoulders and upper arms stretch the suit fabric to its limit. He's hot as hell—all chiseled jaw, scarred eyebrow, icy blue eyes, just-fucked hair, and scruffy five o'clock shadow. His full lips keep moving as he speaks—lips I've often fantasized about. An air of arrogance surrounds him. And, my God, does he smell good. He continues talking to who I now realize is Mr. Collins, and not me. I stumble back, horrified. I thought he was actually speaking to me.

But then I remember that Grayson Maxwell doesn't speak to me. Hell, he doesn't even look at me. Just waves me away, as if me bringing him his obligatory ten o'clock coffee is a nuisance.

Well, fuck him and fuck his stupid scheduled coffee.

I storm away from his desk and can't help but slam the door shut. The sound has several other employees jerking their shocked gazes to me. I give them a scathing glare before smoothing out my hair.

I've had enough.

Nobody here appreciates a damn thing I do. And I do *everything*. Hell, Mr. Maxwell wouldn't be closing on one of his most annoying clients yet if it weren't for my interfering. All it took was a little reverse psychology to have Mr. Collins begging to sell his resort.

I did that.

Not Grayson Maxwell.

Me.

Seven years ago, I could barely look at myself in the mirror. Much less waltz around a corporate office with my chin held high and confident in what I was doing. During the first year after Vaughn, I struggled to find myself. The job I landed at Maxwell was the beginning of that change. I evolved from the broken woman I was into someone strong and capable. I've put in my time. I have experience. This entire office runs like a well-oiled machine because I see to it that it does.

Absolutely nobody recognizes any of this.

I should have been the newest associate. Not weasel-eyed Truman. The kid looks fresh out of college—this is probably his first job. Yet, they're probably paying him double what I make simply because he has a pair of balls between his muscular thighs.

Fuck balls.

Fuck the Boys' Club.

Fuck them all.

"Where are you going?" Darlene, a woman old enough to be my mother calls out to me. She's Jeff Barker's assistant, who's the CFO.

"I'm going home," I hiss over my shoulder. "I'm sick." The lie feels easy on my tongue. I've never taken a sick day. Six years and not once have I called in sick.

"But Mr. Maxwell has the board meeting at three. Who will serve refreshments?" she questions, her voice quivering because, heaven forbid, she have to prance around in that room full of monsters and wait on them hand and foot.

I swallow down the rage threatening to consume me. I

could run circles around Truman, and yet he's the one with the cushy office. With the attention of the board. All I get is to ask them how they like their coffee. I've been here six years too long.

"Violet," Darlene whines, using my full name, probably in a half-assed attempt to soften me. "Please. You know I can't do what you do. They'll eat me alive."

Slowly, I turn around and pin her approaching frame with a fiery glare. "Why do I have to be thrown to the wolves every first Friday of the month?"

Tears well in her eyes at my harsh tone. I've always been nice to her. We've even gone out to lunch on the rare occasion when both of our bosses have been out. I like Darlene. Her grandkids are cute, and I like watching her eyes light up when she talks about them. My misplaced anger at her simmers to a slow boil. I heave out a heavy breath and place my hands on my hips.

"Fine," I concede. "But I am taking an early lunch. I'll be gone for a while too. Make sure you get Mr. Maxwell his one o'clock coffee."

Her head is nodding emphatically like a bobble head. "Of course. Enjoy your lunch, sweetie."

I give her a clipped nod before clacking my heels on the marbled floors toward the elevator. I'm going to finally give in and call back Slante Mortgages. Sean Slante has been trying to recruit me for months now. A part of me suspects it's because he has a thing for long legs and brunettes. But a bigger part of me hopes it's because my résumé is solid.

His reason for wanting me there doesn't matter. The pay is better and at least I'd have the ability to move up in the company. It isn't antiquated. There is no glass ceiling I'd have to beat my fists on.

I'm no longer Violet Simmons, a victim under Vaughn's thumb.

And soon I'll no longer be just another pretty face who makes coffee at Maxwell Subsidiaries.

I'll be a valued employee.

That's all I've ever wanted.

To be cherished and noticed.

"Letty," Ralph Darden, one of the board members, calls out to me. "A refill, please. Not so much sugar this time," he chides. He licks his lips as he shamelessly gawks at my breasts when I bend forward to grab his mug.

When I jerk my gaze along the twelve faces in the room, each and every one of them is buried in their paperwork. Nobody notices Ralph's sexual advances. I wonder if they'd notice if I smacked him upside his balding head.

Just once I wish Mr. Maxwell would look up and notice. I've had countless fantasies of him rolling up his shirt-sleeves and revealing his veiny forearms before landing a punch in Ralph's face. It's stupid. Laughable really. Nobody can save me but me. I proved that seven years ago with Vaughn.

"Mad Max won't rescue you, honey," Ralph murmurs with a chuckle when he catches me staring blatantly at Mr. Maxwell. As much as the nickname for my boss irritates me, I know he's right. That's one of the eccentricities about Grayson Maxwell. He's hyper-focused to a fault. When he's working on a deal, he puts every ounce of his attention into it until it is solid and indestructible. It's what makes him one of *Forbes* magazine's most successful men in America.

Ignoring Ralph, I make his coffee and set it down in front of him with a clonk. He gripes when it splashes over, but I start making my way over to Mr. Maxwell to check on his coffee. We've been in here for nearly two hours as they've been hashing out the Collins resort acquisition. As soon as this meeting is over, I'm going to force Grayson Maxwell to look me in the eyes as I slap my two weeks' notice on his desk.

A phone call to Sean Slante this morning turned into lunch where I finally accepted his offer. Sean is a fairly good-looking man, and in another life, I'd probably have gone after him. He's the type of guy who'd make a good husband and father one day. Successful and handsome. Friendly and polite. His interest in me is obvious, but I want this job to be about my skills, not about anything else. I want to prove to myself that I have what it takes. That I am more than a nice rack and a pair of smooth legs. Thankfully, Sean seemed to have sensed my strictly professional demeanor because he quickly slipped into business mode. By the end of our lunch, I'd accepted a position as a sales associate at Slante Mortgages. It entailed a lot more pavement pounding than I was used to, but I was looking forward to the new challenge.

"Excuse me," a man murmurs as he grips my wrist.

I'm jolted to the present as I glare down at none other than New Guy Truman. His weasel eyes rake over my chest, and he winks. Jesus, he'll fit right the hell in around here. When I start to pull my arm from his grip, he tightens it, forcing me to let out a gasp. *I wonder if I'll have a bruise later.*

"Let go of me," I seethe, under my breath.

Mr. Barker clears his throat and pushes his black-framed glasses down his nose to look over them at us. "Is there a problem?"

Truman releases me and shrugs. "I take Splenda in my coffee, sugar."

My eyes flit over to Mr. Barker's. He wears a frown on his face and darts his gaze between Truman and I, but when Mr. Maxwell begins speaking to him, he turns his attention back to our boss.

Boss.

Not for long.

I almost laugh knowing today will be the last board meeting I'll ever have to serve at. Next month, it will be Darlene, or some newbie, who'll have to endure the sexist remarks and unwanted advances. It will be someone else who has to feel like they've been blasted back to the fifties when women were nothing more than an ornament on a successful man's arm.

Two weeks and I'm gone.

So long, assholes.

TWO

Grayson

"I can't believe he caved. What do you think was the deciding factor?" Bull questions from across my desk. My best friend of thirty-two years sits with his dress shoes propped up on the edge of the solid mahogany surface, a suspicious glare on his face. For a moment, my focus is drawn to the side of his shoe. A scuff discolors the leather, and I wonder how he got it. It wasn't there this morning.

Shrugging, I draw my attention back down to the signed contract and away from his insignificant shoe. "I'm not sure. I've been wooing his ass for months. The prick liked dangling that carrot. I'd planned on taking him to a Knicks game, but before I could even tell him about the tickets, he called and said he wanted to sell." I run my fingers through my dark hair and let out a sigh. "Feels too easy. I don't like it."

He's tense as fuck, so I know I'm not out of line here.

"It's airtight," I mutter as I thumb through the contract. The wheels inside my head click and whir as all of the data flits through. Nothing stands out. But Collins gave in sooner than I anticipated for a reason.

I want to know that reason.

"Come in," Bull hollers.

I didn't even hear anyone knock. He's my eyes when I'm focused on the sole thing in front of me, whatever that may be. We've been this way since we were scrawny little thirteen-year-olds. I was blinded to everything around me by what was right in front of me even then, and he always had my back.

My eyes narrow on the sales price. Fair. Not too high and not too low. Collins and Maxwell Subsidiaries both leave the sale feeling good. Nobody screwed the other. Just business. But that stubborn old fuck has been yanking my chain for months. Milking it for all he could. He knows I wanted that resort. Not because I wanted to plow it down and sell the land. Because I just wanted it. A beautiful New England high-end resort overlooking the glorious Atlantic. I'd stayed there on a business trip and fell in love. I've torn apart the owner's financials, the land records, every single builder who contributed to the construction, the staff, the—

Slap.

I blink away my daze and dart my eyes over to my spotter. His eyes are widened and his feet are no longer on my desk. Something is happening, but I'm so wrapped up in my head I don't even realize it. This is why I need him. I'm vulnerable without him. Always have been.

"Gray," he bites out in a firm tone. "Miss Simmons is here to see you."

I frown at him before dragging my attention to the heavily breathing female standing in front of my desk. Her palm is flat against a piece of paper that she has pinned to the surface of my desk.

My eyes travel up her nicely manicured nails, past her delicate wrist, along her slender arm that's still visible despite the sheer white blouse she's wearing. By the time my gaze is on her shoulder, I can't help but skim across her pert breasts and then up her throat. A strand of old pearls hangs at the base of her neck. These aren't the type of pearls you find at Tiffany's or some other high-end shop. And they sure as hell aren't cheap. These are an heirloom, probably passed down to her. Something my mother would have worn when she was *herself*. Something that would have belonged to her mother, grandmother, and great-grandmother. The pearls are unique and—

"I quit."

Her throat is bright red and her chest still heaves. I skim the rest of the way up, bypassing her feminine features, to meet the fiery, brown-eyed gaze of a woman. *Miss Simmons*, as Bull says.

"What?" My brows furrow together in confusion. This woman, whom I don't even know, is pissed at me. As if I've personally wronged her. I'm careful about the women I sleep with. I have certain requirements. Certain expectations. Not once has that ever come back to bite me in the ass.

"You have my notice," she snaps, her brown eyes narrowing at me. "Two weeks."

Her nostrils flare with anger, and the pieces begin to slot together. She works for me. I think. Why the hell didn't she just take this nonsense to Clint in HR?

"Gray," Bull says in a calm tone, forcing me to drag my attention to him. "This is your assistant. Miss Simmons.

She's been bringing you coffee and doing other administrative tasks for you for six years."

"Unbelievable," she huffs.

Jerking my gaze back over to her, I take in her face more thoroughly this time. She's pretty. Really pretty. High cheekbones dusted in a rouge color that may or not be dark because of her apparent rage. Intense brown eyes that hold a story locked tight behind them. A small upturned nose that fits her face perfectly. And the most succulent lips I've ever seen on a woman. Full. Slightly parted. Painted a color that reminds me of blood. Her silky brown hair has shimmering strands of gold in it. And every time she moves, they catch the light. She fucking sparkles.

How did I not notice her until now?

Bull leans forward and motions for me to look at him. I do. I always do. He knows how I get. And right now, all obsession over the Collins deal is swept to the side as something pretty and shiny takes its place.

"Focus." His one word helps clear my mind. I stare him down as he pops a piece of gum in his mouth.

Smack. Smack. Smack.

"Hello," Miss Simmons says in an exasperated tone, waving her hands to catch my attention. "In case you missed it, I won't be here any longer to bring you your scheduled coffee. I won't be here for the next board meeting where those old pricks get to paw all over me and say crude things. I will no longer be here to save you. If it weren't for me," she motions to the contract still in my fingers, "you'd still be having to take that disgusting old man out to dinners and for rounds of golf!"

Click.

Bull's smacking is helping my focus. The pieces all connect. My constant haze lifts as it always does when I locate my target.

Adjust.

Focus.

Her eyes and mine are locked again. She's furious and I'm...curious. I want to know how her hair smells. I want to know how her voice sounds when I draw pleasure from her. I want to know how the curve of her ass feels with my cock pressed against it.

"Mr. Barker," she huffs and waves toward me while speaking to Bull. "Is there something wrong with him?"

He chuckles. "Please, Letty. Call me Jeff. And yes, there's a whole lot wrong with him." I don't tear my gaze from her but I can sense him smirking at me. Unwillingly, I break my stare from her and pick up her résumé.

Letty?

I don't like the name Letty.

The résumé reads Violet O. Simmons.

Violet?

I like the name Violet.

"Violet," I mutter and bore my eyes back into hers.

Her withering stare falters a bit as her sexy mouth parts open. I want that mouth. I want to taste it and suck it. I want to fuck it, goddamn it.

"Why don't you take the weekend to think on it?" Bull interrupts as he stands. His hand takes her elbow, and she stiffens. As if his touch frightens her. Bull would never hurt a woman, but I don't like the fear rippling from her.

"Release her," I growl. The words are low and threatening.

Bull sends a shocked look at me but lets her go. The tension in her shoulders relaxes. If I weren't paying attention to every single detail on her face, I'd have missed the flicker of gratitude in her eyes. I'd have missed the relief.

"There's nothing to think about," she tells us both, her chin lifting in a brave way. "I'm leaving in two weeks. You'll need to hire someone who can do everything I do for this company. In fact, you'll probably need to hire three people to replace me."

Bull lets out a grunt, but I find my mouth twisting up.

A smile.

Violet Simmons, my little quitter, made my lips do something they really hate fucking doing. And with it, I feel a strange tightness in my chest. I like the way it feels. The foreign ache that matches the one in my cock coupled with the goofy grin on my face has me feeling more alive than I've felt in a really long time.

Oh, dear Violet.

You're not going anywhere.

I'm still staring at her when she storms off toward the door. Her skirt is tight and hugs her curves in a way that leaves little to the imagination. Irritation flits through me that every other male in this building has probably been drooling over what's been mine for six years. And my stupid one-track mind is just now seeing her for the first time.

The door slams shut and it reminds me of earlier this morning. A door slammed. I'd been on the phone with Mr. Collins. She'd been upset then too.

Don't worry, Violet…I see you now.

"Don't."

I blink away the thoughts of her and glare at Bull.

"What?"

"Don't do it. Let her go. That woman has been here for six years busting her ass for you, and you're just now realizing she's here. But it's your dick that finally sees her. Call Elisha. She'll take care of that nosy little dick of yours and you can get back to focusing on shit that matters. Like the Collins deal." He takes his glasses off and scrubs his face as if this entire afternoon is exhausting him.

And I've never felt so refreshed.

I won't be able to sleep until I've learned everything there is to know about Violet O. Simmons.

"You're right," I lie as I gather the paperwork on my desk. "Let me finish going over some stuff. I'll lock up tonight."

He narrows his gaze at me but doesn't say a word in argument as he slips his glasses back on and stands. "Want to grab a beer later?"

I nod and wave him off. I'm antsy. I want my best friend to leave me be so I can do a little research. Twenty long minutes later, I hear his keys jangling against the glass of the front doors of our floor as he leaves.

I'm all alone.

The first thing I do is flip open my laptop. Facebook is where you learn a whole lot about a person. It takes a minute to find her, and when I do, I'm disappointed. She has it locked down. All I'm privy to is her name and her profile picture. Instead of her face, she has a picture of the ocean. Her cover photo is some vague quote.

My past has not defined me, destroyed me, deterred me; it has only strengthened me.—Steve Maraboli.

I'm dying to know what sort of things she posts, but

it's all fucking private. I can't even tell how many friends she has. Does she have friends here at the office? Is Bull her friend? Another blossom of irritation surges in my chest. I've had this stunning woman strutting into my office several times a day and I have never paid one ounce of attention to her. Granted, I don't know ninety percent of the people who work for me, but this feels different. This feels like an injustice. Like I've been duped.

With a huff, I rise and stride out of my office. Her desk sits right outside my door. Everything is neat and in order. Pride swells inside me. My assistant isn't messy or disorderly. She's organized like me. Perhaps that is why she was chosen to work for me in the first place. Bull knows me better than I know myself. I don't deal with the employees or HR. He does and is good at it.

I sit in her stiff chair and let out a groan. The damn thing isn't nearly as comfortable as my plush leather one. I've just sat down and my back already hurts. I make a mental note to order her a new one. Brown. Like the non-shiny parts of her hair. Everything has a place on her desk. A company coaster sits right beside her mouse. All of her pens and papers have been put away. Nothing except her phone and computer and the coaster adorn the desk. One corner is especially empty. I want to fill it. I *will* fill it.

Inhaling, I almost crack another rare smile when I catch a whiff of her lingering scent. A hint of coffee mixed with her sweet floral perfume. I wonder how she would smell the exact moment she spritzes on her perfume and steps out of her bedroom. Would it be intense or faint?

I *will* find out.

Using an age-old trick, I lift her keyboard and am elated

to find a sticky note with her passwords written on it. The same one for all of her logins. SurViV0r.

It only takes a couple of moments to get logged on to her computer. All of her folders are arranged neatly. Her spreadsheets of my clients are all in a manner I approve of. She has many detailed notes from meetings. Meticulous logs of calls made to me and visitors who have come to see me. I also see where she's run data on properties. Checked on sales prices and values. Run comparison analyses. The works. Aside from bringing me my coffee and fielding my calls, I'm not sure what she does for my company. Apparently, though, she does a lot for her own information. None of the data she collects goes anywhere except her spreadsheets.

Skipping over to her email, I'm also pleased to see how neat and organized it is. All that sits in her inbox is an email from HR indicating they've also received a copy of her resignation. Ignoring the annoyance that someone else knows about her attempt to quit, I find a folder in her emails called: Ideas for the Idiot.

I pop it open to find hundreds if not thousands of emails to me. I blink several times to allow what I'm seeing to soak in. These emails are simply saved as drafts. She never sent them. Some are of her telling me off. Those make me crack another smile. Most, though, are of her making suggestions. Or providing analytical details on properties. A lot of her emails could have been really damn helpful.

Why didn't she send them?

I press send on several of the emails that could be useful, especially the data for the Collins venture, before closing out her email and opening the Internet. Once I pull up

Facebook, I type in SurViV0r. I'm immediately granted access to her account.

The first place I click is her friends. I'm dying to know who she's friends with here at my company. I scan through all thirty-six friends. None are Bull. None are Clint from HR. Other than that, I don't know these people.

I'm not her friend, though.

That's okay because I want to be more than friends. I *will* be more than friends with her.

Scanning through her friend requests, I delete all the males who requested to be her friend. I don't like those creepy fuckers. She doesn't have any common friends with them. They're probably just trying to weasel some nude pics out of her. Over my goddamned dead body. Once they're deleted, I check her messages. Most are silly and lame. People sending her jokes or chain letter shit or funny memes. Her Facebook has no real substance to it. All of her posts are motivational memes and the occasional picture of the ocean.

I make my mind up right then to take her to the ocean one day.

I'm scanning through old pictures when a new message pops up.

Sean Slante: Congrats again! I just wanted to let you know we're looking forward to having you join the team. I've already ordered you a computer and Janine has put in an order for your nameplate. If you have any questions about the job, I'm open to meet up for coffee or even a beer. This weekend is pretty open. Hell, I could even see you tonight if you want to talk about how things went today when you put in your notice. You have my cell so

just shoot me a text. Talk soon, Letty.

By the time I finish reading the message, I'm blind with rage. I want to tell the fucker off. Tell him he's not taking my assistant. That he's an unprofessional twit to private message her. That she will *not* be having a fucking beer with him.

Instead, I tamper down my fury and close out of everything. I'll have to play my cards right. Just like acquisitions. I'll put in my time. Analyze the details. Make smart moves.

Violet O. Simmons is mine.

She just doesn't know it yet.

T-minus fourteen days…

THREE

Violet

I feel lighter.

Resolved.

Like I should celebrate.

And that's the only reason I agreed to meet Sean Slante over at an Irish pub for a round of beers. He'll be my new boss soon, and it'll take some getting used to that he actually acknowledges me, knows my name, and recognizes me as an asset.

Unlike *him*.

My thoughts flit back to earlier. When I'd boldly slapped my notice on Grayson Maxwell's desk. How, for the first time in six years, he'd looked *at* me. A shiver courses through me at that thought. His icy blue eyes were narrowed but curious. I felt as though he were peeling off my clothes with every second that passed. With just one look. It was unnerving and a tiny bit satisfying.

I hope he liked what he saw.

I hope he realized what an idiot he was for not noticing what a hard worker I was.

The moment that I had his attention, though, it was strange. Too intense. Too much. Maybe it truly was a blessing that he'd not paid me any mind all these years. I think if he looked at me that way from the very beginning, my job would have been a whole helluva lot harder.

I could have gotten lost in that gaze.

Swallowing down my irritation, I scan the bar for Sean. He's still not here yet. I nurse my beer and worry about my outfit. I didn't want to wear work attire but I also didn't want to appear too casual for my new boss. In the end, I'd settled on a black fitted dress and a pair of trendy matching ankle boots. My long legs are bare, unlike how I wear them to work, but I'm still maintaining some elegance. A part of me had leaned toward jeans but I'm still trying to make an impression, despite my accepting his offer.

"Letty!" a deep voice booms.

When I see Sean, I smile and slip out of the booth. He looks handsome in his dark jeans and powder blue, button-up shirt. The sleeves are rolled up and he's gone without a tie. I let out a sigh of relief that I'm neither overdressed nor underdressed compared to him.

"Hi," I greet and extend my arm.

The friendly man bypasses my handshake and pulls me in for a hug. He smells nice, but I can't tell if it's because he truly does or the fact I haven't been this close to a man in a long time. I give him a polite hug back. When he pulls away, he doesn't release me at first. His lips are pulled up into a half smile.

"I'm so glad you could meet up," he tells me, his eyes flickering with concern. "I know Mad Max. He can be quite the pill sometimes. Was he okay with your resignation? Did the crazy old bastard throw his desk around?"

Again with the Mad Max.

I try not to feel defensive over the man who ignored me for six years. Sean is a nice guy. He's not trying to be catty. If anything, he seems excited to have me, which is a huge change from what I'm used to.

Pulling away, I slide from his grip and sit back down. Thankfully, he plops down across from me. His long legs brush against my own under the table.

"He seemed surprised," I admit before sipping my beer. "I don't think it really sunk in. Probably won't until I'm gone."

Sean smirks and waves over a waitress. Once she takes his order, he directs his green eyes back over to mine. "You're just a number over there, Letty. At Slante, you're a person. Everyone at my company is recognized for their hard work. I know you'll fit right in."

A smile tugs at my lips. "Thank you for taking a chance on me. I know I'm not the most experienced person but I'm a quick learner."

He gives me a wink. "You'll do fine. And if you ever have any trouble, you come see me. We'll sort it out."

When he starts talking about a row of Brownstones he's working on a loan for, something catches my gaze in the window. A shadowed figure leans against a wall between two buildings. It appears to be a masculine figure. He's tall and broad-shouldered. The man simply stares straight at us. Sometimes my imagination plays tricks on me. Vaughn is in my nightmares so it's only fitting he's in my reality too.

But I know he doesn't know where I am.

I've been careful.

Besides, if it were Vaughn, he wouldn't simply sit out-side and watch me have a beer with another man. He'd come in here with guns literally blazing and accost me right in front of everyone.

A shudder ripples through me. When I glance back outside, the figure is gone. Another figment. Always a figment.

"Hey," Sean says with a husky laugh, his knee brushing against mine under the table. "I think I lost you there."

I snap my attention to him. His eyebrows are pinched together as if he's trying to figure me out. He'll never figure out my messy head.

"I'm sorry," I tell him with a forced chuckle. My hand pats his on the table. "It was a long, stressful day."

Mischief dances in his green eyes. "How about we re-solve to have no more of those types of days? I have just the thing to get you on the right foot."

Just the thing turns out to be shots of tequila. And while I was hesitant at first to drink with my new boss, I immedi-ately gave in when he gave me exaggerated puppy dog eyes. Sean is friendly and funny. I've been strutting along for so long with a stick up my ass that it's nice to relax for once. By the third shot, I'm warm and giggly.

Sean disappears to go to the restroom, and I check my phone. I'm not sure why but I'd hoped for some kind of "please don't quit" message from the sexy Grayson Maxwell. Despite his apparent shock and annoyance of my resigna-tion, he sure as hell hasn't tried to get me to stay.

"Miss me?" Sean questions with a chuckle when he comes sauntering back with more shots in his hands. He si-dles into the booth beside me and pushes two shots toward me. "To new beginnings." His grin is wide and flirty. "To new valuable employees."

I swat at him. "Now you're just being ridiculous." But I'm smiling. Truth is, it's nice that he sees such potential in me.

His arm stretches out behind me across the back of the booth, and he leans in. "I'm not. I knew it the moment I read your résumé. Now drink or I'll consider it insubordination."

Laughing, I grab my shot and drain it down.

"Good girl," he teases and runs his fingers along the outside of my arm.

I shiver and pick up the second shot. Once I drain that one, I look at him with a lifted brow. "Who says I'm good?"

It's been ages since I've been out with friends and done something as simple as joke around. Sean's gaze darkens and he doesn't respond. He sucks down both of his shots before slamming them back down on the table. "You're trouble," he says, his voice hoarse.

Warmth surges through me. I'm happy. I am finally leaving a dead end job and running toward a future. After a lifetime of mistakes, I'm going to start making something of myself.

"Thank you," I tell him with a sigh and lean against him. I'm drunk now. The room is starting to swim. This was a bad idea.

His fingers curl around my bicep. "You're welcome."

Sean is warm. Approachable and nice. I wonder what it would be like to kiss someone like him. To straddle his firm hips and ride him right into an orgasm. My panties dampen at the thought of getting laid. It's been years.

Would he kiss me in that soul-consuming way Vaughn used to?

Vaughn was bad for me.

Would he touch me in all the right places like Vaughn did?

Vaughn ruined me.

Would he fuck me like I belonged only to him until the end of time like Vaughn did?

Vaughn was a psychopath.

"Letty." Sean's hissed voice cuts through my confusing haze. I hate Vaughn, but imagining him while I touch myself is the only way I can get off. It's humiliating. "You have to stop or I'll come right here in my pants."

I jolt at his words and look down at my hand that's rubbing his erection through his slacks. Horror threatens to suffocate me as I jerk my hand from him.

"Oh my God," I croak and start to pull from his grip. "I am so sorry."

"Hey," he murmurs against my hair. "This is my fault. I should have fed you before I liquored you up. Please don't think I'm some pervert."

Guilt infects me.

He thinks *he's* the pervert?

I'm the one who was rubbing up on him like a dog in heat.

"Do I still have the job?" I whisper.

His chuckle once again warms me. "Of course."

My eyes close and I think of Vaughn. His blond hair that was long on top and shaved on the sides. The way it would flop into his eyes and stick to his temple when he'd fuck me. The man was terror and beauty molded into one perfectly horrifying package.

"Letty…"

The voice is all wrong.

"I need to call you a cab. Right now. Or else…" A groan. "Or else I think we're both going to regret this in the morning."

When I drag my eyes open, I realize I'm practically in Sean's lap. My lips are pressed against his throat with my fingers tangled in his hair. He has a death grip on my ass. The erection poking into my thigh tells me he really wants me and is barely holding back.

"Shit!" I groan and scramble out of his lap. "I…this…"

"Cab," he says huskily and climbs out of the booth. "God…you have no idea how hard it will be to put you in that car and watch you drive away with this raging problem." He gestures to his cock through his jeans, and a giggle escapes me. This causes him to chuckle too. "Laugh it up, angel. Let's go before we get ourselves kicked out of here."

I vaguely remember him slapping down a wad of cash and ushering me into a cab. Just when he's helping me inside, I hear heavy footsteps. Then, a pop followed by a groan. The car door on the opposite side opens up, but I'm already blacking out. My address is hissed from a familiar voice beside me the moment the car door slams shut. The cab begins to move, but all I can think about are the strong fingers stroking through my hair. The rugged, masculine scent filling my nostrils.

"Shhh," the voice whispers in a possessive way. "I have you now."

Who had me before?

Better yet, who has me now?

His gentle caresses send me right into a slumber without a care in the world.

I have you now.

Sometimes love isn't black or white. Sometimes love isn't even in color.

For me, love is red.

Bloody, dripping, bright, and crimson.

Violent.

Messy but brilliant against my otherwise dull world.

"Tell me you love me," Vaughn murmurs, the slight stubble on his chin dragging along my lower belly. "Tell me."

When our eyes meet, his are bloodshot but not angry. No, right now, he's in a rare mood. Contemplative and borderline sweet. Just Vaughn. Not the unhinged man he's slowly evolved into.

"I love you." *Because right now, I do love him. In this exact moment, it's true. My love for Vaughn changes. Rises and sets like the sun based on his moods. When he's warm and shining his bright smile upon me, I bask in all that's him. But when he clouds himself from me and his features darken, my love flickers and dims. Sometimes my love fades away completely.*

"You know I wish it could be like this always," *he says in a whisper before kissing my hipbone.* "I wish my life wasn't fucked-up chaos."

Boy, do I wish that too.

"You have me," *I tell him with a smile. My entire body is humming with energy. I want him, just like always. Even when he makes me hate him. I always want him.*

His grey-colored eyes turn to hard steel, causing a shiver of anxiety to skitter up my spine. "Of course I have you. I'll always have you."

Not always.

Not when you take away my last breath.

That time is coming.

As if to read my thoughts, he roughly parts my knees. I'm naked and wet and my body accommodates his. Like always. He pushes his thickness inside of me while gripping my thighs. The cold steel in his eyes softens just a bit as he regards my quivering frame. I'm shaking with equal parts desire and fear. The concoction that only Vaughn Brecks can mix up.

His mouth meets mine and his powerful body rubs against me with every thrust. I'm powerless with this man. He's the wicked storm, and I'm nothing but a piece of debris swept up in him. I float in his wake, following him along his path of destruction.

"Sweet Letty," he murmurs against my mouth as his strong hand curls around the front of my throat. My heart rate quickens in my chest, but I don't stop him. You don't stop Vaughn. You simply let it happen. "You're mine. Always mine. Nothing will ever change that." His fingers dig into my pale flesh as he squeezes. My breath becomes lodged in my throat with nowhere to escape to. His soft lips hover over mine as he fucks me while squeezing the ever-loving hell out of my neck. Once upon a time, I fought him. And in those stories, I always lost. But when I don't fight. When I give in to the darkness that swallows me whole. When I let Vaughn do whatever it is he wants to do. I'm free. My mind detaches from my body and drifts off to somewhere else. Someplace

dark and warm. No confusing red. No color. Just muted grey and mine.

"Letty."

When I come to, his grip is gone. His eyes flicker briefly with concern before he chases it away with satisfaction. He's on his knees between my thighs and no longer inside me. Thick, warm cum coats my belly and runs down my side, wetting the bed below. I don't remember him finishing. I certainly don't remember coming.

"Get dressed, Letty Spaghetti," he chirps, melting me with one of his charming grins. "We have errands to run." My melting quickly turns cold. I'm frozen. Errands. Errands mean trouble. Errands mean pain.

"I'm not feeling so well," I rasp out, my voice still hoarse from being choked unconscious.

His glare is severe as he tosses me a pink scrap of spandex material. "It wasn't a request. It was a demand. Make yourself pretty. You're looking like a strung-out whore."

I wince at his words more than his tone. I look like a strung-out whore because he made me that way. If I were to look in the mirror right now, my pale, haunted face would stare back. My normally bright brown eyes would be dull from whatever pill he stuck on my tongue before he stripped me down earlier. Dark circles would ring my eyes from either lack of sleep or from one of Vaughn's "lessons." And my full lips would be chapped from overuse coupled with malnutrition.

I've spent eleven months with this man and I can't seem to pull my head out of the red fog that follows him long enough to straighten out my life. Not that he'd let me go anyway.

His hand tangles in my hair, and I'm dragged out of the bed to my feet right in front of him. Even furious and impatient and on the border of psychotic rage, Vaughn is a glorious vision. He pins me in place with his piercing glare—a glare that promises pain and punishment and, one day, death.

"I love you," he seethes. I believe him. I truly do. "But right now, you're pissing me off." His free hand grabs my bruised and bare ass hauling me against his erection. "We have shit to do, so stop dragging your feet."

I try to nod at him, but his grip in my hair prevents me from doing so. A small yelp of surprise escapes me when he hauls me over to the end table beside the bed. He rummages around until he finds what he's looking for. Little happy pill. I can't help but smile.

"Good girl." He grins back before shoving it into my mouth. I gag but swallow it down. Within minutes, I'm needy, and the dress he helps me put on is too much. Too clingy. Too scratchy. Too much. The urge to seek out pleasure consumes me. I claw at his chest and plead with him to fuck me again. His kiss is gentle but the way he cups me between my legs is not. "You're going to get fucked," he assures me with a cold growl. "I told you we had errands."

I can't find the sadness that usually plagues me. No tears well in my eyes. I'm not even upset as he guides me out of his shitty house to his suped-up sports car that doesn't fit well in the ghetto neighborhood. It's the kind of car that should get jacked or broken into, but nobody touches it. Nobody touches anything that belongs to Vaughn Brecks unless he says they can. Unless they pay him whatever his asking price is. Otherwise, they won't live to see another day.

I'm blitzed out of my mind, squirming and begging the entire drive to wherever it is we're going. He teases me with gentle caresses to my bare thigh and brief rubs against my clit where I'm naked under my dress. By the time we roll up to a high-end condo building, I'm dripping with need.

"You ready to make us some money, sweetheart?" he questions, his grip tightening around my thigh. I'll be bruised, but right now it feels good. Any touch feels good.

"I thought I was yours only," I pout through my haze.

His face becomes murderous. "Of course you fucking are. This is just business, baby. You belong to me. Not this rich fucker who wants to get his dick wet because his fat wife won't put out."

As terrible as they are, his words warm me. They warm me so much that I'm on fire by the time we enter the glitzy condo where the client awaits. Vaughn's grip on my bicep is possessive, but he still hands me over to the man. Accepts a wad of bills and gives me a slight push toward the foreign man with the large stomach. I squint to try and figure out his nationality, but as soon as the door closes behind Vaughn, the man is on me. He paws at me like I'm the first Christmas present he's ever received. And the shit Vaughn gave me has me buzzing with desire. I want to ride this ugly man with the black mustache and beady eyes. I want to grip his greasy hair and fuck him while I think of my boyfriend.

Vaughn's steely grey eyes are at the forefront of my mind as the man manages to push my dress up my hips and bend me over his expensive dining room table. He fumbles with his pants. Then I hear the familiar tear of a condom. Always condoms. At least Vaughn looks out for me. And then the man's thin penis is inside me. He's taking what doesn't belong to him, and I don't care. I let him because he feels good. His reverent touches running up my back. The way his hairy balls slap against my pussy. Nearly inaudible grunts from an un-familiar man.

I come.

I shudder in ecstasy while thinking of Vaughn.

I take the orgasm he wouldn't let me have not an hour earlier.

God, how I love Vaughn.

The man behind me claws at my hips as he groans with his own release, causing slices of reality to bleed inside of me.

God, I have to get away from Vaughn.

FOUR

Grayson

I stare at her as she touches herself between her legs. Her moans cause my cock to twitch in my slacks, but I ignore it for now. For now, I'm concerned about her. How careless was she to go off and get drunk with that asshole, Slante. Christ, he was seconds away from fucking her against the goddamned cab had I not intervened when I did. Violet was wasted. Poor woman slept the entire way to her place, mumbling from time to time unintelligibly. I'd had the cabbie take us to her apartment building where I proceeded to carry her up three flights of stairs because the shitty elevator was broken. When I'd seen she had three locks engaged, fury bubbled up inside me. She shouldn't be living in a piece-of-shit building. Not with what I pay her. After breaking into her computer, I took it upon myself to look at her file in Clint's cabinet. I'm the CEO after all, so her personal file is my business if I say it is.

Address.

Age.

Background.

I found everything I needed, including her salary. Her salary was enough to where she didn't have to live in a shit hole like this. I'll figure out this little mystery. Find out where her money is going. Until then, though, I simply stare at her.

Getting an unconscious woman undressed and under the covers is difficult, even for a fit and able man like myself. Her loose limbs and limp body made for a frustrating twenty minutes. Eventually, I got her naked.

I peel away the covers and take another peek before I go hunting. Her perky tits have the sexiest bitable nipples right in the center of each one. Just looking at them has me nearly coming in my slacks. I'm going to feast on them one day. Not today. One day. Her stomach is flat and her hipbones are showing. The woman could stand to eat a little more. I make a mental note to deal with that problem as well. Her pussy is shaved smooth. The urge to push my finger inside of her is overwhelming, but I fist my hand and ignore the urge.

I notice *everything* about her.

Her smooth brown hair fanned out on the cream-colored pillow underneath her head. Those fuckable lips of hers are parted as she sleeps. Long, dark lashes rest on her pink cheeks.

I want to shake her shoulders and yell at her. To wake her up and explain to her how stupid she's been. A woman who looks like her doesn't need to go off with men she barely knows late at night. Men like Sean Slante could take advantage of her.

A growl rumbles in my throat at the memory of him with his hands on her. I'd watched them through the window of the bar. Sure, he'd played the good guy, but I could see the desire in his eyes. I saw the way he gripped her ass as if it belonged to him.

She does not belong to him.

Violet lets out a moan before muttering a name.

Vaughn.

Who the fuck is Vaughn?

Once again, I fist my hand to keep from grabbing her by the jaw and waking her up by telling her what a naïve woman she is.

Stalking away so I don't do exactly that, I begin to look through her drawers. Everything is neat and has a place. There isn't one ounce of clutter. Just like her desk at the office. It makes me wonder what she's hiding. People who are minimalists do so in order to hide something big about themselves. If they have everything in a place, then they don't have to stress about their past or shortcomings slipping through the cracks amidst the mess. They are able to keep a careful watch on every detail in their lives by keeping it all under the lid where it belongs.

I know this because *I* am this way.

My home is immaculate.

My business is organized.

My entire life is flawless.

The secrets I have stay neatly contained.

But *her* secrets, I *will* uncover. Her secrets are mine. I want them. I fucking crave them. After an annoying search that turns up nothing, I sit at the foot of her bed. Her breathing is soft and measured. If I didn't think she'd flip the fuck out, I'd kick off my shoes and lie down beside her. My luck, I'd fall asleep and she'd wake up to find me there.

Accuse me of things I'm not.

So I don't lie down.

I don't take off my shoes.

Instead, I think.

Where do I hide *my* secrets?

I have an old cedar chest that belonged to my mother. I'd taken it some twenty odd years ago when she first started losing her mind. Before she buried it in her insecurities. I'm not sure she even knows it's gone. In that chest are my secrets. My past that has shaped and molded me. When I think about my past, it reminds me of someone. An error that will follow me for the rest of my life.

Adara.

Her pretty brown eyes haunt me. Hell, I believe they'll haunt me until the day I die. I deserve to be continually reminded of those eyes. I'd made a mistake. It was a mistake that had nearly cost me everything. It altered my life in so many ways, I can't even begin to count them. I'm here, standing right now in this sparse bedroom with a sleeping angel unaware of my presence, because of Adara.

With newfound purpose, I stalk over to her closet. Her suits are pressed and fairly expensive looking, but I know she's not spending all of her money on clothes. They smell like her. Sweet and florally. Mine. I shove the thick coats out of the way and feel around behind the garments. Just like I'd imagined, I find a box. The shoebox, while much smaller than my cedar chest, holds answers about my Violet. I tug it free and bring it with me back into the room. Sitting back down at the foot of the bed, I remove the lid from the box and start rummaging around. Pictures, feminine hand-written notes, a hospital bracelet. The notes aren't hers. I spent hours earlier at her desk and learned her handwriting. These notes are from someone who loves her.

Love you, Letty.

You'll always be my Letty Spaghetti.

Enjoy your lunch, baby girl.

I realize that all of the notes must be from her mother. They're all written on the same type of paper. The lined sheets with numbers at the top and the words "thank you" stamped on the back look like the type that waitresses use to take orders. I make note of the restaurant name imprinted at the top before pushing them to the side. The first picture I look at is of her and a woman who looks a lot like her. When I flip it over, I smile at the handwriting that I know is Violet's.

Me and Momma '04

She's wearing a graduation gown and a smile I've never seen before. Brilliant and hopeful. Proud. Her mother's smile is just as big. Just as beautiful. They make a lovely pair. Sadly, I wonder if her mother died. But then it makes me think of my own mother. Irritation seeps through me, and I shove the picture on the pile of notes. Most of the other pictures are of Violet doing things. Then, I find one single picture of her with a man.

A flicker of hate ignites inside me.

The man with the grey eyes and severe glare with his arm draped possessively around Violet is a threat. I sense it. I can almost fucking taste it. It sours my stomach, and with a growl, I shove everything back into the box. She stirs on the bed, but I put everything back into the closet where it belongs.

When I re-emerge, she's got her hand between her legs

again. In her sleep, she touches herself and moans. There's no rhyme or reason to her movements. Prowling over to her, I loom over her sleeping frame. I crave to push away her uncoordinated fingers and do the job for her. When she whimpers in frustration, I make a decision. I wrap my hand around her delicate wrist and help her along. Using her hand, I give her the speed she needs to reach her climax. Her cunt is probably hot against her fingertips. My dick thickens and pushes against my boxers, begging for its own taste of her.

Later.

This is about her, not me.

With measured movements, I continue my pace, guiding her own hand to push between her pussy lips and massage her throbbing clit. Those sexy whimpers of hers become moans. Louder and louder. Her body squirms and jolts in her sleep as I touch her. When she gasps once before shuddering, I know she's found her release, even in her sleep. With another smile ghosting my lips—a smile only she can bring out of me—I allow myself the very thing I denied myself earlier. A simple taste. I draw her soaked fingers from her body to my lips. Smearing her juices all over my mouth, I grow impossibly harder with the need to push inside her gorgeous body. Instead, I suckle her fingers, removing every trace of her orgasm with my tongue. God, she smells decadent.

I gently rest her hand back on her stomach before covering her back up with the blanket. Her essence on my lips lingers, and I inhale her alluring scent. One day soon, I'll have my face buried between her thighs. I'll feast upon her perfect cunt whenever I want. She'll beg for it. I'll reward her because she's so fucking gorgeous and deserving. With a flick of my tongue, I slowly lick my bottom lip. She tastes like sin. Sweet, decadent sin. My cock aches to sink inside of her, but I ignore him for now. The morning sun is just starting to peek in through the blinds. It's time I leave her be for a bit.

I drop to my knees and then flatten myself against the drab carpet that reeks of renters and stale cigarettes. It takes some maneuvering, but I manage to slide myself under the bed. Once I'm comfortable, with my face pointed toward the closet, I relax. I close my eyes and sleep. And for the first time in months, I sleep really fucking well.

See you soon, Violet.

FIVE

Violet

I wake with a start and jolt upright in bed. The sun blinds me, causing me to groan before shielding my eyes from the bright rays. I'm slightly disoriented and severely hung over. Shame trickles down my spine as I begin to recall fuzzy events from last night.

I'd all but dry humped Sean in a bar booth. Threw myself all over my future boss because I was high on memories of Vaughn and drunk off tequila. Because I haven't been with a man in years, I craved his touch. The liquid courage was the catalyst for a night full of regrets.

But as soon as I'd given in to my desires, they were snuffed out like a single candle in a windowless room. Sean deposited me into the cab and then…

That's where everything really went hazy.

I can't recall a single memory from that point on.

Looking down, I cringe at finding that I'm naked. Panic climbs up my throat but I force it down quickly. Vaughn wasn't here. It was all me. I'd undressed all by myself. A quick look around my room tells me that at least I didn't tear my clothes off before fucking some random stranger either. There are no clues indicating I kept the party going last night. True to myself, even in a blacked-out state, I'd put my clothes away in the hamper. I'd put my shoes in the closet. The need to prove this overwhelms me, so I climb out of bed on wobbly feet. I grab the nightstand for support when the room spins around me.

My pussy feels slightly raw. I must have touched myself in the middle of the night. One sniff of my fingertips tells me I'm correct on that assumption as well. At least I can always count on myself, even when I'm fucked up beyond memory.

A quick peek in the hamper and closet tells me I'm not crazy. I did come home and undress as usual. With a sigh of relief, I take the longest shower known to man. My calves are sore and the rest of my body is achy due to my hangover from hell.

My phone buzzes from my nightstand where I managed to remember to plug it in last night. Now freshly showered and dried off, with a towel wrapped around my wet hair, I walk naked over to the bedside. A chill ripples through me. The feeling of being watched by Vaughn has never really gone away. I blink it away to read my message.

Apparently I've missed several.

Sean: I had fun last night. Sorry if things got out of hand.

Sean: Let me make it up to you. Dinner tonight?

I'm already shaking my head in disagreement. I refuse to spend another moment alone with Sean. I'm already horrified over my behavior last night.

Sean: I wasn't exactly a gentleman so don't go

blaming this on yourself.

I chew on my lip and head back into the bathroom. Pulling my towel off and dropping it to the floor, I look at my reflection. Despite my stupidity last night, I still look like the woman I'd eventually shaped myself to be. I'm no longer *her*. The woman wrapped up in Vaughn's twisted little world. I'm healthy and educated and successful.

Breathe, Violet.

He no longer has his hand around your throat.

I spend the rest of the morning taking my time getting ready. Once my makeup is on and my hair is dried into sexy tresses, I spritz on my perfume and leave the bathroom on a hunt for some clothes.

I get that eerie feeling once again of being watched as I enter my bedroom. The bedroom door is cracked. I squint to make sure nobody is peeking through.

"Stop freaking out," I chide myself. "He's not here." I still shiver as I root around in my closet for clothes. I'll never be able to fully convince myself that Vaughn can't find me. *That I'm safe.* I've taken precautions, but he's a resourceful man.

A click jolts me from my thoughts, and I scamper out of my closet. The bedroom door is now closed. Alarm slices through me. Yanking my robe from the bathroom hook, I quickly wrap it around me and tiptoe over to the door.

Silence.

I try not to breathe.

Another soft click from the living room.

"Shit," I hiss as I engage the lock on my bedroom door. The gun I keep loaded under my mattress is still there when I look. I pull the heavy cold object into my grip and summon up the courage to escape my bedroom prison. My phone buzzes from the bathroom, but I ignore it. Quietly, I manage to check every part of my apartment from top to bottom.

Nothing.

My nerves are eating me alive this morning.

I need protein and sugar and coffee.

I need to snap out of it.

I'm shaking my head at my stupidity when my gaze skims across my apartment to the front door. All three locks are disengaged.

Blink. Blink. Blink.

Confusion causes my blood to creep through my veins like molasses. I never forget to lock my doors. Never. Ever. Fucking never. With three leaps to the door, I snap all of the locks into place before choking out a relieved sob.

Someone was in my home.

Vaughn.

Tears threaten to spill, but I furiously blink them away. He won't own me this time. The heavy gun in my palm wobbles as I imagine myself pointing it at him. A calm washes over me and my hand stills.

If it comes between me and Vaughn, I'll choose me.

Every time.

I compose myself and make my way back to the bathroom. I have another missed text on my phone. But this time it's from an unknown number.

Vaughn.

Unknown: Meet me for breakfast. The hotel on 7th and Madison has a brilliant selection of muffins.

Muffins?

Me: Who is this?

Unknown: It's Gray, little quitter. Let me treat you. We both know I owe you. I have six years to make up for.

Relief floods through me once I realize Vaughn doesn't have my phone number. I went to great lengths to keep this number hidden from anyone I don't want to have it.

Me: I'm more of an omelet and French toast kind of gal. But, sadly for you, I'd rather eat alone.

Despite my reply, I find myself rooting around in my closet for something to wear. I dress professionally for this man every single day, yet he has never once looked me in the eye. Not once has he spoken to me. Not one time has he appreciatively glanced over my outfit.

Except yesterday.

Yesterday he seemed to have realized what was in his face all along.

And now he's, what? Curious. One might even conclude that he feels bad. It makes me want to rub it in his face. Make him understand that I'm not something who can be looked over or forgotten. I am *someone*. Someone special and beautiful and worth knowing.

Unknown: Dear Violet, you'll never be alone as far as I'm concerned. Twenty minutes. I'll be waiting.

His words should alarm me, but right now, I'm attempting to suppress the good kind of shiver that is rocketing through me. Excitement courses through me. I want to dangle in front of him what he can't have. What he was too blind to see all along. Since Vaughn, I've enjoyed any moment when I can make a man feel powerless in my presence. Because it wasn't too long ago that the roles were grossly reversed.

With a skip in my step, I start for a red dress but pause with my hand in the air. Red reminds me of Vaughn. I skim over to a white sweater dress I bought for a date I never ended up going on. Because I'm feeling slightly bitchy, I slide the soft material down over my body sans bra. The nude lace thong is all that stands between my flesh and the cashmere. I find some thigh high boots that hit just below the bottom hem of the short dress. The look is sexy, but I'm also trying to be a little classy so I find a belt to go over the dress and a grey infinity scarf to halfway attempt to hide my bare breasts beneath the fabric. As soon as I step in front of the mirror, I know he won't be able to help noticing me now.

I'll be on the radar of any man with a working dick.

I look hot and I know it.

Smirking, I grab my purse and a coat before leaving to meet my soon-to-be ex-boss. My gun fits in my purse and that's right where it will stay until I make sure Vaughn is still just a figment of my imagination.

T-minus thirteen days until I move on to my newest adventure. But until then, I'm going to make Grayson Maxwell regret letting me slip through his fingertips.

SIX

Grayson

I sit at my usual table wearing my usual scowl. Twenty minutes comes and goes. Then thirty. But, thank fuck, thirty-eight minutes after my text, she shows up at the hotel restaurant looking like she owns the damn place.

Her hair is what I notice first outside the window as she exits the cab. The wind sweeps it up in a lover's grip and the sun catches the gold in her mane. She fucking shines. Brilliant and beautiful. And mine.

I run my tongue along my bottom lip and feel a smile ghosting up on one side. This woman revives dead parts of me. She makes me feel alive. Like smiles and excitement and the thrill of a chase. Her scent lingers on my lips, despite my brushing my teeth this morning, and I can't help the groan that escapes me as I watch her strut toward the building. My cock is rock hard as I imagine peeling off her leather coat and peeking at what she's hiding underneath. I'm already standing by the time she enters the restaurant. Her eyes light up when she sees me. I jerk my head to signal her in my direction.

"Fancy seeing you here," she says, her words breathless.

I inhale her floral scent. Just like I promised myself I would, I got a good whiff of her as she exited her bathroom earlier. Even from my shitty position on her awful carpet, I could smell her. Her perfumed scent killed the disgust of the floor and instead replaced it with...her. I hadn't wanted to leave her but my stomach—after not having eaten dinner in my quest for knowledge of her—had started to grumble. Loudly. I didn't want her to find me sprawled out under her bed with a ten-inch boner. Plus, I needed to shower and change clothes.

I stand to greet her as she approaches. "You look radiant," I tell her, my voice low and husky. Radiant doesn't even begin to describe how gorgeous she is.

Her brown eyes narrow at my choice of words as she sheds her coat. The moment she slips it from her shoulders, my cock hardens. Her nipples are erect underneath her sweater. I can see the faint pink outline of them beneath the soft cashmere.

"Jesus fucking Christ," I hiss as I yank her chair back. "Where's your damn bra?"

She chuckles and it has a musical quality. "I don't like wearing one with this dress. You can *see* it."

"I can *see* your tits, Violet," I seethe as I sit across from her. My gaze sweeps over the lingering late breakfast crowd, but thankfully nobody is paying either of us any mind. Her tits are safe from the leering eyes of the other patrons for now.

"Those are choice words coming from my boss. Hmmm," she bites out before sniffing the air. "Do I smell a sexual harassment suit?"

Rolling my eyes, I hand her the menu in hopes she'll cover her perfect tits from any onlookers. "If anyone is sexually harassing anyone, it's you harassing me. I came here for breakfast. The show was free."

Our eyes meet and hers flicker with challenge. The defiant look in them has my cock engorged with blood and the need to push inside her is all I can think about.

"What do you want, Mr. Maxwell?" she demands, her voice saccharine sweet.

I stretch my leg out under the table, settling it between hers once I've pushed her ankles apart with my foot. Her eyes widen but she doesn't try to move away. Just the thought of her thighs spread slightly open has my jaw clenching. I wonder if she's wearing panties. My mouth is about to blurt out some shit that isn't ready to come out. She's not ready for what I have to say. So instead, I stare at her. Blatantly. I eyefuck her because clearly that's what she wanted when she put that dress on. Her throat moves as she swallows and she shakily lifts the menu as if to hide those tits from me.

With my finger, I push the menu back down to the table and then sweep my gaze over her gorgeous mounds. I linger my stare before licking my lips and then give her a smug smile.

"W-What do you want?" she asks again, this time minus the hidden venom.

My eyes sear into hers. "Isn't it obvious what I want?"

"I've made my decision and will start at Slante Mortgages in less than two weeks," she mutters and picks up the water glass on her side of the table. She downs it in a few unladylike gulps. "I'm leaving your company."

As long as she doesn't leave *me*.

Once I have my sights set, I acquire my target.

Violet O. Simmons isn't going anywhere.

"Sean Slante is a sleaze ball," I grunt as I flick at the button on my sleeve of my dress shirt. Suddenly I'm fucking hot. And pissed. After I roll both sleeves up my forearms, I thread my fingers together over the table and look back up at her. Her brown eyes are staring at my arms. She swipes her pink tongue across her bottom lip before lifting her gaze.

"So are you," she challenges with a lifted brow.

I smirk. "I'm not the one forgetting to wear parts of my wardrobe to meet my boss. Perhaps you're the sleaze, Violet."

Anger surges through her and her nostrils flare. "Are you always such an asshole? I'm glad you ignored me until now to be quite honest."

Ignore isn't the right word. I simply didn't *see* her until yesterday. Now, she's *all* I see.

The server interrupts our tense moment to take our order. When she can't decide what to eat, I abruptly instruct the man to bring one of everything on the breakfast menu. Watching her neck heat to a perfect crimson color has another one of those rare grins tugging at my lips.

"So not only are you a sleazy asshole but you're also a chauvinist pig who orders for his date," she snaps. "Got it."

I lift a brow. "Date?"

This gets another blushing reaction from her. It also gets me a frustrated sigh. "You know what I mean."

"Actually, I don't. Do you want this to be a date? Because if it were a date, I'd find a way to get you out of that dress later," I tell her as I motion to her perfect tits on full display beneath the fabric.

She crosses her arms over her chest. "Not a date. And you will not be seeing what's under this dress."

Oh, but I already have, sweetheart.

I let her win for now and change the subject. "Where does all your money go?"

The smirk on her face is wiped right off. Fear flashes in her eyes briefly before she steels her gaze. "What are you talking about?"

"I looked up your address." And then I napped under your bed while you slept. "You live in the fucking ghetto."

Her lip curls up. "Did I seriously dress up on a Saturday morning for my soon-to-be ex-dickhead-boss to berate me about every single part of my life?"

"Just answer the question. The rent on those places is like two hundred bucks a month or some shit. Scum lives there. Not…" I wave at her as if to imply exactly what I mean. Diamonds like her don't belong in the rough. Diamonds like her need to be polished and cared for. Diamonds like her are meant to shine without fear of always getting dirty. "Not people like you."

She casts her gaze out the window. Her jaw flexes as she desperately clenches it closed as if to fight off emotion within her. A tear hastily snakes down her cheek but she discreetly wipes it away. With her eyes elsewhere, she responds, her voice ragged. "I like it there, okay? Can you drop it?"

No.

I can't drop it.

Not until I know why.

"Are you hiding from someone?" I demand.

She jerks her head to gape at me. "Why would you ask that?" Then, her nervous gaze flits across the restaurant. As if she's looking for the very person she's hiding from. I notice because it's in my nature to notice these things. That and because I now notice everything about her.

"That building accepts rent in cash only. Month-to-month lease. The superintendent is a scummy asshole who doesn't like to pay taxes. I know this because I called." Of course I called. I attempted to pull more information from him. According to the raspy voice over the phone, he didn't know shit about the snobby lady in three-twelve.

"You're a stalker," she huffs.

If she only knew.

Before I can reply, the server comes back with several loaded plates. They all won't fit on one table, so he drags another one over to us. For a good five minutes, Violet stabs at her food making sure to keep her mouth full, probably so that she doesn't have to talk. When she swallows, I speak again.

"Where is all your money going?"

She glares at me. "This is none of your business. Thanks for breakfast, but I need to go."

Earlier, I rifled through her desk at home while she slept. I'd flipped through her bank statements. Tracked where her money went. During each pay period, she pulls out over a grand in cash. Twelve hundred dollars of her hard-earned money every two weeks. I know at least a few hundred of it goes to the scuzzy building she rents from. The rest…I need to find out. My eyes narrow as she stands and yanks her coat from the chair. I know where she's going.

To the farmer's market near the office. Like clockwork. Her receipts show a purchase from there every Saturday.

"Violet." My voice is husky with regret. I don't mean to upset her, but she's a pretty puzzle I've just gotten my hands on. I want to put her together and see the picture she makes.

"Mr. Max—"

"Gray."

Her brown eyes harden as she shrugs her coat on. "Just let me be. Two weeks and I'll be out of your hair. I'd appreciate it if things went back to normal. Back when you didn't even know my name."

Guilt surges through me. For as long as I can remember, I've been this way. I'm not like most men. I don't do relationships. I don't mingle and try to get along with people. Everything I do has purpose. Everything has reason. All of the other bullshit along the way is just complicated and messy. Highly unnecessary.

But Violet?

She's necessary. For what? I'm not sure. All I know is that I need to know every detail about her. If I don't unravel all of the parts of her, I'll go fucking crazy. Usually, when I get hyper-focused, it's on a project. A deal. An assignment. I analyze data and zero in on my target. I make shit happen. My focus has only ever been on a woman once before. And that was Adara. When I made it my mission to know her so that I could complete one of the most difficult assignments I'd faced in my life. I picked her apart. Studied her. Then I used her.

But she wasn't supposed to die.

My thoughts are dark and raging by the time I realize

Violet is gone. I catch a glimpse of her shiny hair before she slips into her cab. An empty feeling settles in my gut. I feel an actual sense of loss without her shooting scathing glares at me.

I'll get her to warm up to me.

She'll see I only want what's best for her.

I wave at the server to bring the check and I pull out the extra key I swiped from one of her drawers. A key to her apartment. Today I'll have a copy made and then put this one back before she notices. Then, I'll be able to keep a close eye on her. My mind flits back to the way her naked body writhed with the need to orgasm when my phone buzzes.

Bull: You're too quiet. I don't like it. Thanks for standing me up last night.

I scrub at my face and let out a sigh.

Me: Remember Adara?

Bull: Is this a trick question? Of course I fucking remember Adara. She almost got your ass killed.

Me: I have to know her.

Bull: Violet is leaving in two weeks, man. You don't have to know her. Just forget about her.

Her sweet scent lingers in the air, and I'm already craving to see her again.

Me: That's impossible. You know this.

Bull: Not saying I like it but I have your back. At least come to the house and have dinner with Sadie and I. Joshua misses his uncle.

He's trying to distract me. There's no point.

Me: Give the family my love. I'll see you Monday. I have some work to do.

Bull: Try not to get arrested.

At this, I smirk.

Me: Wouldn't be the first time you've had to bail me out.

I'm still smirking but it quickly turns into a scowl. Bull has always had to look after me in some way. The day when shit went south with those Saudi Arabians, he saved my life and pulled my unconscious body to safety. My thoughts drift into the darkness.

"Want to watch MTV?" the peppy nurse questions. "Music videos all the time. Can you believe it? The hospital finally got cable. I've never had cable before so the only time I get to watch is while I'm at work."

I drag my gaze from the book I'm reading to glare at her. "I'm reading. Go away."

She laughs at me and strolls into the room anyway. Last nurse that came in, I had her close the blinds. This fucking woman yanks on the cord to allow the sun to stream in. I squint against it and toss my book to the floor.

"Close the goddamned blinds," I snap.

Nurse Fucking Annoying ignores me and flips through her chart, humming some semi-familiar song I'm sure she heard on her beloved MTV. "Looks like it's time to change your dressings."

I wince because I fucking hate this. Not only is it painful as hell but it's also a stark reminder of everything that went wrong. "Fine. But don't be so damn eager."

"I do love to see a man howl in pain," she teases. "But I'll tamper it down just for you. Sound good, big boy?"

I flip her off and bury my face into the pillow. But when I close my eyes, I think of her. Adara. Her wide, innocent brown eyes. The way she stood at the exact moment I pulled that trigger. She was supposed to stay seated. Everything revolved around her remaining in her seat. The wound would have hurt, but she'd have lived. It was meant to be a simple graze—a distraction. If only she'd have stayed in her goddamned chair. That one small variable was the catalyst for everything that went wrong.

Nurse Fucking Annoying Giggling Sadist happily spends the next hour removing the soiled dressings on my back, buttocks, and legs. I black out a couple of times from the pain. When I come to, she ruffles my hair. "Need a little something for the pain, soldier?"

I grunt and soon something cold enters my vein. At least Nurse Fucking Annoying Giggling Sadist puts me out of my misery for a couple of hours. But despite my drug-induced haze, I can't ever seem to shake the image of those brown eyes, belonging to the teen I so brutally shot. It was an error. I don't make errors. But that day, I did.

I'll never make a mistake like that again.

SEVEN

Violet

Before heading to the farmer's market, I stop by my apartment and change into something more comfortable. I'm still shaking with fury. How dare he suddenly become so damn nosy about my life! I've worked hard to keep certain things to myself. And now, I feel like he's prying into something that needs to remain shut. If he pulls open the parts of my past I keep contained, I'll lose my mind.

I don't want to remember the years I spent with Vaughn.

I don't want to recall how he went from possessive boyfriend, to monster, to my worst nightmare. I don't want to think about the things he made me do. Things that still embarrass and horrify me. Things that would tear apart everything I've worked so hard to achieve if they ever got out.

Hot, furious tears are spilling from my eyes. I hastily swipe them away as I leave to do my weekly shopping. Gray, my stupid boss, has grabbed my now normal life and given it a hard shake. I don't like that he's rattled some memories inside me that I prefer to keep hidden.

In an effort to block his annoyingly handsome face

from my mind, I think about my new job. I'm eager to learn something different. On the way to the market, I pass by the post office where my PO box is located. I check it but don't find any correspondence. That both hurts me and relieves me. The last few cards I sent, I foolishly included my PO box address. I pull the sealed envelope that holds ten crisp one hundred dollar bills inside a funny card out of my purse and slip it into the outgoing box.

Just once I'd like to receive a letter back. To be acknowledged. But that would invite problems. Problems I don't need, no matter how much my heart aches.

The walk to the market is cold. I doubt we'll have snow, but it looks like a chilly rain is imminent. I'll need to hurry with my shopping today.

Normally, I spend several hours at the market as I take my time and enjoy the day. But today, I'm too wound up. My tension is like the cold wintery rain that will most likely hit before I make it back to my place. Whipping all around me and stressing me out. I grunt all the way back to my building with my haul.

It's times like these when I wish I had actual friends. People I could chat with and talk about my day. A girlfriend to groan to about my annoying boss, my terrible drunk night with my future boss, the fear my psycho ex will hunt me down, and all of the other awful things in my life.

Unfortunately, I don't.

The moment I feel the first drop of cold rain on my forehead, a shudder of defeat ripples through me. In this big bad world, I'm all alone. By nature, I'm not normally a crier. But today, I let it go. I sob as I run three long blocks through the soaking rain with my arms full of groceries.

My teeth are chattering by the time I reach my building. Out front sits a shiny white Range Rover that seems to sparkle in the pouring rain. I suddenly wish I owned a car. I suddenly wish I lived somewhere with a garage, reliable heating, and tenants who aren't drug dealers.

I stomp through the puddles and seek refuge in the dilapidated building. Gray was right. I live in the ghetto. This place is all I can afford by the time I send away most of my wages. It's sad. My entire life is just pathetic.

Eventually, I make it up to the third floor but I'm exhausted and soaked to the bone. So when I see a familiar face, I'm too tired to fight. In some stupid way, I feel a sense of relief.

"What are you doing here?" I mumble as I rummage through my purse for my keys.

Gray frowns at me. He's holding a folder tucked under one arm and a dripping umbrella in his other. The man still looks every bit as sexy as he did at breakfast. Too bad he's such an asshole. "Can we talk a minute?"

Letting out a sigh, I unlock my door and gesture for him to come in. My place instantly smells like him. Clean and masculine. A hint of cinnamon.

Once inside, I make a beeline for the kitchen to drop my bags. He follows me into the small space making it seem even smaller with his imposing presence.

"Let me unload those while you take a hot shower and change. You're turning purple, Violet." At his silly pun, he smiles. The man is ridiculously good looking and it makes me angry. I hate that I react so easily to him. My stupid heart patters away in my chest just from the way he looks at me. As if he'd like to lick away every droplet of the rain.

I suppress a whine because that sounds a lot better than I want it to.

"Thanks. I'll be back in ten minutes. Don't steal anything," I threaten.

He chuckles as he starts unloading the bag. "I wouldn't dare."

Eighteen minutes later, I'm dressed in a warm hoodie and a pair of yoga pants. My slippers cover my frozen toes and I've pulled my wet hair into a messy bun to keep it off my neck. When I enter the living room, Gray is sitting in the middle of the only piece of furniture I own as he sips on some coffee. He looks like he belongs here. Like this is his place. The thought irritates me.

"Make yourself at home, why don't you?" I grumble.

He winks at me and points to a steaming mug on the coffee table. Swallowing down my irritation, I sit down next to the big man with the intense gaze and take his peace offering. The coffee tastes good. I'd expected it to be the way he likes it. One cream. Two sugars. A bit of cinnamon. But it's the way I like it. Black with a hint of sugar.

"How did you know—"

He cuts me off. "I need your help."

My brows shoot up. "This is work related?"

His fingers run through his dark hair, messing up the gel, and a lock falls down over his eyebrow. It gives him a boyish quality, despite his age. I know he's at least fifteen years older than me. Vaughn was much older too. I shudder at that thought.

"I wanted you to take a look at this property. Tell me what you think," he says, his voice gruff as he scratches at his jawline. I'm mesmerized by the way his long finger absently scrapes along the hair that's just beginning to grow in there.

He hands me the file, and I blink away my daze. "This is the Collins property. I thought you already acquired it yesterday."

He nods but his brows pinch together. "I did. It's a resort a little up north. Do you think it was a good purchase?"

I feel like this is a trick question. Or maybe he's just toying with me. Either way, I don't like how he suddenly feels the need to include me in on business. Maybe it's about Mr. Collins. What if he's here to gripe at me for pushing the old man into selling?

"Sales price was fair for the market value," I say slowly as I scan the documents. "It's quite beautiful actually." I stare at the picture of the ocean view.

"Very beautiful," he agrees.

When I glance at him, his penetrating gaze is on me and not the picture. It sends a quiver of excitement rushing through me. I quickly scold myself internally and drag my eyes back to the file. "Everything looks fine to me. Looks to be a good investment."

He lets out a sigh that has me glancing at him again. "I agree. How did you learn all of this? You're working as my assistant and yet you know all of these things. I was searching for a document and the IT department granted me access into your computer. You have so many emails…"

Horror washes over me. And shame. As much as he pisses me off, I never intended for him to see my drafts in my inbox. Some of those emails I typed up were when I was angry. Not just at him but at the entire world. He always bore the brunt of my fury. Thankfully, I was smart enough to never send them. I never dreamed he'd ever read them.

"I'm sorry—" I start, my voice but a whisper. I wonder if he's come to tell me I can just quit without working my last two weeks. That stresses me out, considering I just mailed out my most recent paycheck—well most of it— back home. I'm sure Sean would let me start early, but I already feel humiliated by how I acted around him last night.

"Don't be. I know I'm difficult to understand and apparently difficult to work for." He turns his sharp gaze on mine. I see the way his eyes dart over my face, inspecting every feature closely as if I'm on display under a microscope. It unnerves me, yet I find my body heat rising from his close inspection. "Tell me how you know these things, Violet."

I stiffen my back and let out a small sigh. "I'm perceptive. One of those watch-and-learn personalities. Also, I research a lot of things. If I'm interested, I try to learn more about it. I even took some night classes. Most of them were business related. Some touched on the economy and investments. I can't really say I learned it all from one place. It was more or less a culmination of many things." His eyes are on my mouth as I speak. I like how focused on me he is but at the same time, I'm disgusted.

Vaughn kept a close eye on me and I hated it.

I sip my coffee, directing my attention to the window. The rain pours outside. I should send Gray out in it and hope he gets drenched for being such a prick earlier. As if in tune with my thoughts, he speaks.

"I'm sorry about breakfast. I didn't mean to pry…"

"But?" There's always a but.

He scrubs his face and regards me with a vulnerability

I've yet to see from the powerful Grayson Maxwell. "But I'm just so curious about you right now."

His honest answer has me regarding him with gentler eyes. I know I can be a cold, hard bitch sometimes. Maybe part of the reason I don't have any friends is because I refuse to let anyone in. My walls are always erect and impenetrable.

"I just don't like talking about my past or my reason for doing things," I admit as I set my mug down.

He mimics my actions and gives me a crooked grin that sends a swarm of butterflies fluttering around in my stomach. "Can we start over? Can we be friends?"

With him sitting in my living room, looking like he belongs, and turning on the charm, I feel some of my inner ice thawing. "I'll only be around for two more weeks, Gray. Maybe being friends isn't such a good idea. I'll be gone before you know it, no longer in your hair."

His eyes darken and I notice a tick in his jaw. "There usually isn't a timeline on friendship. Maybe I still want to be your friend, even after you leave."

I chew on my bottom lip for a minute contemplating his motives. There really is no hidden reason why he would want to be friends. I mean, maybe his definition of friendship leans toward the fuck buddies territory, but I can thwart his advances. He knows I'm leaving and hasn't necessarily tried to prevent me from doing so.

"Please." His word isn't a plea but more of an olive branch.

"I'm afraid I would be a terrible friend," I admit with an embarrassed smile. "I don't have any because I never really wanted any."

He regards me, his eyes doing that strange thing he does now—ever since he seemed to snap out of Mad Max mode yesterday—where they skim over every part of my face as if he's trying to memorize each freckle on my flesh. "I'm the worst friend you'll ever know. Just ask Bull." He winces at the name, which only makes me want to know why.

"Who's Bull?"

"Jeff."

I crack a smile at the sheepish way Gray is behaving. Normally, I see the powerful, arrogant, one-track minded madman who runs the company I work for. I've never seen other sides of him. Bashful and vulnerable. Playful and grinning.

"What exactly do friends do?" I question, changing the subject. "We're not sleeping together."

A beautiful smile curves his lips and his entire handsome face lights up like never before. Just one look at him like this has me chiding myself. *Don't lie to the sex god, honey. We both know you're eventually going to let that man into your bed.*

His eyes narrow as they drop to my throat. The heat is painted on my skin—I can feel it. I clear my throat and tap the paper to distract him. "Have you been to the resort?"

"Once before. The moment I settled into my suite with a glass of brandy and sat in the armchair that overlooked the chilly Atlantic, I knew I wanted it for myself." His hand covers mine as he draws it away from the picture. He's looking down at the stunning boutique resort, but I'm focused on the way his large hand lingers on mine. I swear my heart is thudding so loudly he can most certainly hear it.

"Do you just take everything you want?" My words are meant to tease but they come out in an accusatory tone.

He leans into me as his hand squeezes mine. Warm lips brush against the shell of my ear, and hot breath tickles me when he speaks. "Always. When I want something, I do whatever it takes to get it."

We're not talking acquisitions anymore.

Or maybe we are.

"And what happens when you finally get it?" I can't help but poke him a little more.

He lets out a heavy exhalation that sends shivers of need coursing through me. If he asked me to get naked for him right now, I probably would.

"I don't let it go," he says finally. He pulls away and takes the folder from me. I'm frozen in place, assuming he's about to scoop my melted body up and take me into my room where he'll spend hours ravishing me. I'm disappointed when he stands and clears his throat. My eyes drift to the large erection bulging in his slacks.

"Are we done here?" I murmur before reluctantly pulling my gaze from his dick to meet his hardened glare.

He runs those long fingers again through his now messy hair. I could think of a good use for those fingers…

"For now. I'll pick you up at seven for dinner." He doesn't wait for a response before he stalks toward the door. "Take a nap until then. You look exhausted."

I rise on shaky legs and follow after him. "Dinner? I thought we were just friends."

"Friends don't eat dinner together?" he implores with an impish grin.

I roll my eyes at him but I'm smiling too. "Last meal we

had together went badly. You were an ass."

His smile falls and a fierce stare finds me. His hand raises to cup my cheek. "I'm sorry. I was out of line. It won't happen again. You just…" He drops his hand and looks off behind me toward the windows. "You just looked too damn pretty to be prancing around without a bra on for all those perverts to see." His eyes snap to mine and fire flares in them. I'm definitely melting again under his glare.

"Oh."

"Wear something casual. Jeans or something," he says.

"And a bra?" I taunt, my lips turning up to give him a wicked grin.

His laugh is charming and it shaves years off his age. "Clothing is always optional when you're around me. I may have to beat some motherfuckers down for looking but I'm not opposed to the idea, little quitter."

He's already turning on his heel and pulling the door open.

"Bye, Gray." Hours ago I hated the very ground he walked on, and now, I don't want him to leave.

"Bye, Violet."

EIGHT

Grayson

The day started out shitty but having Violet bend to my requests earlier certainly made it better. I'd also successfully managed to return her key while she showered. She's already softening toward me. Soon, she'll soften beneath me as she takes every inch of my hardness. I can imagine her pouty lips begging. *Please fuck me, Gray. Oh God...*

My eyes slam shut as my release spurts out in the shower against the slate-tiled wall. There was no way I'd be able to walk around with my cock at half-mast through dinner. I don't like how my body responds as though I'm fifteen again and getting my dick wet for the first time. And yet, this is the most exhilarated I've felt in two decades.

I quickly dress, attempting to keep it casual. Dark jeans and a pale grey cashmere sweater. I'd told her to wear jeans but I'd love to see her in a dress. To slide my rough palm up her smooth, bare silky thigh and—

"Gray!"

I'm jolted from the hot-as-hell vision by the soft

feminine voice on the other side of my bedroom door. Guilt sluices through me. I've been hiding from one of the few people in my life who matters anymore. Lying to her. Telling her I've been inundated with work.

Sauntering over to the door, I do my best to plaster on an easy smile. When I open it, I find the other part of my heart staring up at me with curious blue eyes. Kind, sweet, innocent. I'm everything to her.

"Gwen."

The little sprite of a woman launches herself into my arms. She's much shorter than me and only comes up to the top of my chest. Her wild chestnut hair has been somewhat tamed into a bun. Paint speckles her hair, and when she looks up at me, I see it's on her freckled nose as well. "Work must have been a doozy. You never came home last night." There's a hint of accusation in her voice. Once again, the guilt floods through me.

I pet her hair and shrug my shoulders. "Just unexpected was all. How did you fare last night?"

She tugs away and plops down on the bed with a sigh. "It was lonely without you. I had to eat dinner alone. You know," she grumbles. "A phone call would have been nice."

I keep my expression impassive. It's hard to call when you're hiding under a woman's bed. "I lost track of time." Mostly the truth.

Her eyes narrow as she searches for answers. We've been this way for as long as I remember. Me, dutifully caring for her but never letting her see past my own barriers. I'm the man of this house and I intend on keeping my weaknesses shielded from her. Always.

"I thought maybe we could have dinner tonight and

you know…" she trails off, her cheeks turning rosy. I know what she wants, but she won't ask for it. She wants me to go *there* with her. I suppress the shudder that threatens to overcome me. Until she asks, I won't offer. I don't miss the love flashing in her eyes, pleading for me to give it to her.

I cringe at the very thought.

Absolutely disgusted.

"I actually have plans," I lie. "Work stuff."

When her bottom lip wobbles, I weaken. "What sort of stuff?" she questions, a slight pout in her voice that I've never been able to resist. "Maybe I could tag along."

My chest tightens at the thought of Gwen and Violet in the same room. It's too much. Too emotionally crippling. I scrub my face with my palm. "Another time." My voice is gruff.

"You're hiding something from me," she declares as she rises from the bed. She stalks over to her favorite place to annoy me and plops down. Her legs are crossed as she attempts to decode the numbers of the lock that's attached to the cedar chest. "Who is she?" she demands with her back to me.

"Enough of this, Gwen," I seethe as I pace at the end of the bed. "We'll spend the day together tomorrow. Just give it a rest."

She gives up on the lock, like always, and stands. "I have a part of you inside of me. You seem to forget. It links us, Gray. Some weird kind of sixth sense. I feel it. Something is wrong. You're hiding something from me. You promised you'd never do this to me."

We glare at each other for a long couple of minutes before I relent. "Fine. Meet me at Bull and Sadie's. Joshua hasn't seen you in ages. He's into *Paw Patrol* now so make sure you've googled the lingo because he's going to talk your fucking ear off."

She squeals before launching herself into my arms. I hug her to me and inhale her comforting scent. "Thank you. I was going crazy cooped up in this house."

"Always so dramatic," I tease before ruffling her hair. "Make sure you wash this mess before tonight. We'll have one of my employees dining with us as well. Don't overshare."

She snorts and bounds away from me. "Who me? Overshare? I would never."

"I mean it," I call out to her even after a door slams shut behind her.

Her voice is muffled. "No, you don't."

A tiny smile plays on my lips.

No, I really don't.

Gwen's stories are sometimes the only breath of fresh air I get in an otherwise suffocating world. I just hope things don't go too haywire with Violet. That woman is the exact opposite of Gwen. If you look at them side by side, you'd deem them as opposite as two women can be.

And yet…

Some part of me hopes that they'll like each other.

On the way to Bull and Sadie's, Violet and I chatted about safe topics. Turns out she likes to read but her Kindle's broken and she never thinks to go to the library until she's in bed wanting to read. She loves breakfast food and sometimes makes it for dinner. And she can sing. In Latin of all languages. Her choir teacher in high school had a thing for Latin songs. I'd pressed her to sing me one but she'd just laughed and waved me off. The drive was light and fun.

I haven't been this relaxed in ages.

And her scent filling my car had me wanting to reach across the console to thread my fingers in her hair so I could taste her pretty mouth too.

Like a gentleman, I refrained from mauling her in my car. Instead, I stole glances. Tonight, she's wearing jeans, like I'd requested, paired with some knee-high boots. Her sweater is fitted but she is clearly wearing a bra underneath. I am both annoyed and thankful for that. I'm dying to peel away her clothes and sink my cock into her hot body but I know women like Violet are worth the wait. When I finally do get my opportunity, it will be that much sweeter.

"We're here," I tell her as I pull into the driveway beside Gwen's Camaro. That shiny red sports car was my present to her for her thirtieth birthday.

I climb out of the Range Rover and make it over to Violet's side just as she's opening the door. Our eyes meet as I hold it open for her and offer my hand.

"So you *can* be a gentleman," she teases. Even though she's smiling, I don't miss the nervousness that's rippling from her. Her brown eyes dart down the street—both ways—before returning to mine. One day I'll find out who she's looking for. And if the fucker has hurt her in any way, I'll harm him too.

Once I close the door, I don't let go of her hand until we reach the door. I'm not about to advertise my interest in Violet in front of Gwen. Not even going to go there tonight. I knock on the door and soon Sadie answers.

"Well, if it isn't my favorite guy," she gushes as she steals a hug. "But don't tell Jeff. You know he gets jealous."

We both chuckle.

"Sadie," I introduce with a wave of my hand. "This is my…" I trail off. I don't want to introduce her as my girl, even though she is and just doesn't know it yet. But "assistant" feels cold. We're friends I suppose but I don't like that one either. In the end, I choose the safest option. "She's my Violet."

Sadie's eyebrows raise. "Your Violet, huh?"

"Violet Simmons," Violet rushes out and extends her hand. "I'm Gray's assistant at the office."

Sadie lets out a laugh. "Okay, that makes more sense. I thought I recognized you. I meet Jeff from time to time for lunch. You might remember my son bouncing through there, terrorizing everything and everyone in sight."

Violet smiles politely at her, but I can tell she feels uncomfortable. "I believe I've seen you a time or two."

"I'm hungry. What're we having?" I question as we follow her inside. The Brownstone they live in is decorated well. Sadie does interior design. She's the one who came through and turned my masculine home into something more livable. Gwen certainly doesn't have the touch—not like Sadie.

"Jeff marinated some steaks. Everything's just about ready. We were just waiting for you to get here before we threw them on the grill," Sadie chirps as we make our way toward the kitchen.

Joshua, their rambunctious six-year-old, is sitting on the bar playing on his iPad. But when he sees me, he screeches before launching himself off the counter like a spider monkey. I catch him with a grunt as the growing boy nearly tackles me. "Uncle Hawk!"

Violet's gaze narrows at me as she eases to the side of the kitchen.

"What have you been up to, buddy?" I question as I set him to his feet.

He starts telling me about *Minecraft*, droning on about creepers and some guy named Steve. I have no idea what he's going on about so I just nod and smile. Eventually he grows bored. "Where's Aunt Gwen? She promised to play with me."

Sadie answers for me. "Aunt Gwen is out back with Daddy. Tell them Uncle Hawk is here." Sadie turns to me as she grabs the plate with steaks. "I'm going to run these out. I'll be right back. Help yourself to some wine."

She knows I don't drink often for my own personal health reasons but always offers anyway. I do, however, pour a glass for Violet, who has gone tense with nerves.

"Relax," I tell her as I hand the wine to her.

Her brown eyes are cold as she stares back at me. "What sort of game are you playing, Gray?"

Frowning, I push the glass into her palm. "What do you mean?"

She gulps down the red liquid and sets the glass down rather roughly so that it makes a clang. "This"—she gestures around us—"bringing me here. I thought…" Heat creeps up her neck and she shakes her head. "Never mind."

"We're friends, Violet. That's what you wanted, right?"

She glares at me. "That's what *you* wanted. But yes. That's *all* we are."

When voices resound in the other room, Violet once

again stiffens. A moment later, two familiar arms hug me from behind. "There you are. Late as always," Gwen says with a laugh. Violet's eyes are on mine, and I sense that she's hurt. It makes my chest squeeze.

"Hi," Gwen greets, peeking around me to offer her hand. "I'm Gwen Maxwell. You must be the work associate he was telling me about."

Violet blinks several times before reaching for the wine. I watch her with a lifted brow as she fills it to the brim, ignoring Gwen's outstretched hand. Instead, she waves and gulps half the glass down.

Gwen drops her hand and looks up at me with a frown. Her feelings are hurt and her brilliant blue eyes shimmer with unshed tears. Before I can do damage control, Bull comes up beside Violet and tugs at her hair before leaning in to whisper loudly. "Just because your boss is an asshole doesn't mean we are. You can't help who you love. Ain't that right, Gwen?" He flashes her a silly smile before regarding Violet. "But we're not like him." He points at me, and I flip him off. "We're a nice lot once you get to know us."

Violet seems to relax toward Bull but won't meet my gaze. She's a tough nut to crack. But I will crack her. I'll get inside of her in every way that I can, and she'll never be able to get me out.

NINE

Violet

Gwen Maxwell.

I can't believe the nerve of that prick.

Parading his would-be mistress around in front of his wife.

The pain searing through me is similar to the first time Vaughn informed me he was going to share what I thought was sacred between us with another man. I was devastated. Furious even. But when I balked at his request, I'd learned who the strong one was in our relationship. Vaughn brought me to my knees that night with the back of his hand. And through my tears and not-so-silent begging, I'd pleaded for Vaughn to wake up and see what he was doing to me. To us. In one single night, he tore the hard-earned love from my heart and replaced it with something dark and sick.

"You're a quiet one," Sadie, the attractive blonde woman, murmurs as she grabs my now empty dinner plate. "Want to help me in the kitchen?"

I'm eager to escape the dining room where their child

babbles about cartoons I know nothing about, and Gray's wife stares at me as if I'm something rotten. She'd been all smiles until I couldn't bring myself to shake her hand. How does one shake the hand of another woman when moments before she was lusting after her husband?

Bile creeps up my throat, and I wish I had more wine to wash it down with. Thankfully, once in the kitchen, Sadie seems to sense my stress levels. She pulls a bottle of rum from the cabinet and pours some into a coffee mug. Then, she starts the Keurig. Hot coffee pours into the mug along with the liquor. We're quiet as it fills. Once it's done, she pushes it along the counter to me.

"You like Gray," she says softly.

Usually, I like a sprinkle of sugar in my coffee but tonight I'm after the numbing liquid that will have to suffice as a substitute. "He's my boss," I murmur as politely as I can manage despite the fury raging inside of me. And I don't like him. Not at all. Especially now.

"He doesn't bring women around. Ever. So you must be special," she tells me and offers me a small smile.

I clench my jaw and try desperately not to say anything I'll regret tomorrow. "I don't feel very special. I feel horrible and embarrassed. Poor Gwen." Even though Gwen seems to hate me, I can't help but feel remorse for her. Her husband is a cheating asshole. There was heat and desire in his eyes. The man wanted to nail me, and had I let him, he would have.

"Oh, so you know?" she questions, her brows bunching together. "Don't you feel sorry for her?"

"Well, if I had to live with Gray, I'd feel sorry for me too," I hiss at the seemingly nice woman. My anger is misplaced. I want to grab him by his stupid collar and shake him for leading me on.

"He's not so bad," Sadie teases. "Even if he is a bit of a neat freak. I think that's what bothers Gwen the most."

I gape at her as if she's lost her mind. Neatness is Gwen's problem with her husband? What about his eager dick? The damn thing was hard for me.

"You girls having fun without me?" Gwen questions in a cool tone behind us. We both jerk around to stare at the small woman. Sadie glances at me and guilt shines in her eyes.

"I'm not feeling so well," I tell them both as I abandon the steaming mug of hot spiked coffee. "I think I'll catch a cab home."

Gwen narrows her eyes at me. "I could have sworn you rode in with Gray. Is he not taking you home?"

Swallowing, I shake my head. "Nope."

At this, she scowls. "Well then I'm taking you home."

Before I can argue, she stomps into the dining room and announces it to the two men. I can hear her and Grayson arguing in hissed tones. Sadie simply offers me a sympathetic smile.

"I'm sorry you're not feeling well," Sadie says and pats my hand. "Please come over again."

I nod that I will as I snag my coat from the hook. The voices in the dining room grow louder, and I slip out the front door to escape them. Moments later, Gwen comes clomping down the steps and hits the fob, making the lights on a red Camaro light up. When I steal a look at the house, Gray stands in the doorway with his arms crossed over his massive chest. He's pissed yet he has no right to be. If it weren't for not wanting to cause a scene, I'd run right over there and give him a piece of my mind.

Gwen and I don't speak aside from me pointing her in the direction of my building. When she pulls up in front of it not twenty minutes later, she turns off her car. I reach for the door handle but she touches my arm to stop me. Turning, I meet her gaze and fear for a moment that she'll slap me for something I didn't do.

"I'm sorry," she says and bites on her bottom lip. The move makes her seem young, childlike almost.

"About what?"

"About getting off on the wrong foot. I was being grumpy and that wasn't fair. He sort of blindsided me by inviting you. Work associate my ass," she grumbles but waves me off when I start to speak. "Clearly, I love him. I just want him to be happy. I wish he would have told me about you—that he was dating you—"

"We're not dating," I argue.

"Fucking. Whatever. What I'm saying is—"

"We're not fucking!" I screech, horrified to even be having this conversation.

She laughs and that confuses me. "Down girl. All I'm saying is that if he likes you, then I want him to do what makes him happy."

I gape at her, my mind attempting to process her words before I snap out of it.

"Whatever kind of sick relationship you two have is your business. In two weeks, I'll be out of your lives. I'm sorry I almost got involved in the middle of your…your… your whatever it is. Goodbye, Gwen," I blurt before stepping out of the car and bolting to the building.

The car door slams and she shouts after me. "Violet! Wait!"

Ignoring the crazy woman, I rush into my building. I catch sight of a man leering from the shadows and I stop dead in my tracks.

Vaughn?

Panic slices through me, and I let out a garbled sob as I inch backward toward the door. I nearly knock down Gwen in the process.

"Stay away from me!" I screech at the man hiding in the shadows.

When he emerges, I flinch and cover my face with my hands. *No! No! No!* Gwen makes what sounds like a battle cry. Then, some man starts yelling. "My eyes! You bitch!"

I jerk my gaze to see that now the man has fully come out of the shadows. It's not Vaughn. Just one of the usual lecherous men who hang around these parts. She grabs my elbow and ushers me into the stairwell. Once the door closes behind us, she urges me up the steps quickly.

"What just happened?" she demands when we get to the first landing.

"Third floor," I croak and point up. "I thought he was...I thought he was someone else."

"Grayson?"

I blink at her in confusion. "No." It won't hurt to tell her. "I thought it was my ex. His name is Vaughn."

Understanding flashes in her bright blue eyes as she helps me to the third floor. My knees are wobbling, and I'm shaken up badly. She tugs my jangling keys from my grip when I can't seem to fit the key into the slot. Once we step inside, I hastily snap all of the bolt locks in place. Her wide blue eyes are staring at me as if I'm an injured animal that might bite the person trying to help them.

"Is this Vaughn character stalking you?" she questions, concern painting her pretty features. I want to hate her, but right now she's the only person I've got.

"No. I just…" I trail off and a shudder ripples through me. "I thought he might have found me, and it's been stressing me out. I'm sure it's all in my head. He can't know where I am. I've made sure."

Her eyes flit around the dumpy apartment as she comprehends my meaning. "Can I make you something to drink?"

Tears well in my eyes as I regard her. Hours ago her husband was on my couch making himself at home. Now, she's in here, offering to serve me as if I'm her guest and not the other way around.

"Vodka. Freezer," I clip out.

She nods and disappears into the kitchen while I plop down on my sofa. The afghan on the back was one my therapist made for me. I jerk it around me and attempt to warm up. I'm shaking from the inside out. When she returns, she has two glasses filled with what looks like ice water. I know better. I can smell that gasoline from a mile away.

"Thirsty?" Her eyes flicker with a slight wickedness as she hands me my glass.

I sip my vodka on the rocks and make a face. But the fire running down my throat instantly warms me. "I'm sorry about all of this." I wonder if she can smell her husband's scent lingering in my apartment. I can and I'm annoyed that I still like the smell.

"So you're having a bad day," she says with a laugh and plops down beside me like we're best friends. "I have them often." Her eyes darken and she looks away from me. Guilt surges through me. I wonder how many other women Gray has been with while married to this woman. There's nothing wrong with her. She's beautiful and feisty. Why would he step out on her?

"Why do you stay with him?" I ask, my throat suddenly choking up.

Confusion swims in her eyes. "With Grayson?"

I nod and her gaze softens.

"Because I love him," she says as if that's enough reason. "And because I don't cope well on my own."

"Cope?"

"When I was a kid, I suffered from kidney issues. My left kidney was dying and trying to poison me in the process." We both eye the alcohol in her hand and she sets it down on the table. "I'm not supposed to drink that." She laughs and tears shine in her eyes. "There are a lot of things I'm not supposed to do now. But I wouldn't be here if it weren't for Gray." Pure love is reflected in her gaze.

"That's why you put up with his…" I can't even say the word.

"Shenanigans?" Another laugh from her.

I chug the vodka while she composes herself.

"Slow down there, killer, or I'll be cleaning up vomit. My brother would have a fit if I got his girlfriend shitfaced." She snorts and steals the glass from me. The room spins as I gape at her.

"Wait. What?"

Her lips quirk up on one side and she reminds me of a

certain crazy man who's recently decided to disrupt my entire life. "Grayson's my older brother. I was the 'oops' baby my parents had fifteen years later."

I'm so stunned, I have no words to say.

Brother.

Brother.

I've made a fool out of myself because I thought Gwen was his wife.

"Oh my God…" I groan and clutch my stomach that truly is roiling. "But you were so mad at me."

"You were eyeing me like I was a venomous snake!" she argues with a giggle and swats my thigh. Warmth shoots through me. My friend Lisa from high school used to be that way. A knee slapper is what we called her.

"Because I thought Gray brought me on a date to meet his wife!"

This sends her into a fit of laughter that has her doubled over. Once I make sense of the stupidity of it all, I start laughing too. Then we're both trying to talk with tears streaming down our cheeks.

"You h-h-had the bitch look!"

"You were s-so p-pretty and I thought you were his wife!"

"I thought my brother found himself a mega bitch!"

"I thought I was going to have to castrate him in front of his wife!"

We're both laughing so hard when someone pounds on the door. We ignore it at first, but when the pounding gets louder, we both fall silent.

"You stay there," she instructs as she fumbles for her keys. She holds up a can of mace that's on her key ring as she starts toward the door. Must have been what she got that creepy dude downstairs with. Suddenly, I want to hug this girl and never let her go.

When she stands on her toes and peeks out the peep-hole on the door, she lets out a snort. "Oh, God. Do you want to talk to him?"

"Why are you here, Gwen?" he growls from the other side.

She looks at me and rolls her eyes. "Consoling your girlfriend. You hurt her feelings."

"I'm not his girlfriend," I hiss but she just winks at me.

"I don't know what the hell happened," he roars from the other side. "One minute everyone is hunky-fuck-ing-dory and the next my baby sister runs off with my…" Silence falls, and Gwen and I seem to be holding our breath.

"Violet," he finally says with a huff.

"Your Violet?" Gwen challenges with an arched brow my way.

I shake my head at her. "I'm not his." But warmth spreads throughout my body by that notion.

"Let me in so I can make sure she's okay," he pleads.

Something in the vulnerable way he says it has me chewing on my lip and nodding. As soon as she unlocks the last bolt, he pushes through the door past her and drops to the sofa beside me. His icy blue eyes seem to swirl with hurt and concern. It causes my heart to flutter. Stupid heart. His warm hand envelops mine and he squeezes.

"Everything okay?" His voice is husky and raw.

"Yeah."

"What happened?"

Gwen tosses her keys back in her purse. "A miscommunication."

Gray frowns at me but doesn't press the issue any further. "Do you want me to stay with you?"

"I'll be fine. I've just had a long day. Truly. You two should go. I appreciate the…" I stall because I don't know what to call this intense pair.

"In the real world, they call it friendship. Glad we became friends," Gwen chirps, wearing the same shit-eating grin her brother wore earlier today when he made a declaration of friendship as well.

My eyes dart to Gray's, and he's smirking at me. "We'll leave but get yourself to bed early."

"So it's not just me he bosses around," Gwen says behind him.

He flips her off but his eyes never leave mine. I like the way they wash over me. Assessing my emotions. It's nice to be someone's focus.

"I'll call you and check up on you tomorrow," he says finally. I can hear the reluctance in his voice, but he stands anyway.

Gwen walks over to me and hugs me. "Talk soon, *friend*." Her smile widens. "I'll get your digits from my brother."

Grayson ruffles her hair and then proceeds to poke at her until she makes her way to the door. Now that I'm not freaking out over her being his wife, they're actually a cute pair of siblings.

"She's a stalker," he mouths to me. "You're going to have to block her."

She punches him in the arm but wears a smile that she

regards me with. "Don't forget to lock up, Vi."

I give them a wave and follow them to the door. Grayson gives me a long penetrating stare before mouthing the word "bye" and stalking after his sister.

Two friends in one day.

It only took seven years to make all two of them.

TEN

Grayson

Sleep is for pussies. At least that's what I tell myself on night two of no shuteye. After I made sure Gwen made it home safely and we watched a movie together, I slipped out of the house to go see Violet again. When I left her earlier this evening, she was shaken up and slightly drunk. It took everything in me to leave, but the only reason I left was because I knew it would only be a matter of hours before I came back.

Click.

I twist the knob and push the door inward after disengaging all three locks. The apartment is dark and quiet. Slipping inside, I make sure to close the door as silently as possible. For a moment, I remain still with my back pressed against the door. I'm patient. I count the seconds. Then the minutes. And eventually, it rolls into an hour before I feel comfortable to proceed. I slip out of my shoes and pad through the house. Last night and earlier today, I learned so much about her. Tonight, I intend on finding more out. If I don't find anything, it will be worth just seeing her sleep again.

Her bedroom door is ajar, and the room is dark. I want to turn on a light to look at her, but from the sounds of her soft breathing, I don't think she's in a heavy sleep like the night before. With slow and silent movements, I tug at the curtain until moonlight shines down upon her bed from the window. I'm disappointed to see that she's sleeping in a T-shirt rather than in the nude like last time.

I'll have to fix that.

Prowling through the room, I make my way over to her bedside. She looks angelic in the moonlight as she sleeps. So delicate and perfect. Fragile like a porcelain doll. The thought of anyone breaking her has fury bubbling up inside me. Earlier, when I'd probed Gwen about what they'd talked about, she'd kept her lips zipped. Despite my annoyance over being left out of the loop, I couldn't help but feel a sense of pride that my Violet was able to pull forth a sense of comradery from Gwen. My sister doesn't have friends. Her issues make it difficult for her to make or keep them. Boyfriends are non-existent. My sister is unable to take care of herself, much less others, which is why she relies so heavily on me. The fact that she seemed to have this desire to look out for Violet—even so much as protecting a secret—was huge for Gwen.

Maybe Violet's neatness would rub off on Gwen.

The very thought of Violet wading through Gwen's mess has me suppressing a shudder. Gwen is too much like Mother. She teeters on that edge between sane and lost. It terrifies me. I attempt to tether her to me so if she falls, I can reel her back in. From time to time, I do just that. But what worries me the most is that our connection won't be strong enough. That one day she'll fall and it will simply snap. My sister will be just as gone as our mother.

I sit down on the edge of the bed and brush Violet's hair from her brow so I can see her eyes. They're closed and her mouth is parted. She sleeps soundly. With a smile, I peel away the blankets and regard her perfect form. Who needs sleep when you get to spend the night staring at this vision? I begin a slow, subtle pulling of her T-shirt. Tiny movements that won't be felt as she slumbers. Carefully, I bring her arms through the holes of her shirt and then eventually remove the shirt altogether. Her tits are absolutely divine in the moonlight. With a sigh, I carry her shirt over to the hamper and dump it inside. Then, I make my way back over to her. Pale pink panties are the only thing she wears now. I want those gone too.

My fingers tug at the fabric and I'm able to gently slide the soft material down her thighs. Once I get them past her knees, she makes a soft sigh. I pause in my efforts as my heart jackknifes in my chest. If she found me like this, undressing her, things could turn bad very quickly. Her breath evens out, though, and I set to sliding her panties off the rest of the way. Instead of relinquishing the lingerie, I keep it as a token. I inhale the fabric, my mouth watering at her unique scent before I shove them into my pocket.

My cock is hard in my pants, but I ignore it as I settle for digging more into her life. I snag her phone from the charger and take it with me into the kitchen. In the dark, I rummage around until I find a bowl of fruit on the counter. I settle at a bar stool and begin peeling the orange as I flip through her phone. She has no pictures saved, which I find strange. But when I hunt through the deleted folder, I find a few selfies she took. So beautiful when she smiles. I also find some screenshots of the ocean. There's even a screenshot of a woman's Facebook page and I connect this woman as her mother. From her phone, I text all of the pictures to my phone. Of course my phone doesn't buzz from my pocket because I turned it off before my little recon mission. I delete the trace of my sending them to me from her phone.

Once I finish peeling my orange, I eat the wedges unrushed as I snoop through her phone.

Her texts are basic. I'm in her contacts along with my office number. She also has that fucker Sean Slante on there. I'm not sure where all of her friends are but they're not here on her phone. Popping up her messages with Sean, I read through everything they've chatted about. Apparently he's very apologetic about last night. The motherfucker should be. He took advantage of her. She eventually responded back to him in a very polite manner, saying she'd talk to him later. He'd responded back with some other flirty bullshit. And my girl never replied. I smile and it doesn't feel as foreign as usual.

From her phone, I decide to take matters into my own hands and pretend to be her.

Violet: What you did was sleazy.

It satisfies me knowing he'll read that and shit his panties. It's late but apparently, the fuck is awake because he replies.

Sean: Are you drunk again?

His tone boils my blood. It's as if he assumes she gets wasted all the time. I don't know Violet well but I am perceptive enough to realize she doesn't do this often. Her life is too orderly to get out of control on a frequent basis.

Violet: I'm clear headed. How do I know that when working for you, this kind of thing won't be a regular occurrence? I was blacked out, and had that nice man not saved me, you'd have probably fucked me in that cab.

His response is immediate.

Sean: Whoa. Calm down, Letty. We both got a little wasted but the last thing I would ever want is for you to think I would take advantage of you. I'm not like those guys at Maxwell. You know this.

I stiffen and glare at the glowing screen as I shove the last orange wedge in my mouth.

Violet: What do you mean?

While he types, I scoop up all of the orange peelings and hide them at the bottom of the garbage can.

Sean: You mentioned last night how they touch you against your wishes. I may have drunk a lot but I didn't forget what you said. And last night, you wanted me to touch you. It was extremely unprofessional and I'm sorry. I don't want us to get off on the wrong foot.

My blood boils and I nearly crack the screen in my brutal death grip. Who the fuck has been touching her against her wishes at Maxwell? I'm raging with fury but I attempt to quell it. I'll get to the bottom of this on Monday. Whoever thinks they can fuck with my girl is going to pay.

Violet: Please keep things professional from here on out.

Sean: Of course. I'm sorry.

Once I'm certain he isn't going to respond anymore, I delete all of tonight's correspondence before pocketing her phone. I give my hands a quick rinse in the sink and then

I'm back to check on her. She's still sleeping soundly, but this time naked like she belongs. My cock aches for her. In the moonlight, her perfect round tits are on display. I want to mark her up and stain her with all that is me. Those sorts of thoughts don't help my dick.

Before Violet, whenever I'd feel the need to fuck, I'd give my friend Elisha a call. She'd come over and let me use her however I needed to. Then, she'd leave, her purse a little heavier than it was when she showed up.

But now…

The thought of being inside any woman who isn't Violet is repulsive. Violet is mine and she will continue to be mine. I'll make her mine in every way that I possibly can. There's no way I'll be able to peacefully sleep with my cock throbbing so painfully. I carefully undo my belt and pants before sliding them to my ankles. With my foot, I kick them under the bed. I peel away my sweater and have it join my pants as well. Once I'm standing beside her in nothing but my boxers and socks, I stroke myself through my underwear.

God, I fucking want her.

I push my boxers down my thighs so that my heavy erection bobs out. When I take it in my grip, it's hot and pulsating. I'm dying to push into every single one of her holes. To draw out pleasure and pain from her. I want to own every part of her.

Fisting my cock feverishly, I attempt to keep my grunts stifled. With each tug, I get closer and closer to release. Desire for her alights every nerve ending from my skull to my toes. I push the sheet away from her so I can see all of her creamy flesh. Her sweet cunt looks good enough to eat.

The thought sends me over the edge, and I spurt my heat all over her lower stomach. I groan as the last of my orgasm drips from the tip of my cock onto the edge of the bed. With a sated smile, I run my fingertips through my release on her body. I drag my seed along her taut stomach to the curves of her breasts. I smear it all over her nipples and my dick jolts with excitement when they harden in response. With my wet fingers, I give in to the urge to touch her cunt. I'm satisfied when a small moan escapes her the moment my cum-covered finger slides along her seam and rubs at her clit. Last night she had her own fingers. Tonight she has me. She'll always have me.

Her body squirms in her sleep. I'm dying to pry her legs apart and suck on her perfect nub until she screams my name. But her breathing has slowed, and I don't want her to wake. Reluctantly, I remove my finger and simply stare at her. My cock has gone flaccid, but I know if I keep staring at her wet tits, I'll come all over her again. With a soft sigh, I use the sheet to clean away my spent seed. Eventually, a yawn escapes me. I decide a small nap is in order. Her breathing is regular again, so I walk around to the other side of the bed. I gently slide into the covers beside her.

She's warm and smells delicious as fuck. I'm completely addicted to her. My dick lurches when it rubs against her smooth side. I can't help my greedy fingers. They want to touch her all over. I settle with running soft circles around her peaked nipple. My nostrils flare with every breath she takes. I want to inhale her deep inside of me and never release her.

Sweet Violet…you'll never have to worry about men like Sean, or whoever messed with you at the office, because I'll always take care of you. I'm going to embed myself so far under your skin, you'll die if you ever try to cut me out.

Sleep steals me away but not before I press a kiss to her temple.

Goodnight, lovely.

I wake with a start. Early dawn is peeking in through the windows, and I let out a yawn. A smile tugs at my lips to find Violet wrapped around my naked body. She's still sleeping but she clutches onto me like a lifeline.

Soon.

Soon every night will be like this, and she'll want this as much as I do.

I don't want to leave her side, but having her wake up like this would be bad for our budding relationship. With the patience of a saint, I slip out of her grip and off the bed. She rolls over onto her side with her back to me. I'm just about to walk over to the other side of the room to grab my clothes when her alarm starts buzzing.

I freeze when she leans forward to turn it off. I'm standing there, staring at her, buck-ass naked when she slips out of the bed and hobbles toward the bathroom. Quickly, I drop to my belly and slide under the bed. I can hear her peeing in the bathroom. I'm hard just imagining her squatting on the toilet. I bet her hair is messy and her face is scrunched up with sleep. One day, I'm going to fuck her mouth while she pees. I'm grinning like a fucking idiot when the toilet flushes, and I hear the sink. But something catches my eye. My boxers are sitting on the floor beside her bed.

Panic seizes my chest, and I scoot toward the edge. I snag the boxers, yanking them under the bed with me just as she exits the bathroom.

"Oh, God," she groans. "It's too early for this shit."

I roll onto my back and am thankful when the springs squeak as she settles back on the bed. My heart is thundering in my ears and I wish it would quiet down, so I could hear her better. She fidgets and squirms.

"Gray," she murmurs. "What have you done to me?"

I freeze and it takes a moment to realize she's talking to herself. Then, I hear her bedside drawer open. When a buzzing sound fills the room, I grin up at the mattress. She's masturbating…to the thought of me. The thought elates me. Soon, she won't have to. I'll give her every orgasm she never knew she wanted.

"Mmmm," she whines.

I stroke my now rock-hard cock as I imagine her naked squirming body beneath mine. Her scent clings to me, which makes the visual even better.

"I want you inside me." The setting on the vibrator increases, and the entire bed seems to rattle. "I bet you're bigger than this." Even though she is talking to herself, I pretend she's talking to me. I stroke my cock harder and faster but am still careful not to be too noisy. The sound of a cap being popped open has me biting back a groan. I've snooped around in that drawer. I know she has several vibrators and a bottle of lube. My sweet Violet was correct—I'm much bigger than anything she owns in that drawer.

"Oh, God, yes," she chokes out. A slurping sound indicates she's fucking herself with one of her toys. I'm jealous of the damn thing and wish it were my dick instead. But my envious thoughts are snuffed out when she utters my name again. Her breathing grows heavier and ragged. Every time she moans, I swear I'm going to moan with her and give myself away. Eventually, though, she puts us both out of our misery when she comes hard. "Gray!"

A small grunt escapes me as my cum jets up across my toned stomach. She's still moaning and writhing as she milks another orgasm from her inadequate vibrator so she doesn't notice my sounds. After a moment, she stills and the room goes silent.

"I need to get laid," she says with a chuckle and slips back off the bed. Soon, the shower is running, and I can hear her humming inside.

Quickly, I slip out from under the bed. I throw on my clothes but then take a moment to grab her vibrator off the bed. It still glistens with her juices. With a wolfish grin, I snag it up and suck on the rubber. It still tastes of the lube, but mostly it's her. She tastes fucking delicious, and I can't wait until I can tongue her essence straight from her cunt myself. I lick off all of her taste before dropping the dildo back on the bed.

I don't want to leave her but I know I must. With silent steps, I sneak the bathroom door open and prowl inside. I'm playing a dangerous game but I can't help myself with her. I need to see her. From the sliver of an opening between the shower curtain and the wall, I can see her eyes are closed as she washes her hair. Her tits are soapy and look hot as hell. I allow myself one second longer to look at her before slipping out undetected.

With a quick sweep, I check to make sure I haven't left

any clues. I make it to the door and slip on my shoes. Then, I exit her apartment. With practiced efficiency, I engage all of the locks in seconds.

I want my girl to be safe.

There are all kinds of freaks in this world who would die to be inside this apartment with her.

Lucky for her, she has me to protect her.

There's only room for one freak in her world.

And I take up a lot of space.

ELEVEN

Violet

I'd set my alarm for Sunday morning just like I do every Sunday morning. I call it my reset day. The day when I try to calm myself a bit before subjecting myself to a week of frustration at work. Normally, I pull on some yoga pants and head off for some Pilates before wasting my time at Starbucks for a couple of hours, planning vacations I'll never take.

But today…

Today feels different.

I feel different.

Last night, I dreamed about Grayson Maxwell. Fantasized that we were intimate. Thought about him warming my bed. It felt safe. For once in a very long time, I wasn't absolutely terrified of being close to a man. I'd woken up with his scent still stuck in my nose from seeing him the night before, and I masturbated to him. For once, it wasn't Vaughn—that sick bastard—that I thought about while I got off. Perhaps I'm not as broken as I thought.

The thought thrills me. I almost bet if I were to thaw

a bit, Gray and I could have that delicious rumble in the sheets. But I'd already friend-zoned him.

A girl can still dream about her sexy-as-sin boss who she'd like to fuck if this were another life and she wasn't herself.

"Excuse me," an irritated woman utters, dragging me from my daydream. "Is that seat taken?"

I'd been so lost in my thoughts, I'd forgotten that I skipped Pilates altogether and went straight to Starbucks after a long shower where I ended up using the showerhead to ease another ache. They seem to keep coming. Literally.

"Oh, uh—" I start but a masculine voice interrupts.

"The seat is taken."

I jerk my gaze over and find myself staring into Gray's ice blue eyes. His hair is wet, as if he just showered, and his chest is heaving as if he ran all the way here. The woman waddles off when he drops into the seat across from me.

"Fancy seeing you here," he says with a laugh as he sips on his coffee.

I can't help but beam at him. "Are you stalking me?"

His eyes flicker with amusement. "I wish my story was as glamorous as that. I was actually in the neighborhood on my way to this market I recently found out about. Thought I'd grab a coffee first. You'll never believe the hottie I ran into."

With a snort, I shake my head at him. "You're relentless. Were you really in the neighborhood?"

He flashes me a shy grin. "I was, but in all honesty, I was coming to see you. You were upset last night, and I wanted to make sure you were okay." His cheeks turn slightly pink. The boyish gesture has me thawing.

I chew on my bottom lip as I take in his appearance. He's slightly disheveled. It makes me wonder if he was in a hurry to come see me. The thought is a warm one. How is it that this guy was cold and in his own world Friday, but by Sunday he's someone I don't mind spending time with? "I'm fine. That's sweet of you to check up on me. Although," I say with a slight shake of my head. "You're a far cry from the prick I handed my notice in to on Friday."

His smirk has the room feeling as though the temperature has risen. "Let's just say someone pointed out my flaws. Now I'm trying my damnedest to make her realize I'm not a complete asshole."

Even though we're surrounded by a ton of people on this busy Sunday morning, I feel as though we're all alone. Lost in our own little world.

"This whole having friends thing is weird," I admit with a chuckle.

His long leg brushes against mine under the table and a spark of electricity darts its way to my core. I try not to shudder in pleasure.

Friends.

We're just friends.

"I want to get to know you, Violet," he murmurs, his hand boldly covering mine on the table. I stiffen but then relax when he adds. "As friends."

A smile plays at my lips. "Okay. I don't see the harm in that, I guess."

"Come with me to the resort on Wednesday," he murmurs and leans closer, his leg once again brushing up against mine.

My cheeks blaze crimson as I recall my dreams last

night. Dreams where he touched me and held me. Dreams where we were naked and tangled together. "I, uh…"

He chuckles. "Down girl. I meant as colleagues. I've needed to travel out to the property now that I've acquired it from Mr. Collins. There's some business stuff I need to take care of. I'll require the aid of my hardworking assistant."

Embarrassment floods through me. Of course he wants to look at the property. I assumed he meant he wanted to take me away for a romantic weekend. God, I'm such a flake around him. If he wasn't so damn good-looking, I wouldn't get so tongue tied. This whole friends thing will take some practice. I'd guess that most friends aren't as severely attracted to the other, like I am to him.

"Yes, I'll go. I knew what you meant," I tell him firmly, despite the burning heat still lingering on my cheeks and throat.

He flashes me a crooked grin. "Come on. Grab your coffee to go."

Once we're outside in the cold drizzle, he pops open an umbrella and holds it above us. It's small, so I have to lean into his side to keep from getting wet. Together, we start walking down the busy sidewalk.

"Gwen and I watch football on Sunday nights. She likes to cook. Spends hours making all this finger food, even though we're the only ones there to eat it," he says with a chuckle. "You should come over tonight and watch the game. As friends of course."

My gut instinct is to tell him no but then I remember I'm attempting to try new things here. Friendship is one. And I'd be lying if I said I didn't want to try and get to know Gwen a little better.

"Okay," I concede. "What should I bring?"

He guides me over to his white Range Rover. "Yourself. That's all I want." The husky way in which he says it has me frowning at him.

"Gray…"

Pulling open the car door, he laughs. "Stop reading so much into everything. We both want you there." I slip into his vehicle, that smells just like him, and ponder what I'm even doing right now. This was not a part of my Sunday plan.

"Where are we going?" I question once he slides into the driver's seat.

He shrugs as he zips down the road. "I need to do a little shopping. You up for a quick visit to the mall?"

Considering we're now going in the opposite direction of my home, I can't help but agree. It would be rude to make him turn around to take me home. "Yeah, the mall sounds fun."

The seat warmers in his car have me feeling relaxed as ever. I'm enjoying the passing sights and the music that's playing and the comfortable quiet between us. So much so that it isn't until a song that Vaughn used to play when we were fucking comes on the radio, that I feel ice begin to creep into my bones. I hadn't realized how little I think about him when I'm with Gray until now.

"Can you change it?" I ask, my voice breathless.

My eyes close and I can almost feel the weight of Vaughn as he pins me to the mattress. The way he'd wedge his knee between my thighs until his cock was settled against me. How he'd hold me down and fuck me slowly at first. I'd get lost in his gentle touch until he'd turn dark on me. Until he'd hit me or choke me unconscious or do something equally brutal.

"Violet, babe, you're scaring the hell out of me right now," a voice growls.

I snap my eyes open to see Gray glaring at me at a stoplight. My hand shakes as I swipe a lock of hair away from my face. Not meeting his gaze, I say, "Nothing. I was just daydreaming."

The song has long since been changed and the light has turned green. This time, the silence inside the car is thick and heavy. I can sense him brooding about what just happened. Sickness roils in my belly.

"You can talk to me, you know," he says gruffly. "That's what friends do."

Not about this.

I can't ever talk to anyone about this.

"Maybe one day," I lie as I twist my fingers in my lap.

He reaches over and covers my hands with his much larger one. His pinky innocently grazes against my clit through my yoga pants, causing me to jolt. I sneak a glance at him. His jaw clenches as he maneuvers the road with ease, his attention ahead of him. My nipples harden, and I know my panties are now damp.

What is wrong with me?

I'm a pervert.

He's trying to comfort me, and all I can focus on is how his pinky rests against the seam of my sex. My breathing is heavy. I try desperately to calm it. His thumb rubs over the back of my hand in a comforting manner. I wish it were his other finger, though, doing all the moving.

"I need help picking out a chair," he tells me as we pull

into the mall parking lot. "They have one of those ergonomic office stores here. Ever been?"

I shake my head because I can't manage words with his finger on my pussy. He gives my hands a squeeze which makes a thrill shoot straight to my core from where his finger innocently rubs against me again.

"There's a spot," I choke out, pointing to an empty parking space. I jerk my other hand out from under his and run my fingers through my hair. Instead of pulling his hand away, he settles it back on my thigh. That naughty pinky of his seems to fit right up against me as if it belongs there.

He pulls into the spot and tugs his hand away to put the car into park. I let out a long breath I'd been holding. His full lips curl into a lopsided grin when he regards me. My entire body buzzes with electricity that seems to be linked to him.

"Ready?"

I bolt from the car and stalk toward the mall. Soon, he catches up to me and places his palm on my lower back. The rain has stopped, but it looks like the bad weather will continue throughout the day.

"Your ass looks nice in those pants, little quitter," he says with a grin.

I huff and glare at him. "Boss. Boundaries."

He snorts and gives my ass a swat. "Friends get to say these things."

I'm pretty sure friends aren't this touchy-feely, but what do I know. What I do know is that it is fucking with my head. Gray is too hot for him to be playfully touching me all the time. One of these days he's going to get me so worked up that I pounce on him.

We spend the next hour trying out office chairs. He says he needs a new one and insists I try them all out to tell him which is the most comfortable. When I sit a little longer than necessary in one of them and close my eyes, he snaps his fingers.

"I want this one," he tells a salesclerk.

I turn my attention to see him watching me with his muscular arms folded over his solid chest. He looks good today. No surprise there. He looks good every day. But now that his focus is on me, he seems especially handsome. His eyes seem to never leave mine. The way his gaze follows me everywhere reminds me of Vaughn. But with Vaughn, I'd always felt like a mouse caught in a trap—and he was the cat about to eat me.

Gray stares at me as if he's trying to memorize every freckle and expression.

He watches me with a hunger that promises so much more than friendship.

"Stay there," he tells me. "I'm going to go pay for this."

When he disappears, I let my mind wander. I remember shopping with Vaughn early on in our relationship. Back when he'd only started becoming possessive. At the time, I thought it was sexy.

"Try this one on," he says with a wolfish grin. He holds up a skimpy dress fit for going to a club.

I frown because he'd promised he'd take me to buy more jeans. After growing up in a household where my mom scrimped and saved so we'd scrape by okay, it is nice having a boyfriend with money and who wanted to splurge on you.

Problem is, I don't ever feel right to ask him for what I need. I just let him buy what he wants.

And today, he wants a red dress two sizes too small.

He flashes me a smoldering grin that has me tugging the fabric from his fingers. I walk to the dressing room with a frown playing at my lips. Sometimes Vaughn is everything I ever wanted in a boyfriend.

Other times, he's intense.

Too intense.

With each passing day, his like for me turns into something borderline obsessive. And while I think it's hot when he glares at other guys for looking at me, I don't always think it's hot when he lashes out at me for it.

"I'm coming with you," he growls from behind me as he grabs my ass through my dress.

I shiver and look over my shoulder. His grey eyes are hard like steel, and that perfect jaw of his is like stone. I push through the dressing room and hang the dress on the hook. He locks the door behind him and sits on the only chair.

Vaughn is hotter than any guy I've dated. Not that I've dated tons. He's definitely way out of my league. I'm simple and plain and fairly on the innocent side. Vaughn is far from simple. He's complex and layered and tricky. And he eats innocent for dinner.

My gaze falls to his sculpted chest that's barely hidden behind the stretched white fabric of his T-shirt. I know that hiding behind the shirt just over his heart is an anatomically correct tattoo of a black heart with my name in the middle.

I'd been horrified when he showed me the tattoo just three weeks after we started dating. My mother was always against tattoos. I grew up getting lectured that you should never permanently mark up your skin. Especially not with someone's name. If she knew Vaughn had 'Letty' scrawled across his flesh forever, she'd have a coronary.

I jerk my eyes to the red dress and turn my back to him. He watches me with narrowed eyes in the mirror. I try not to focus on him but become distracted by the dark bruise on my throat I'd tried desperately to cover with makeup. It's times like these that I begin to regret my two-month relationship with him. As much as I love him buying things for me and showing my body pleasure it's never known, I can't help but feel slightly trapped.

I mean, he has my name inked up on him for crying out loud.

"Babe," he growls. "We don't have all day. I have business shit to take care of later."

I flash him a quick smile in the mirror that doesn't reach my eyes as I begin peeling off my jeans and shirt. By business, he means drugs. I know he sells the hard stuff. I've tried to stay out of it but on occasion, he's done deals in front of me.

I pull the red material up my body and situate it. It's a tube-top dress and molds against every curve on my body. I look like a skank. My lip curls up to tell him this, but then his heat is up against me from behind. His erection pokes into my back as he grabs my breasts. Our eyes meet in the mirror and his smoldering one weakens me.

"You look so fucking hot," he praises.

"It's a little tight," I breathe.

He smirks and I loosen up. But that's until I start to worry about other men seeing me dressed this way. He hates when they look at me, which is why I don't fool around too much with my makeup or cute outfits. Vaughn thinks I'm beautiful when I'm plain and boring. I don't need to doll myself up for other men.

His palms slide up the outer sides of my thighs and he urges the dress up to my hips. When he starts to pull down my panties, I let out a nervous laugh.

"Not here, Vaughn," I hiss, my throat heating with embarrassment.

His eyes become hard in the mirror. He pinches my tit through the material causing me to yelp in pain. My eyes well with tears. From time to time, he gets rough with me but it usually ends with him kissing away the hurt and being super sweet. He grabs a handful of my hair and yanks my head back. His hot breath tickles my ear as he spits out his word. "Here."

His other hand yanks my panties down my thighs. When he starts to bend me forward, I fight against him. What if someone hears and they kick us out?

Crack!

My forehead slams against the mirror and I black out. When I come to, he's fucking me from behind. A massive headache is thundering in my head and my sex hurts from not being wet when he entered me. With shaky hands, I press them against the mirror and push away to regard my face. Blood trickles down from the left side of my forehead down over my eyebrow. A wave of dizziness washes over me. I start to collapse but Vaughn's powerful arm holds me up. He grunts and then pulls out at the last minute. His cum shoots against the dress as he hisses in pleasure.

I can't look at him.

What he just did is…

That's rape, right?

My boyfriend just raped me?

Again.

Bile creeps up my throat and a tear slips out of my eyes. I'm still staring at my haggard face when I hear fabric ripping. He shreds the dress as he pulls it from my body. I would be horrified but I'm too dizzy to think too hard about it. He twists me around so I'm forced to look into his cold eyes. They quickly soften as he uses the red dress to wipe away the blood from my wound. It's his tongue he uses to wipe away my tears.

"I'm sorry," he murmurs, his hot breath against my cheek. He trails soft kisses to my parted mouth. His kisses are sweet and apologetic but I'm numb. I don't understand why he keeps doing this to me.

"I…I…why?" I ask, a sob caught in my throat.

He leans his forehead against mine and strokes my hair. "Sometimes I love you so much I lose my head. My mind turns black."

His simple confession has me softening. He loves me. I sort of thought he did, but this is the first time he spoke of it.

"Vaughn…"

"Babe," he whispers as he hugs me tight. "Let me love you. Don't fight it at every turn."

I sag against him. My heart hurts because the person who is able to single-handedly destroy me is also the person to fix me. I'm warm and safe in his loving embrace.

"You hurt me," I accuse, more tears leaking out.

"I'm sorry. You know that." He pushes his hand into his jeans pocket and retrieves a pill. "Here," he coos. "Take this to take the edge off."

I'm not one to do drugs but my head is throbbing and my heart aches so badly. I open my mouth and swallow the acrid pill dry.

He's gentle as he helps me redress. Him being tender right now is almost as worse as him being rough. He once again wipes away some lingering blood with the dress that got us into this mess and then pulls my hair down in front of my eye to cover the wound.

"So pretty," he praises. He tosses the soiled dress onto the floor, and I'm thankful I won't have to ever look at it again.

With a firm grip on my elbow, he guides me out of the dressing room. Several women shopping stare at us as he all but drags me through the store. We start to pass by the racks of red dresses and bile rises up. Thank God I won't ever have to look at them again. But then he jerks one off the rack before hauling me over to the register. The cashier won't make eye contact as she rings up the dress.

"I thought you didn't like it," I murmur, tears once again threatening.

He releases his death grip on my elbow to pull out his wallet. "But you look downright fuckable when you wear it, baby," he says with a wide grin that an hour ago would have made me crazy with need. Now all it does is make me shudder.

"Thank you," I breathe.

The cashier makes a sound of disapproval but I don't meet her stare. I can't. I'm ashamed and embarrassed. If my mother knew he treated me this way, she'd probably kill him.

The medicine begins to work its way through my system on my empty stomach and the room spins. When I wobble on my feet, Vaughn chuckles and pulls me against him.

"I've got you, Letty. I will always have you."

TWELVE

Grayson

After I pay and give the clerk the address to my office, I search for Violet. Her eyes are haunted as she stares straight ahead. She's stiff-shouldered and her skin is pale.

What the fuck?

I stalk over to her and kneel right in front of her. Her pretty brown eyes are lost. Those plump pink lips are positively kissable, but she's in a zone. Trapped in a memory. I know far too well how that feels. It fucking sucks.

I cradle her face with my palms and tilt her head to look at me. "Violet, sweetheart, what's wrong?"

Her eyes shimmer with tears, and a sound of despair groans from her throat. Without thinking, I press a kiss to her cheek and then her nose. Then to her forehead against a pale white scar. When I drag my nose against hers, her breath hitches. Our mouths are so close to kissing it makes me crazy.

"Gray," she murmurs, her voice so damn soft.

I pull away and regard her with a frown. "What just happened?"

Her entire body shudders as shame crosses over her features. She darts her gaze past me while she worries her lip between her teeth. "Nothing."

Fucking liar.

I refrain from rolling my eyes.

Instead, I indulge her.

"Okay," I say with a sigh. "Let's go grab some lunch."

She doesn't balk when I take her hand in mine and guide her out of the store. I want to take her someplace nice but the nicest place at the mall is a Mexican restaurant. Thankfully, they find us a round booth in the back corner away from everyone. I'm able to sit close to her with my hand still clutching hers.

I hate how zoned out she is. Whatever her past holds, I intend on shaking it out so I can inspect it. Someone hurt her. And I will hurt that someone.

It isn't until after I've ordered our food and drinks that she seems to snap out of it. Her hand tries to pull from mine, but I grip it.

"You're okay," I assure her and give her hand a squeeze. "You're safe now."

Her eyes dart to mine and her cheeks blaze red. "Oh my God. I am so sorry for that."

"Panic attack?"

She bites on her bottom lip and shrugs. "Something like that."

I let out a heavy sigh and reach forward for a tortilla chip. "Friends open up to one another."

This time, she's the one letting out a heavy breath. "Some things are better left locked up in the past. Some monsters belong there."

I'll free her monsters.

Because once they're free, I can find them and kill them.

"What's his name?" I probe.

She shudders and jerks her hand from my grasp. "He was nobody."

"He was somebody. I have a sneaking suspicion he's the reason you go to great lengths to protect yourself. That shitty cash-only apartment is one of those ways."

Her body stiffens. "Vaughn."

The name on her lips is like ice. Cold and bitter. Whoever this Vaughn fucker is has hurt her badly. I need to know how he hurt her so I can fix it.

"Was he your boyfriend?"

She darts her head toward the rest of the restaurant and skims the growing lunch crowd as if she's searching for someone. When she doesn't find said person, her body relaxes.

"Ex, yeah. Things didn't go well toward the end."

I want to ask her more but don't want to sour our date. "Do you have any family?"

My sudden change of subject has her jerking her head up. Tears swim in her eyes and her bottom lip quivers. "My mom."

I smile at her. "Feel free to elaborate."

She smirks, and I'm glad to see her mood lighten. "She gave birth to me."

"Smartass," I growl.

A cute laugh escapes her. She grabs for a chip and shrugs again. "I don't know. She's just Mom. Works at a diner back home. I love her and miss her dearly. Haven't seen or spoken to her in years."

"Did you have a falling out?" I probe.

She bites the chip and shakes her head. "More complicated than that. I just wanted her to be happy. And with me"—she sighs—"it was impossible."

I can tell she doesn't want to talk about it because she starts babbling about some real estate news she read about this morning in the paper. I focus on her face. A storm brews in her brown eyes, but she keeps it at bay, her face a picture of calm. Those juicy lips move rapidly as she speaks, and I want them. All over my body. Between my teeth especially.

My gaze drops to her slender throat. I imagine suckling the flesh there and turning the cream to crimson. Would she pant softly or moan my name? My cock throbs in my pants. One day I will have her. But my Violet is like a frightened stray. I need to feed her with affection and gain her trust before I slap a collar on her and declare her mine.

"So what does Gwen do for a living?"

I jolt from my daze and scowl. "She's an artist."

Her brown eyes light up with excitement. "Really? That's amazing."

I down my water glass to keep the violent words from spewing. "Yep," is all I manage.

"Now look who's being vague and strange," she admonishes softly. When her palm rests on my thigh, I stiffen. Everywhere.

I turn to look at her, and she stares at me with an expectant look. "Gwen has issues."

She frowns, and I like the way her forehead crinkles between her brows. It makes me want to rub the wrinkles away with my thumb until it's smooth again so I can kiss it.

"Feel free to elaborate," she throws back at me with a smirk.

"She's a lot like our mother. Mom is clinically depressed." And clinically insane. "The depression bleeds into all aspects of her life."

Her eyes dart over my face in confusion. "But she's so sweet and…" Her nostrils flare. "Normal."

A harsh laugh escapes me. "Is she?"

We're silent for a moment before I rest my hand on hers that still sits on my thigh. "She's on one of her highs right now. The lows are dark and abysmal and fucking scary."

Understanding flashes in her eyes. "I suffered from depression years ago."

I quirk up a brow and my full attention is back on her. Her cheeks and throat have turned pink again. "After him?" I ask.

She gives me a clipped nod before turning her head back to the increasingly crowded restaurant. Her gaze sweeps the room for a moment before she looks down at her lap. "He did a number on me."

White-hot anger surges through me and it takes everything in me not to slam my fist on the table. I hate this fuck, whoever he is. I'll find him. Until then, I'll find out what I can about him from her.

"You're safe now," I assure her. I fucking dare him to even look at her.

She snorts and her tone is cold. "I will never be safe."

I'm about to drill her with more questions, but the server brings us a giant sizzling plate of chicken and steak fajitas to share. The rest of lunch is light and easy as we share not only food but also laughs.

Once lunch is over, and we're walking back to the car, she lets me hold her hand again. I know I told her we'd be friends but I can barely refrain from pushing her up against the closest wall, tearing a hole in her yoga pants, and fucking her until we offend everyone at the mall.

My cock likes this image because it thickens in my slacks. I swear all I do is get hard in her presence.

"I can't believe the weekend is nearly over," she groans once we're back on the road. "My boss is a real prick."

I smirk and shoot her a smoldering stare. "I bet you'll find that once you get to know him, he's not so bad."

I don't miss her smile before my attention is back on the road. She lets out a sigh and stares out the window. I like how serene she is right now. Most of the time, she's wound up tight. But not now. Now, she's relaxing and letting me look after her. As it should be.

"Do you want to change before we go to my house?"

She laughs. "Am I really coming over?"

"As if you have any choice in the matter. Once Gwen and Gray Maxwell hook their claws into you, you can't get away," I tease. "Friends aren't really our thing so when we make one, we don't like to let go."

Her chuckle is sweet, but I can tell she likes the idea of being our friend. I like the idea of my cock deep inside her wet cunt better. Baby steps.

Once outside her ghetto building, she runs upstairs. While she's gone, I pull up the Internet on my phone and start scouring the web for anything to do with Vaughn. Without a last name, I'm helpless. I'm still grumbling fifteen minutes later when Violet returns. Her brown hair is down and even the glum rain clouds can't take away her shininess. The gold strands in her hair glisten and sparkle just like her. My gaze falls to the scoop neck of her dress. She wears a leather jacket over the jade-colored dress. Her black boots and tights complete the sexy look. Her eyes are darker with mascara and her pretty lips shimmer.

My cock aches for attention, but she's stolen the show. I can't look away from her. She pops open the door and laughs.

"Take a picture. It'll last longer."

Don't mind if I do.

I'll wait until you're asleep and naked, though.

The girls chat on the sofa as the game drones on. My gaze is fixated on Violet as she chomps on some pretzels. Gwen came through and made enough food for an army. I'd be annoyed about her wasting so much food except that cooking is something that draws her out of her rooms. Those rooms are a chain keeping her from total freedom. When she cooks, she's free for a little while.

My phone buzzes, jerking my attention from my woman.

Bull: That fumble was bullshit.

I barely register that the football game is on.

Me: I slept under her bed.

His response is immediate.

Bull: WTF. You have issues.

I snort and my eyes find Violet's. She's drawn her attention from my sister's babbling to regard me curiously. I flash her a panty-melting grin that makes her throat flush red. When she turns back to Gwen, I reply to Bull.

Me: She's so fucking beautiful. I'm going to make her mine soon.

Bull: Fuck.

I dart my eyes back over to her and my gaze lingers on her creamy thighs that are visible now that her dress has ridden up. I'm dying to taste her there—to taste her everywhere.

Bull: Maybe you should call Elisha. You're losing touch here.

I grumble and tap out my response.

Me: Elisha is nothing compared to her. Nobody is.

Bull: Why can't you just date her like a normal person? Is it necessary to stalk her?

Me: I'm trying. And until then, yes.

She stands and asks Gwen where the bathroom is. Gwen directs her, and I stare after my woman as she walks away. Her ass is round and fucking delectable in her dress.

Bull: You do realize if she ever finds out, you're fucked. Like seriously fucked. Like you could lose your company and go to jail fucked.

I smirk.

Me: She's worth getting fucked over.

He responds with the hand flipping the bird emoji. Gwen starts cleaning up her mess in the kitchen, so I stand and shove my phone into my pocket. I stalk down the hallway because I want to steal a moment alone with Violet. She's been teasing me in her sexy little dress all night. But when I approach the bathroom, the door is ajar and she's not inside.

Fuck.

I rush into my room first because I worry I've left my chest open. Once I realize it's still locked, but she's not there, dread fills my chest.

Oh, God, no.

I take off down the hall to the other side of the house. The side I never want Violet to see. No other woman I've ever brought home has dared leave my bedroom or the living room. They were there for one reason only. But since Violet is here "as friends," I guess she's taken it upon herself to explore.

"Violet," I holler as I stalk down the long hallway of my giant house. There's a reason why Gwen stays on the other side. When I near her rooms, the stench hits me. I hardly ever come over here, and the housekeeper has been forbidden to step foot past my bedroom. Bile creeps in my throat when I find that one of the doors is open. Her bedroom. The fucking worst.

I pull my shirt up to cover my nose and mouth. Violet stands just inside the doorway. Her entire body is frozen stiff as she stares.

"Fuck."

THIRTEEN

Violet

Gray's voice is muffled as he curses behind me. My stomach roils as I take in the scene before me. Madness. Absolute chaos. I'm so shocked because the other parts of the house are immaculate and pristine. But this… this is sick.

"Violet," Gray hisses as he grabs my elbow.

I jerk my arm from his grip and stare at the dump. *Dump* is a nice word. It's an absolute shithole. I'd barely gotten through an episode of *Hoarders* once a few years back. After they found a dead cat under some debris in an old woman's house, I shut it off and scrubbed my bathtub until I could see my reflection.

This is worse.

The stink is sickening. Rot. Mildew. Sour…something. Yuck. The potato skins I ate moments earlier, before I went exploring, threaten to make a reappearance. From floor to damn near the ceiling, this room is piled high with junk. Not just junk but trash. Trash! Somewhere in the middle of the chaos is a bed. Shit has been piled up on the bed as well. Only a small portion remains uncovered. *Where that person sleeps.* Whose room is this?

"Gwen," Gray mutters as if to answer my unspoken question.

He told me she was sick, but not like this. This is something else. I see something run across her bed and I let out a scream. A strong hand covers my mouth from behind. I'm dragged out of the room and the door slams shut. The stink lingers in my nostrils, and I feel like I'll throw up at any second. I fall limp in Gray's grip as he retreats quickly down the hallway. I expect him to drag me back to the living room but instead, he pulls me into what must be his bedroom, hence the familiar masculine scent. I inhale it in hopes of ridding my nose of the disgusting stench from Gwen's room.

My body trembles and he hugs me tight against him. With my back pressed against his chest and his strong arm around my middle, awareness prickles through me. Slowly, he peels away his hand from my mouth.

"I'm sorry."

Guilt rushes through me. "I-I overreacted."

He nuzzles his nose against my hair and groans. "You didn't. It's…it's not something that people besides her and I see. I didn't prepare you. It's disgusting. I'm sorry you had to see it."

"*Things* were living there," I hiss, my voice quivering on the line between hysteria and calm. I'm pretty sure it was a big mouse but I can't be certain.

"I know," he growls. "Trust me. I pay a fucking exterminator to come out every week to try and deal with it."

"You pull it all out and throw it away. That's how you

deal with it," I exclaim.

He releases me, and when I turn to look at him, his palms scrub over his handsome face in frustration. "If it were that easy, the shit would have been hauled away a long time ago. This is…this is something she's learned. It's been ingrained in her since birth."

I frown at him when he stalks over to a chest in the room. He sits on it and then regards me with a despondent look.

"Our mother is worse," he murmurs, shame coating his features.

Big, powerful, neat-as-hell Grayson Maxwell is surrounded by a family of hoarders.

"Your father?" I ask, my voice soft.

He shakes his head. "He's the cause, honestly. Mom always collected things in our basement. But when Gwen got sick, she started trying to record and save all her moments. Both of them became obsessed with collecting things. It drove my dad crazy. He ended up spending more and more time at his apartment in the city near his office. Eventually, he never came home."

My stomach roils when I imagine his mother's house. How could it be worse than that?

"So, they're divorced?"

He sighs. "No. He paid off the house and always saw to it that she had enough money." He pauses and his eyes shift away, but I don't miss the storm brewing in them. "She won't ever leave the house, though. I've taken over paying utilities and sending groceries to the house. Dad won't come see her. They're married, but he hasn't seen her probably in twenty years."

I gape at him. I suppose everyone has skeletons in their closets. His are apparently full of hoarded skeletons.

"She needs help," I tell him softly. "That can't be safe."

He stands and prowls over to me, anger written all over his face. I flinch when he raises his hand. The action makes his hard features crumple. Vaughn has ruined me forever.

"She used to see a therapist each week but eventually got angry with Dr. Ward and quit going. We've tried everything. At first, it was just her room. Then, she took over two more rooms. I refuse to let her take over anymore. Sometimes, she brings her things to Mom's. They find room in that shithole somehow."

I swallow and close my eyes when he touches my cheek. His other hand grips my hip and he drags me closer. I love that his masculine scent is quickly chasing away the horrible one from Gwen's room. He rests his forehead against mine, and it grounds me. Something about this guy affects me.

His mouth is so close to mine, and if I were to tilt my head up, I'd be able to kiss him. I want to kiss him. But a kiss will lead to more. I'm certainly not ready for more with him.

"I should go," I murmur, trying to ignore the way his thumb rubs my hip.

"I wish you didn't have to."

I place my hands on his firm chest that I'd love to explore more and push him away. "Can you take me please?" I bite on my lip and frown. "And please don't tell her I... saw."

He shakes his head. "I won't. It would send her into a tailspin that I can't afford to mentally deal with. I have too much else on my mind."

It reminds me that he's a successful businessman who spends his day acquiring hotels and businesses left and right. But a small part of me hopes that I'm also on his mind.

"Let's go then," I breathe out.

His gaze falls to my lips and he clenches his jaw before nodding his agreement.

I wake up in a cold sweat.

And naked.

Why do I keep undressing in my sleep? Am I sleep-walking again?

Dread consumes me. It's been years since I've had the night sweats where I would find myself in various places around the apartment. What's triggered this? Is it Gray?

I squeeze my eyes shut and will myself to sleep. But then I hear it. A ping. I jolt upright in bed and still my breath. Then a creak.

Holy shit.

The hair sticks up on the back of my neck. Someone is in my house. I slide out of bed and snag my gun from under the mattress. I keep it loaded and ready to fire. Once I have it in my grip, I call out in a shaky voice.

"Who's there?"

Thud. Thud. Thud.

The footsteps are heavy and a scream gets lodged in my throat. He's coming for me. It's Vaughn. He's here and he's going to drag me back home with him by my hair.

No!

I stumble backward until my bare ass hits the wall with the gun wobbling out in front of me. It's dark aside from the moonlight pouring in from the open curtain.

The front door swings open and crashes against the wall before slamming again. My heart jackknifes in my chest. I bolt through the apartment and then twist all the locks into place. As soon as the last one engages, I start to cry.

He was here.

It had to have been him.

I'm panicking. I don't know what to do. I can't call the cops because he'll kill me and my mother. That was something he always told me he would do. At times, I didn't care about me, but it wasn't fair for my mother.

My hand trembles, but I keep hold of my gun while I hunt for my phone. I dial Gray and pray he'll wake at this ungodly hour. He answers on the fourth ring, his voice thick with sleep.

"Yeah?"

"G-Gray, h-he was h-here," I sob as I start frantically turning on every light in the apartment.

He growls. "Who?"

"V-Vaughn. It had to have b-been him. I heard him s-slam the door shut when h-he left." My teeth begin to chatter as another jolt of fear slices through me.

"Lock yourself in the bathroom and don't come out until I call to tell you I'm there," he instructs as he shuffles around. "I'll be there in twenty minutes."

We hang up, and I rush to the bathroom. I yank my robe off the hook and sling it on before locking the door. Twenty minutes feels like twenty years. But in sixteen minutes, a loud bang on the door causes me to scream.

Gray: I'm here.

I toss the phone down but I'm still too afraid to relinquish my gun. I unlock the bathroom door and run to the front one. Once I peek through the hole and make sure it's him, I disengage all three locks. When I barely have the last one unlatched, Gray's pushing in with a frantic look on his face.

"Violet," he hisses as I all but jump into his arms. He's warm and safe and here to protect me. That's what friends do. "It's okay, baby," he coos. "I'm here now." His voice cloaks me like a safety blanket. He pulls away briefly to lock up the apartment and to gently pull the gun from my grip. Then, he wraps an arm around me and guides me to the sofa. Together we sit, and I practically crawl into his lap seeking security.

"Tell me everything that happened from start to finish," he tells me, his voice tense.

I launch into how I woke from a nightmare and heard a sound. I leave off the embarrassing fact that I don't know how I got naked. I'm certain it wasn't Vaughn who got me that way. He wouldn't have been able to undress me and resist touching me. I'd have awoken with his cock deep inside me if it were him that had taken off my clothes. That was all me.

"The nightmares are back and now..." I trail off and shudder.

"And now what?" he questions, his fingers finding my chin to tilt my head, so I can see him. His handsome face is screwed up in concern as he regards me. I get lost in his fierce, icy-blue gaze before my eyes drop to his mouth.

"Vaughn is back."

"Vaughn who?"

I shudder just thinking about him. My eyes close, but then I see him staring at me with hate in his eyes so I quickly reopen them.

"We can't go to the cops," I whisper. "He'll kill my mother. He'll kill me."

His eyes bug out of his head for a moment before a murdercvvous scowl washes over his features. "He won't touch you, but I want his name."

When I start trembling again, Gray grabs my hips and guides me farther into his lap. The lines of friendship are blurring because I straddle him over his thighs. His palms cradle my face as he searches for answers.

"Brecks. His last name is Brecks," I murmur. "He can't know where I am. Ever."

A quake ripples through my body as another sob catches in my throat.

"Come here," he growls and slides a hand to my ass to pull me closer. The silky robe hardly hides the fact that I'm naked. His palm remains on my butt as he rubs me in a comforting way. I bury my face against his neck. God, he smells delicious. My breasts are pressed against his firm chest, and it feels good to be against him like this.

His other hand rests on my bare thigh and he runs circles with it just under the robe. My entire body starts quivering for a different reason. The adrenaline coursing through my body has channeled into something else. Something hot and hungry.

"How do you think he got in?" I question, my breath hot against his flesh.

His cock begins to harden beneath me, sending ripples

of need coursing through me. I'm pressed against his very impressive length in his jeans.

"Those locks are cheap and easy to break into," he tells me huskily. "I'll call my locksmith we use for the office tomorrow and have your door fitted with something impenetrable."

I sit up so I can look at him. His blue eyes have darkened with lust. I wonder if mine mirror the look. He lets go of my ass and boldly tugs at the rope holding my robe together. It falls open and a gasp of shock rolls off my tongue.

"Gray," I murmur in warning.

He arches a brow and it makes him ten times sexier. "What?" he questions, feigning innocence.

A smile tugs at my lips. "Friends don't try to undress friends."

He chuckles and it warms me all the way to my core. I find my eyes fixated on his full lips.

"I need to kiss you," he admits, his voice thick with desire.

I dart my eyes back up to his. "A kiss isn't what friends do either."

His fingers slide to my neck and he curls them around the back of my head. "Maybe I don't want to be friends. Maybe I want to take care of you in so many ways that go beyond friendship."

When I'm tugged forward, I start to protest with my palms against his chest. But then his other palm cups my breast in a gentle, reverent way that has me whimpering. I end up meeting him in the middle and pressing my lips against his. The kiss is soft and sweet at first. All it takes is one moan from me and he slides his tongue into my mouth, seeking something deeper.

My clit throbs with need and my nipples ache to be touched. As if he has direct access to my thoughts, his thumb rubs across my erect nipple, causing me to shiver.

"I see you, Violet," he murmurs against my mouth, his teeth nipping at my bottom lip. "I see you."

His words turn me on. After so many years of existing as a mere shadow—*in his shadow*—I love that I'm in his spotlight. Shamelessly, I grind myself against his erection, which makes him groan with pleasure.

"Gray," I moan as I rock against him. "We should stop."

He laughs and it reverberates down to my core. "Why would we want to do that?"

"Because we're friends," I try but then decide I like kissing him better than talking. My mouth devours his.

His palm slides down my side, dangerously low on my stomach, and my breath hitches.

"Friends can still fuck," he growls.

I let out an embarrassing sound when his thumb grazes against my clit. The pleasure from such a simple touch sears through me like hot fire. He massages my clit in a slow torturous way that has me jolting with each movement. An orgasm decides to take hold of me out of nowhere. And, holy hell, is it delicious. Electric pleasure shudders through me just as he pushes a finger inside my wet center. The sudden intrusion coupled with the high of my orgasm sends another orgasm right on its heels. I throw my head back and cry out in pleasure. When my body stops shaking, he slips his finger back out and leans forward to press a kiss between my breasts. The tickle of his hair reminds me of Vaughn, and I scramble away from him with a scream falling from my lips.

I don't toss a look his way until I'm safely on the other side of the couch. He still sits with his powerful legs slightly spread apart and his erection blatantly obvious through the denim. His hair is messy—I must have grabbed hold of it at some point—and his chest heaves. The lust in his eyes is enough to almost have me crawling back into his lap.

"I-I can't," I mutter, tears threatening.

He reaches over and clutches my bare ankle. "It's okay." His gaze darts to my bare chest before he clears his throat and pulls his hand away. "I'll stay over tonight to make sure he doesn't come over again. Do you have a pillow and a blanket?"

I swallow and nod as I stand. With quick movements, I tie my robe back up. "Thank you. And I'm sorry." My eyes drop to his erection, and I frown.

He laughs. "I'm fine, little quitter." Heat and amusement glitter in his eyes, effectively diffusing the awkward moment. "Get some sleep. We'll talk more in the morning."

I locate some bedding and practically throw it at him before shutting myself in my room. As soon as the lights are turned off and I'm back in bed, I slink out of the robe and slip a hand between my thighs. I'm still soaked from the orgasms he gave me. I run the wetness up between the lips of my pussy and let out a hiss of pleasure. I still tingle but all he did was make me crave more.

Silently, I massage myself into one more orgasm.

I hope he didn't hear his name as it shamelessly moaned its way out of my mouth.

The more time I spend with Gray, the more I like it. Is this his plan? To woo me into staying at the company? I have less than two weeks to get my head back on straight and focus on my career. Not men. Not my past. My future.

T-minus twelve days…

FOURTEEN

Grayson

"*Grayyyy.*"

The way she said my name last night behind her door had driven me wild with lust. I'd already been jerking my cock for relief under the blanket so when I heard the moan, it sent me over the edge. We'd been so close to fucking, but then something spooked her.

"New client I want to talk about later, once my assistant gathers some more information when she gets here," Bull grunts from my doorway.

I wave him in. "Close the door."

His brows furrow together as he shuts the door and stalks over to the chair in front of my desk. Violet isn't due for another half hour. I left her house early this morning upon her demand. She was back to her fierce self and promised she'd shoot anything that came through her door.

The only reason I left her was because it wasn't Vaughn who had been in her house. It was me. I'd been rifling through one of her other closets when I heard her voice. She didn't rouse when I slipped into her apartment. She didn't wake when I undressed her. And she didn't wake when I rubbed her pussy while I jerked off. *Again.* It was like the night before. Until it wasn't.

I'd almost been caught.

"What is it?" Bull asks.

"She almost caught me."

His features darken. "Under her bed?"

"I was looking through her front room closet. She thought it was Vaughn, her ex. Apparently, he was quite a psycho," I growl.

Bull laughs. "She really knows how to pick 'em."

I flip him off. "Fuck you. I've already called the locksmith to change her locks out, but, man, she was terrified. I want you to call Dusty and have him see what he can drum up on Vaughn Brecks. Everything, no matter how big or small. I want to find this fuck."

All humor is wiped from Bull's face. We only call our ex-military buddy, Dusty, for emergencies when we need info on a big client. This is a fucking emergency.

"You're taking shit far," he says with a groan and tugs at the knot on his tie.

"I know. I want her. I want all of her. We have a connection. Both conscious and subconscious. Her body responds to mine. We belong together," I clip out.

His eyes regard me almost sadly for a moment before he shakes away the look. "Fine. I'll check it out. Be careful."

I nod and then let out a heavy breath. "I also want you to shake down every sick fuck who has put his hands on Violet and bring them to me."

His eyes widen. "Like her entire life?"

I growl. "Here."

He clenches his jaw and nods. "I have a couple of names right off the top of my head. I'll get you a list starting with our VP, Brent Adams."

"I want him gone. And the fact that there is a 'list' has me wanting to go fucking postal," I seethe, my hands fisting tight. Who the fuck is Brent Adams, anyway?

"I've mentioned it to you before but—"

I glare at him. "What?"

"Do you remember when I fired, Jack Langston?"

The name rings absolutely no bells.

"He only worked here for three years," he tries.

I shrug. "Don't know him."

"Well, I saw him slap Letty's ass once in the break room, so I canned him. To save her from embarrassment, I told the employees he got a job elsewhere."

"Her name is Violet," I growl.

He holds his hands up in defense. "Fine. Violet. Anyway, Truman replaced him but apparently, Clint hires shitty guys because he's number one on the list right beside Brent Adams."

I slam my fist on the mahogany desk and glare. "I want Adams and Truman gone. But not before I talk to them."

Bull's eyebrow lifts and he smirks. "You can't kick their asses."

"No, but I can scare the shit out of the little pricks."

He sighs and stands up. "I guess it's high time we cleaned house around here."

"We have eleven days to make her stay," I tell him, my mind whirring with ways to make that happen. I'll be goddamned if I let her go to Slante who is no better than Adams or Truman or any of these other fuckers.

"What if she doesn't want to stay?" he challenges.

My nostrils flare. "That's just not a fucking option, man."

After I place an order to the flower company, I start a little recon on my own. I start with Facebook first. I sift through her friends list looking for connections and cross-reference most of them as women who work for me and their friends. Nobody traces back to the town where her mother works. I'd looked up the diner name on the paper I found in her closet. My Violet is far from home.

Vaughn Brecks doesn't come up on Facebook but he does have a rap sheet a mile fucking long. Mostly for drugs, assault and battery, and pimping and pandering. My blood pressure rises as I wonder if he pimped Violet out. The thought makes me borderline fucking crazy. I'm going to find this guy and make him bleed.

Unfortunately, he's not showing up anywhere when I try to hunt him down. No addresses. No legal jobs. Nothing. And he isn't dead because there isn't any record of that either. He's flying low under the radar.

But now that I have my sights on him, I'll find him. I'll put my crosshairs on his motherfucking head and blow his brains from here to Connecticut.

After I send an email to Dusty with what little info I have, I check on an Amazon order I placed this weekend while I was chilling under Violet's bed. I have a surprise coming in today that I paid expedited shipping for.

Now that she's practically mine, I want to shower her with everything. Love. Attention. Gifts. Cum.

People start filing in. Normally I don't notice them but today I have my door open. I'm waiting for her. It's been just an hour since I've last seen her, and I'm going nuts. This weekend she was semi-casual and I'm dying to see her in some sexy office attire. Goddamn, I need this woman.

My ears perk up when I hear the name Truman outside my door. A douchebag-looking motherfucker stops to talk to Clint from HR. They chuckle and discuss last night's game. When a woman walks by, Truman's narrowed gaze follows her ass.

Rage bubbles up inside me.

Violet was right. This place is crawling with sexist pigs. Because of me. Had I laid down the law in the beginning, these assholes would know how to act. But since they know they can get away with this shit—because human resources clearly doesn't have a fucking issue—they continue to abuse the situation and my female staff.

They abuse my Violet.

I stand from my chair and fist my hands.

Bull is going to gather the men and we'll have a big fucking meeting later this afternoon. Until then, I need to let Truman feel my fury. I stalk out into the hallway. His gaze turns from leering to friendly as he regards me.

"Mr. Maxwell," he greets with a grin.

Clint turns and stares at me, shock in his eyes. "Sir."

I tilt my head to the side and size up Truman. Clint is a pussy because he murmurs that he has work to do and retreats. Truman, the dumbass, opens his mouth like we're fucking chums.

We. Are. Not. Fucking. Chums.

"I need coffee," I clip out, my voice short but calm.

He frowns at me in confusion. "What?"

"I need coffee," I repeat, stepping into his personal space. "I need coffee now."

His stupid beady eyes dart over to Violet's empty desk. Before he can open his mouth and say something stupid, I growl startling him.

"I need *you* to make my coffee. *You*, Truman."

A flash of anger flickers in his eyes. "Don't we have people for that?"

"Two scoops of sugar. One scoop of creamer," I seethe, my chest bumping against his. "And don't forget a dash of cinnamon."

His jaw clenches as his eyes challenge me. I fucking dare him to challenge me. Finally, he bites back his reply. "You got it, boss."

He storms into the kitchen and starts slamming shit around. A smile tugs at my lips but it turns full blown when I hear the clack of heels. I jerk my gaze to see my gorgeous, confident woman striding into the office. Her long, brown hair is like pure silk hanging in front of her perky breasts. She's paid a lot of attention to her makeup today because it's perfect—like she's headed for a photo shoot at a magazine, not work. My gaze roams down her sexy little body. Today, she wears a white button-up blouse that hugs her round tits and is tucked into a slate grey pencil skirt that seems a tad shorter than the one she wore Friday. I drag my eyes along her long legs to a pair of snakeskin stilettos in the same shade as her skirt. When I finally find her eyes again, she's smiling.

Goddamn, she's beautiful.

"Did you need something?" she asks with an arched

dark eyebrow. "Coffee perhaps?" The challenge in her voice gets my dick hard.

"You don't make coffee anymore," I growl as I prowl toward her. Panic briefly crosses her features, almost as if she fears she's in trouble. She's in trouble for not giving me her pretty pussy last night. But I'll punish her later with my tongue. As far as this job goes, she's doing much more than I ever realized. I quickly analyzed the data she collected on the Collins property, and it helped me with some decisions that needed making. Violet is smart—too smart to be making coffee and answering the phone. And as if a light bulb goes off in my head, I know what I'll do. Later. It is the answer to a lot of my problems.

"Gray," she murmurs when I near. Her brown eyes do their own little field trip down my body. I'd worn one of my expensive suits to impress her. It fits well and shows off my build. I need to drive her just as fucking crazy as she drives me.

"You look good, little quitter," I say with a lopsided grin.

She laughs and waves me off as she starts for her desk. "Back at ya, Gray."

Pride fills my chest as I follow her. The skirt hugs her ass perfectly. My fingers twitch to grab the hem and slide it up to her hips so I can see which panties she's wearing. I've pulled them all out of her drawers and inspected them. I have my favorites—favorites that I didn't steal for my own personal Violet souvenir collection in hopes that I'd get to see her in them one day.

"What is this?" she asks suddenly, drawing me from my thoughts.

"Mmmm?"

She snaps around and glares at me. Her pert nose flares with anger. I bite the inside corner of my lip as I stare at her pouty parted lips. God, I need those lips like I need air. They tasted like sweet honey when we kissed last night—

"Gray," she hisses. "Focus."

Focus.

Focus.

My eyes are on hers.

Locked.

She's in my sights.

And I'm coming straight for her.

I'll obliterate her heart.

She's my target and I'm the motherfucking bullet.

Mine to pierce and lodge myself into.

"Gray." Her voice is softer this time. Those dark brows are no longer furled in anger. They pinch together in concern. "Why did you buy me a chair? I thought this was for you."

I flash her a smug grin. "You practically fell asleep in it. Why do you think I had you test it out? Just don't go falling asleep on the job. My methods for waking you up are…" I scratch at my jaw with my finger and narrow my gaze at her as I lick my bottom lip. "Unconventional. Probably illegal."

Embarrassment paints her cheeks and throat as her eyes quickly dart around to make sure nobody heard. I simply shrug. Who's going to tell on me? I'm the fucking owner.

"Gray," she murmurs, her voice thick with an emotion I want. Something that my ears equate to need and lust. I want to bathe in the way she says my name. "I'll be leaving in less than two weeks. You shouldn't have bought me a chair."

As if cold water splashes me awake, I jolt at her words. "Nonsense. The chair you had was crap. You deserve it."

Her cheeks turn slightly pink as she sets her purse down on the desk. "You shouldn't have."

"I did," I challenge in a low tone.

She flashes me a smile that makes my heart nearly thud out of my chest. When she sits down and leans back, she lets out a sigh of approval. "Okay, so maybe you should have like six years ago."

I smirk and sit down on the edge of her desk. "After you get situated this morning, we're having a meeting."

Her brows crash together as she frowns, and I instantly hate the loss of her smile. "What sort of meeting?"

"One that's long overdue," I tell her with a sigh.

"Sir," Truman grits out as he approaches carrying a steaming mug of coffee. "As requested."

I don't miss the slight intake of air from Violet. Pride fills my chest that I'm already making changes that will make her happier. And making this dipshit do menial tasks will make her fucking giddy.

"Thanks," I grumble as I accept the coffee. I take a sip and it kind of sucks but at least she didn't have to make it. "Oh…"

Annoyance flits in his eyes but he wisely clenches his jaw to keep those words locked up tight. "Yeah?"

"Violet needs coffee this morning too."

His nostrils flare as he regards her. "How would you like your coffee?"

She sits up and leans forward plastering on a bitchy smile I've never seen before. "I take Splenda in my coffee, sugar."

I narrow my eyes at her. I know for a fact she doesn't take her coffee that way, but something tells me she's saying something that is intended to piss him off. And, boy, does it work like a charm. He lets out an angry huff and storms away.

Her smile turns into a beautiful one I'm familiar with and her brown eyes glitter with triumph. I love this look on her perfect face.

"Let me guess," I say, my eyes lingering on her pouty lips I'm desperate to nibble on. "Truman likes Splenda in his coffee."

She laughs, the sound reverberating its way straight to my cock. "He's an asshole. Serves him right."

"You let me know if he so much as gives you a funny look," I tell her in a firm tone. "I want to know everything."

Relief morphs her features and it once again makes me feel like a fucking blind prick. She's been dealing with this shit for six long years. I could have stopped it. All I had to do was notice…

"I'll be in my office. Come see me when you're settled," I instruct before stalking unwillingly away from her.

"Your mother wants you to stay with her so she can look after you," my father says from in front of the hospital window. His arms are folded across his chest and he refuses to look at me.

"Dad," I grunt, wincing at the never-ending fire that seems to rip across my back each time I move, despite the

fact I've been here for weeks recovering. "I can't go there. You know I can't."

He turns, a heavy sigh on his lips, and regards me with disdain flickering in his eyes. It's a direct blow to my heart. No matter how hard I've tried to become my father—to fuck- ing please him—it's never enough. I'm never enough.

"Well, I sure as hell don't have the time to take care of an invalid," he snarls, his normally cool features screwed up in anger.

An ache forms in my chest but I ignore it. "We can hire a nurse. Please don't make me stay there. You're never there anymore and—"

"Because I have to work my ass off to provide for this ungrateful family!" he roars.

I blink at him in shock. My newest nurse, Sasha, peeks her head in and asks if I'm okay. Once she's gone, I glare at my father. "She's not ungrateful," I hiss. "She's sick. You need to call a therapist."

He huffs and shakes his head. "Your mother isn't sick. She's just a shopaholic and she babies you kids. It's not a sick- ness, it's a personality flaw."

I tremble as if I've been struck by him. "She loves us. Last time I checked, loving your children and husband wasn't a personality flaw. It's called 'normal.' But what isn't normal is you staying in the city all the time. Gwen doesn't understand."

Guilt flashes in his eyes for a brief moment. My baby sis- ter just turned five and is sickly. Mom tries to say it's some- thing to do with her body but my father always argues that it's my mother's filthy housekeeping that's making her sick. Regardless, nobody has discovered yet what it is that's mak- ing her ill.

"Gwen is just a girl. She doesn't understand these things," he grits out.

"But I'm not. You don't explain anything. Why won't you come home to them?"

His lip curls up slightly. "I already told you. My company is in the city. It's time-consuming. I don't have time to run home at every turn and take care of them. I'm able to take care of them financially so that's what I do. Your mother doesn't need a therapist, she just needs her own space."

"Dad, it's a cop out," I snap.

He glares as he storms over to me, his finger wagging in my face. "Don't come at me acting like you know everything, Grayson. I've been married to that woman for over two decades. Trust me when I say it works better this way. She can do…she can buy…she can collect whatever the hell she wants, and I can work. We stay out of each other's hair and everyone is happy. Nobody needs fucking therapy."

I stare up at him in disbelief. How can he even convince himself that all but abandoning Mom and Gwen is okay? Mom's becoming more and more obsessed lately with online shopping. She buys all these things to make Gwen happy. Together, they pick stuff out online and act so fucking happy when shit comes in the mail. But it's weird. It's not normal. And it's starting to collect.

"We're a family," I murmur. "We're supposed to stick together."

He growls. "You're a grown man now. Discharged from the military due to your injuries, sure, but you have a bright future ahead of you that doesn't have to involve the military. You're smart and you'll continue your education. I did what I could to set you down the right path. Gwen is your mother's

problem. They're too much alike. I'll never know how to han-
dle that little girl. It's high time you accept they're happier just
the two of them and eventually move on with your own life."

"A life that doesn't involve you," I clarify, my voice shaking with anger. "You want Mom to nurse me back to health
only for me to abandon them just like you did once I'm well?
Just making sure that's what you want me to fucking do, Dad.
Will that make you proud? A chip off the old block—"

Fire explodes across my back as my father strikes me. An
agonized scream rips from me, and tears roll out of my eyes
on their own accord. Dad stares at me in shock for a moment
upon realizing what he just did. I writhe in excruciating pain
as he stalks out of the room, barking at a nurse to come see
me on his way out.

Fuck you, Dad.
Fuck. You.

"Gray," Violet grumbles as she steps into my office, dragging me from my memory. "You sent me flowers? And a
Kindle?"

I shake away the dark thoughts and grin at her. "Do
you like them?"

Her plump lips purse together as she closes the door
behind her and leans against it. "This is too much. You're
going overboard." She lifts her chin in a brave way—as if
she's been practicing this little speech all morning.

I stand from my chair and drink in her appearance. I
could stare at her shiny long legs for hours. Run my tongue
along the smooth flesh—

"Focus," she snaps, her hands finding their way to her

slightly curved hips. "You can't do—" she waves her hands around her for effect "—whatever it is you're doing here. People will notice."

Who gives a fuck if people notice I'm finally appreciating her for all that she is?

"Listen," I say as I stalk over to her. I love the way her breasts jiggle beneath the fabric as she takes in a harsh breath of air. "I owe you. I owe you so much."

Her body relaxes when I reach her and cup her jaw with my hand. I love how small she feels in my powerful grip. Soon I'll be able to worship every perfect part of her from sun up to sun down. I step closer to her until her full breasts brush up against my chest. My thumb strokes along her jawline as I look into her big brown eyes that no longer hold fury in them. There's heat flickering but it's the kind of heat that I want to get burned by.

"I'm going to kiss you," I murmur, my eyes dropping to her now parted lips. "I'm going to kiss every part of you one day."

A small mewl rattles from her chest. "Gray…"

I rub my nose against hers and inhale the lingering coffee scent on her breath. I want to know if she tastes as good as she smells. "Is this harassment? Is this unwanted?"

"N-No," she admits. "I like this. Too much."

My lips brush against hers, and she grips the lapels of my suit jacket as if to ground herself. *I've got you, little quitter.* I slide my free hand to her hip and press my hard body against her soft one. When she lets out a small moan, I drown it with a kiss. A soul-consuming kiss.

My tongue dives into her mouth. I expect hesitation or resistance. Instead, her tongue eagerly meets mine. She kisses me back just as hungrily. My cock is hard as stone in my slacks and I can't help but press it against her, so she can feel just what she does to me. This sends another pleased moan rippling from her. I take it as an invitation to grind my erection into her stomach as I kiss her deeply enough to steal her breath.

"We shouldn't," she whimpers, turning her head to break our kiss.

I smile as I go for her neck instead. I nip at the flesh and then run my tongue up to her ear, enjoying the way her body trembles in my grip. "You know we should."

"I can't have sex with you here," she utters, her voice but a whisper.

I chuckle and nip at her earlobe this time. "When I take you for the first time, it sure as hell won't be a quickie in my office. I'm going to pin you down in your bed and give you so many orgasms you'll forget your name. And then, I'll slide my cock inside your wet cunt."

She lets out another strangled sound. "You're so confident I'll sleep with you."

I grin and pull away so I can look at her. God, she's so fucking gorgeous. "I'm confident your panties are soaked."

At this, she arches a sculpted brow at me. "Confident, huh?"

"You're practically trembling with the need to fuck me," I assert with a shit-eating grin.

She rolls her eyes. "And if my panties are not 'soaked,' then what?"

"Your panties are soaked. But if they aren't, hypothetically, I'd say I'd owe you something."

"Lunch, perhaps?" she challenges.

I laugh because either way, I'm winning. "Of course."

With fire in her eyes, she grips my wrist and guides it to her thighs. Our gazes stay locked as I take over on my path to her drenched panties. I kneel down on one knee and look up at her to make sure she's still okay. Her swollen-from-our-kiss lip is captured between her teeth as she watches me with hunger dancing in her eyes.

I lean forward and inhale her. From this position, I can smell her arousal. My cock is going to rip through my slacks at any moment.

"Lift your skirt," I command, my voice husky.

She grabs the hem of her skirt with each hand and slowly inches it up, baring more creamy flesh to me. Right before she gets to her pussy, she stops. "This is going too fast," she breathes.

I shoot her a smoldering glare. "Not fast enough."

At my comment, she smirks and her confidence returns full-force. She slips the skirt up past her pussy to her hips. When I drag my gaze from her pretty browns to between her legs, I stare in shock.

"You played me," I growl, my eyes fixated on her smooth bare pussy.

"You were so sure of yourself," she says with a laugh. But her amusement dies down when I grip her thigh and place it over my shoulder. "W-What are you doing?"

I slide a finger along her wet slit and tease her clit softly. "I'm about to get you back."

A moan rushes from her the moment I push a finger into her tight body. Now that her skirt is scrunched up on her hips, she abandons the material to grip my hair. Slowly, I fuck her with my longest finger. Her body reacts beautifully. So fucking responsive. She seems to quake and tremble with the slightest of my movements. I wonder how she'll respond when I'm buried deep inside her cunt and tearing at her smooth flesh with my teeth.

I'm desperate to taste her, so I lean forward and use my free hand to spread her pussy lips apart. My tongue is on a mission to annihilate her with pleasure. The moment it runs across her clit, she nearly collapses. Her grip tightens in my hair. "Oh, God," she chokes out. "Gray…"

I suck on her clit and begin an assault on her that makes her seem to drip with more arousal. The moment I hook my finger inside her and graze her G-spot, she cries out loud enough for people to hear. I don't give a fuck, though. This moment is worth whatever consequences may follow. I suck on her clit and revel in the way she explodes with pleasure. I don't stop my tasting and sucking until she starts wobbling. Then, I pull my finger from her and stand quickly to capture her in my arms. Her slender arms hug my middle, and I don't miss the way she inhales me.

"Did you like that?" I question with a smile and kiss her soft hair.

She nods. "That was so bad. We shouldn't have done that here."

"I do what I want around here," I tell her with a chuckle. "There's so much more I want to do with you. You just have to let me."

"I wasn't exactly fighting you off just then," she says with an annoyed huff. "What's gotten into me?"

I slide her skirt down her hips and back in place and then press a kiss to her pouty mouth. "Not me. Yet."

She laughs at my crude joke and gives me a small shove.

"I'm here to work. Not…"

"Get your pussy eaten by your boss?" I quip.

Her brown eyes widen and her cheeks and throat blaze crimson. "Yeah, that."

I hold my hands up in surrender but flash her a conspiratorial grin. "You ready to get to work now or do I need to make you come one more time?"

FIFTEEN

Violet

I'm flustered and hot and turned on. I can barely focus on the file in front of me as Gray happily rambles on about land values. Two hours ago, he went down on me. In his office. At work. And I let him.

I'm mortified but mostly I can't stop replaying it in my head.

He was so good at it. His tongue and—my God those teeth—knew exactly what they were doing. I remember enjoying oral sex with Vaughn but I'd been half fucked up out of my skull whenever he'd do it.

This was different.

This was real.

I enjoyed every second of it no matter how wrong the location was.

"I can see someone's a little distracted," he says with a smirk from across his desk.

At having been caught, I feel my cheeks heat. "Sorry. I was just thinking about lunch."

He gives me a knowing wink before leaning forward. "I

could eat again."

"Honestly, Grayson," I huff but I can't keep the smile off my face. "You're so crude!"

His chuckle is warm and reverberates its way to my core. "I've been called worse. Seriously, though, what's wrong?"

I miss the way your lips kissed mine. I was thinking of how the inside of my thighs are raw from where your cheek stubble scratched me. My pussy has been throbbing ever since you gave me that orgasm.

"Nothing."

He reaches across the desk and takes my hand. "I want to do that again soon. Your taste is addictive, little quitter."

A couple of days ago, I bristled at the pet name but it's starting to grow on me. Especially coupled with the words before it. "I think I want that too." My eyes drop to our hands that are now threaded together.

"I want so much more than that too, though," he tells me, his voice deep with insinuation.

I chance a glance at him. His icy blue eyes are sharp and focused on me. I love the way he seems to zero in on me. It's as though I'm his primary focus. After everything that went on with Vaughn, you'd think I would be opposed to that kind of attention. But…apparently I have issues because I like it.

"How much more," I breathe, unable to refrain from baiting him into more naughty words.

His eyes drop to my lips. "For starters, I can't wait to feel those pouty lips around my dick. I'm not sure your little mouth can even take my cock." He flashes me a smug grin that has my thighs clenching. "And I can't wait to strip you bare so I can taste every inch of your flesh. I want to run my tongue along every dip and curve you own. I want it in every single hole."

My eyes widen. I'd done anal plenty of times with Vaughn, but I never had his tongue in my ass. The thought both disgusts and delights me.

"I also can't wait to spread your sexy thighs apart so I can look at your needy cunt. I bet it'll always drip for me," he muses and scratches his stubbly jaw with his free fingers. "I know you'll want me to wear a condom, because you don't know me, but I'm fantasizing right now about how you'd feel bare. I bet my cock would slide right into your tight pussy and you'd come just from the way I stretch you out to capacity. I can almost see your juices running down my shaft and—"

"S-Stop," I breathe and squirm in my chair. "I can't think about that right now."

"My dick inside you?"

I let out a sharp breath. "Yes. Oh my God. Stop talking about it." My voice sounds whiny but really it's because I'm needy for all those things too. "Please."

His blue eyes darken with lust, but he nods. "We'll pick this conversation up later tonight."

The promise of pleasure sends excitement coursing through me. "Later," I agree with a smile. "Now let's talk numbers."

After four hours of me showing Gray my many ideas on how to improve not only the way he does things, but the company overall, he announces he's taking me to lunch.

He stands and then offers his hand to help me out of the chair once he's rounded his desk. I take it but immediately hate how affected I am by his touch. All thoughts dissipate as he becomes my only thought. My mind reels with all of the things he said earlier—all the things he wants to do to me. God, how I want them too.

He guides me over to the door, and when I attempt to pull my hand from his, he turns to frown at me. "What's wrong?"

"We can't leave this office holding hands," I tell him, my voice shaky.

He scowls. "And why not?"

"Because you're my boss!"

I'm pulled against him, and he attacks my lips with his. Within moments, I'm lost in his deep kiss. He eventually pulls away and regards me with a dark expression that sends a chill skittering down my spine. "Fuck all of them. You're mine." His lips are back on mine. Owning me. The possessiveness rippling from him should scare me. I should be running for the hills. How is it that I find myself attracted to these severely intense people?

He's not like Vaughn.

At least I hope not.

"Listen to me," he murmurs against my lips as he strokes my hair in such a reverent way I think I might melt. "I'm going to take care of you now. Just let me in, baby."

God, how inviting that sounds.

"This is all too much," I whisper.

He drowns out my words with a kiss that has me dizzy and weak. Once I'm putty in his hands again, he nuzzles his nose against mine. "You deserve everything. It'll never be enough."

Years and years of loneliness threaten to tear my heart wide open. For the first time since I ran from Vaughn, I feel the desire to be with someone else. I don't have to be so hard and guarded around Gray. Around him, I feel relaxed. Safe even. And considering Vaughn could be stalking me at this very moment, I am glad to have Gray's presence cloaking me.

"I'm scared," I admit with a frown. "And Vaughn could be—"

A growl silences me. "He is not a threat to you. Not while I have a say in it. You have to trust I'll take care of you."

I stare up at his serious blue eyes. His jaw clenches as if he truly believes he has the power to protect me from my psycho ex. I almost laugh because Vaughn will stop at nothing. I hope to God it was an intruder from my crummy building who broke into my apartment, and not him. If it truly was my ex, I'm more than screwed. Even big, powerful Gray wouldn't be able to save me.

"How about we start with you buying me lunch first?" I tease in an attempt to lighten the mood. Intense is good in the bedroom. But sometimes intense is too much for everyday life. I worry Gray has those same tendencies as Vaughn. The obsessive ones. However, Gray doesn't share the empty, soulless gaze Vaughn always had. Gray's eyes dance with secrets and curiosity about me and desire. I feel like those are normal for a budding relationship between two people. And they probably mirror my own.

"Lunch first," he agrees with a bright grin that has my

thighs clenching. "But I'm holding your fucking hand."

I'm still laughing at his fierceness as he drags me out the office door. He's on a mission, but my eyes lock onto Truman's, who happens to be standing near my desk. His eyes narrow and he shakes his head in disgust.

Gray doesn't notice him and hauls me out of the building in no time. Once we're outside, he slings an arm around my shoulders and pulls me to his side as we head down the sidewalk. It feels good being like this with someone. It's hard for me to believe that a few days ago, Gray didn't even see me. Now, I feel like I'm all he sees. I'm not stupid. They don't call him Mad Max for no reason. But his eccentricities are endearing now that I'm on his radar.

"Where are we going?" I question as we stroll down the street.

"Someplace good." His tone is sure and smug. I can't help but laugh.

When we walk up to Ziggy's, the city's most popular pizza parlor, I stop in my tracks. The heavenly aromas of garlic and other deliciousness invade my senses. "Ahh," I groan and glare at him. "You're so mean to tease me with this place. You know we can't get in. There is always a three-hour wait." I gesture at the long line of people wrapped around the building to make my point.

He chuckles as he grabs my hand. "Good thing I know people."

"No," I gasp, excitement flitting through me. "Tell me you can get us in."

He steals a chaste kiss and waggles his brow. "I can get us in."

I squeal all the way past the line, ignoring the annoyed

glares, and nearly die when we step inside. The place is small with only a few booths lining the walls. Every seat is packed except a booth in the corner. When he starts for it, I panic a bit. "Are you sure?"

"Positive," he tells me, flashing me another smug grin.

We slide into the booth together on the side that faces the wall, rather than the crowd of people, with me on the inside and him on the outside.

"Someone was probably waiting for this booth," I tell him, my nerves still eating me alive.

"The owner was," he says with a shrug as he grabs a menu from the table.

"We should go then—"

"I'm the owner."

I jerk my head to gape at him. The shit-eating grin he wears so well is sometimes annoying. Okay, so it's not annoying at all. What's annoying is how I melt every time he does it. "You own this place?"

"And this is my booth. Bull and I come here all the time. They know to keep it open for me," he tells me, mischief glittering in his gaze.

"Wow," I utter and steal the menu. "You're full of surprises, aren't you?"

His palm rests on my thigh just below the hem of my skirt so that his fingertips graze my sensitive flesh, sending quivers of desire dancing through me. "You have no idea, little quitter."

The rest of lunch goes amazingly well. He wasn't lying when he said he owned the place. The wait staff knew him and seemed eager to please him. We were brought Gray's favorite items, as well as a few things I wanted to try. By the end, I was stuffed.

"I'm so full," I groan and pat my stomach.

His palm covers my hand and he leans forward, his hot breath on my ear. "I could still eat."

Desire washes through me and I squeeze my thighs together. "You're crazy," I breathe but don't stop him when he slides his palm under my skirt, between my legs. His mouth kisses me slowly along my earlobe and along the side of my neck. All of his touches are making me lose my mind. "I wish we didn't have to go to work," I admit as I tilt my head to the left to give him more access to my throat.

"We can go home," he suggests, his teeth grazing along my tender flesh.

God, how I want to.

"Baby steps," I remind him just as his fingertip grazes along my pussy. I jerk my gaze over to see if anyone can see us. From our position, we're hidden from prying eyes. Which is exactly why I find myself parting my legs. A mewl escapes me the moment his finger is back inside me. "Too fast," I tell him. "All of this is too fast."

He sucks on my neck and then presses a soft kiss to my skin. "I can't slow down with you. Everything in me screams to devour you. I won't stop until I've had all of you, Violet."

His finger slowly fucks me, which drives me borderline insane. My entire body shakes with the need to orgasm right here in a restaurant full of people. He's corrupting me.

"Gray..." I bite my lip to hold back a moan.

"Give me what I want," he growls and then flicks his tongue at my ear. Coupled with his hot breath in one of my most sensitive places and the way his finger owns me, I come like he wants. I come hard and not-so quiet-ly. Thankfully, the restaurant is fairly loud and my sounds are drowned out by forks clattering on plates and people talking. When I come down from my high, he slides his finger out of me and drags my wetness along the inside of my thigh.

"I'll clean that up later," he assures me before pressing a kiss to my cheek.

I'm in a daze as he pays the tab. Nobody is aware this man—my boss for less than two more weeks—just finger-fucked me in this booth. I'm almost giddy from my orgasm and the fact that we just did something super naughty. Gray appears cool and composed whereas I feel as though every-one in the restaurant knows what we were up to. He takes my hand, his finger still wet from my juices, and tugs me from the booth. His blue eyes are dark with lust and hun-ger. I wish I could repay the favor.

Tonight.

I shiver at his promises. He wants to continue this later. In my bed. I'm nearly delirious with the thought of hav-ing sex after so long. After everything that happened back then, you'd think that I'd be opposed to sex. And maybe, for several years, I was. But after some intense therapy, I was able to work through the things Vaughn made me do. I'm normal again.

"What's wrong?" Gray questions once we're back out-side. The sky has darkened as a storm starts to brew. Wind howls between the buildings and I shiver. His brows crush together as he shrugs out of his suit jacket and wraps me up in it. It smells just like him, and I inhale the masculine scent.

"I was just thinking about…" I trail off.

He stops and pulls me up against a building to block the wind. His palm cradles the side of my neck as he regards me with concern. The look in his eyes causes my heart to flop. I could easily fall for Grayson Maxwell. "We're friends," he tells me, his eyes searching mine. "And we're going to evolve into more. We already are. I want you to tell me things."

I swallow and chew on my lip for a moment to draw up the courage. "It's horrible."

"There are things about me that are horrible. Tell me."

My curiosity is piqued but I decide I'll probe more on his horrible secrets later. "Vaughn…he…he prostituted me out."

Gray's face becomes murderous. "He fucking did what?"

My bottom lip trembles as I desperately fight tears. I'd gone so long without even thinking about it regularly. But just saying it out loud, to someone other than my therapist, makes it all come crashing back down around me.

"H-He made m-me have sex with men for m-money," I chatter out. I'm not cold, just overcome with emotion.

He pulls me to him in a brutal hug that sucks the air out of me. When he starts whispering assurances into my hair as he strokes my back, I collapse in his grip. Gray is strong and fierce and holds me against him so I don't fall on my ass.

"I'll kill him. I'll fucking kill him." He chants this over and over and over again as if those words have the power to heal me. And magically, they do. I feel myself latching on to the furious way he says them—so sure and confident—that

I believe him. I believe if he has the chance, he'll do it. God, how I want him to. But Vaughn is a ghost when he wants to be. Nobody is taking him out. Not even the beautifully intense man who is holding me together.

"Are you okay? Did they hurt you?" he demands suddenly, pulling back slightly so he can see me.

I tilt my head up and admire his chiseled jaw and fiery eyes. His nostrils flare and if he grits his teeth any more, he might break them. "Mostly it was just sex. And on the occasion when someone hurt me, he hurt them." I shudder. "I just…I didn't want to do it." More tears well in my eyes. I feel dirty and used and disgusting—just like when I confessed it all to my therapist. But instead of seeing pity or sadness, like I did in her eyes, I find hate and vengeance in his.

"I'll find him and I will end him, Violet. I swear it on my own life," he vows in a low growl. "Oh, sweetheart." His forehead rests against mine and we both close our eyes. Despite unloading one of my most embarrassing secrets, I feel better. Lighter and freer.

"Thank you," I murmur, my voice catching.

"For what?"

I let out a sigh. "For everything. You're slowly chipping away parts of me that I didn't realize were weighing me down. Thank you for that."

His palms find my cheeks and he tilts my head up again to look at him. "You deserve to be free of all of it. I'll do whatever I can to make that happen."

He presses a soft kiss to my mouth.

Everything is going too fast, but somehow I can't find it in me to care. I'm getting sucked into his vortex but I feel like that'll be okay because he'll keep me in the eye of his storm. Nobody will hurt me as far as Gray's concerned.

And what if the storm becomes too intense?

I've survived much worse.

As soon as we got back from lunch, Gray got caught up on a phone call so I busied myself with some cost analyses. Despite him telling me I didn't have to make him coffee, I can't help but notice the time. A scheduled coffee time. And normally, I'd resent every second of having to go into the breakroom to make it for him.

Today is different.

I *want* to make him a cup of coffee.

He has been nothing but good to me since I turned in my notice Friday. Doting and attentive. A good friend. And...*more*. A smile tugs at my lips as I walk into the breakroom and pull a mug from the cabinet.

When heat cloaks me from behind and two hands rest on the countertop on either side of me, I let out a surprised squeak.

"I see you're back to doing your job," Truman seethes.

I freeze and glare at him over my shoulder. "Get away from me."

His eyes are manic and furious. Terror claws its way up inside me, but I squash it down. He is not Vaughn. Nobody will ever be as frightening as Vaughn.

"So help me if you don't step away from me, I'll scream bloody murder," I threaten.

He pins me against the counter and his mediocre erection presses into my ass. I'm stunned for a moment as to what to do. "You scream and I'll deny everything. You think they'll believe the office slut who's clearly banging the boss to get out of doing her damn job?"

I elbow him in his gut and he stumbles away. When he starts for me again, I twist and crack the coffee mug against the side of his face. We both stare at each other for a long moment in surprise. Then his fingers touch his eyebrow. The moment he pulls them away, I realize they are smeared with blood.

"You fucking hit me," he hisses in disbelief.

I grip the handle of the mug and ready myself to use it again. "You fucking touched me," I bite back.

I'm still pressed with my ass against the counter and my arm poised to swing if necessary when I sense a comforting presence. My senses are right because a second later, Truman is shoved away from me.

"What the hell is going on in here?" Gray thunders, his body between Truman and me. With his back to me, I can't help but feel as though he's chosen this stance as a protective one. My heart cracks and breaks because I can't take his kindness. It's too much. Too addicting. I'm going to crave it like an alcoholic needs her booze to survive. I want to get drunk off him. To let him hold me and fight all my battles that I'm too tired to fight anymore.

"She hit me," Truman accuses in a venom-filled tone as he snags a paper towel from beside the sink. "With a coffee mug."

"Boardroom," Gray booms. "Both of you."

I stiffen and want to choke Truman when he shoots me a satisfied smirk before he storms out of the room. Once he's gone, Gray turns his murderous attention on me. I almost cower beneath his hard stare, but soon he softens and strokes my cheek.

"You okay?" he questions, his blue eyes assessing me.

I nod and hold up the mug. "I had a little help from my friend."

"I'm so sorry." His apology is a knife to my heart. It guts me.

"He got handsy and threatening. I took care of him," I tell him, confidence bleeding back into my voice. "This is not your fault."

His fingers run through his messy hair and he growls. "It is but I'm going to make up for it. I swear." Then, his gaze falls to my lips for a moment. "Let's get to the boardroom."

"Am I in trouble?"

"Fuck no," he snarls. "We have a meeting. A meeting you're going to want to be a part of."

"What?" I stare at him in confusion, but he grabs the mug and sets it down, his gaze narrowing.

"You won't be needing that because you have me." His lips quirk up on one side in a sexy, playful way. "Now come on."

I let him take my hand, no longer concerned about people seeing. I won't be here after two weeks anyway. Besides, he's the owner. What are they going to do about it? I smirk at Clint from HR when I pass him in the hallway.

I grow nervous, though, when we enter the boardroom. Eight men are seated around the table. The eight men I hate most at this company. But then my eyes lock with Jeff's—or Bull as Gray calls him—and he gives me a reassuring smile that has all the air in my chest rushing out in relief. He's one of the few I don't hate. Gray pulls out a chair at the head of the table—his chair—and motions for me to sit. All eyes are on me as I take my seat. I flit my gaze up to him and give him a questioning look.

Instead of answering me, his voice thunders as he addresses the group.

"You all were called here today because we have something very important to discuss. But first, I want to ask you all what Violet Simmons does for Maxwell." His voice is low and deadly.

Jeff winks at me before turning to regard Ralph Darden at his left. "What do you think, Ralph?"

Ralph huffs and shrugs. "She's a secretary. Grayson's secretary."

Gray crosses his arms over his chest and walks over to Ralph. "Wrong."

At this, I scrunch up my nose in confusion but I don't dare interrupt. Whatever it is that's going on, I know Gray has my back. He wouldn't treat me the way he's treated me all weekend and today to suddenly throw me under the bus.

"She does special favors for the CEO," Truman quips, disgust in his tone.

Gray's fist slams so hard down on the table beside Ralph, it's surprising that he doesn't break his bones or the table. Everyone gapes at him in shock. Then, he places both palms on the mahogany and leans forward to glare at Truman from across the table. "That," he clips out in the coldest tone I've ever heard, "is sexual harassment."

Truman's eyes widen in surprise and Ralph starts to protest.

"No!" Gray thunders. "You all will listen really well. Jeff and I became aware that many of you are sexually harassing our employees. Specifically, Violet Simmons. And in case you didn't know, sexual harassment will not be tolerated at my company."

Clint peeks his head in the doorway and clears his throat. He looks scared as hell. "That's right," he says in a wobbly voice. "According to our HR policy, many of you have violated the rules."

"This is ridiculous," Ralph hisses. "Just wait until the board hears—"

Jeff slides a piece of paper over to Ralph. "Actually, the board already knows. The motion has been approved to remove you via telephone conference earlier today. As of now, you are no longer an active board member."

"You've got to be kidding me," Brent Adams, the VP utters.

Gray rises to his full height and pins the VP down with a vicious glare that has him hunching in his chair. "I don't joke about sexual harassment."

Brent has the sense to shut his mouth. His face turns bright red. I have to bite back a smile. That asshole has been one of the biggest thorns in my side here.

"Ralph, you may leave," Gray says dismissively. "As far as the rest of you, you're fired."

A roar of arguing voices all start up at once, but Gray once again silences them with a fist slamming down on the boardroom table.

"This is not up for negotiation. Clint and Mr. Barker will handle it from here. I want you gone within the hour," Gray hisses, his fiery glare meeting each and every one of them.

Truman, the arrogant prick, just can't leave well enough

alone because he stands abruptly and points an accusing finger at me. "Sexual harassment isn't okay but it's okay for this bitch to suck you off in your office. Double standards, man."

Gray starts around the side of the table, a loud growl rumbling from him, but Jeff stands and blocks him.

"Enough, Truman," Jeff bellows. "Talking shit after you get fired isn't changing the fact that you no longer work for this company."

Gray shoves past Jeff and pulls my chair out before offering me his hand. Once I'm standing, he addresses Clint this time.

"Violet is now our VP. *That* is what she does for this company. I'll send you an email with the details, but understand this," he tells the wide-eyed HR guy. "She *is* your boss. You report to *her*. And if any more of this sexual harassment bullshit slips through again, it'll be *your* job next."

He gapes at Gray but nods like a bobble head. "Yes, sir."

I'm still in shock, even after we make our way back to his office and he closes the door. "What just happened?"

He stalks back and forth in front of his desk like a caged lion. "I did what I should have a long time ago."

I swallow and stand in his path. His solid chest bumps against mine. A hot glare is affixed on his handsome face. When I reach up and run my fingertips along his jawline, his gaze softens. "I don't know what to say," I murmur, my lips tugging into a frown.

"There's nothing to say," he says gruffly. His palm finds my shoulder and he grips me gently. "They shouldn't have lasted as long as they did."

"But me? I don't know, Gray…" I trail off. Why promote

me right before I leave anyway?

"You're more qualified for that position than anyone in this damn office," he argues, his jaw ticking.

"Won't they think…that…I don't know…"

"That we're fucking?"

I gape at him. "We're not, though."

His eyebrow quirks and he flashes me a smoldering grin. "Not yet."

SIXTEEN

Grayson

I've been counting down the minutes till five ever since I fired a bunch of losers and promoted my girl. And like the hard worker she is, she's taken her new responsibility seriously. She's been tapping away at her computer for hours now. I've been trying to focus on work-related shit, but my mind keeps drifting back to lunch.

It had been perfect. I got to taste her—willingly on her part—before lunch and then had my finger back inside her before lunch was even over. I'd been looking forward to the moment I'd have her alone until she broke apart on the street.

That motherfucker prostituted her out.

I will put my crosshairs on his goddamned forehead and blow his head off.

"Is murder on the agenda today?" Bull questions in a teasing manner from my doorway.

I shrug. "Maybe."

His eyes widen and he closes the door behind him. "I was kidding, but apparently you're not. Who are we killing?"

I can't help but grin at my best friend. Always willing to go into battle with me no matter what. "Vaughn Brecks."

He stiffens and gives me a clipped nod. "Thought so." He drops a file down on my desk. Dusty's familiar handwriting is scrawled on the outside. Three possible addresses. I flip open the file and stare at the pictures inside.

"He took these photos?" I demand, a menacing growl in my throat.

He shakes his head. "No, but he's doing more digging. The first address is the one he thinks he's at. A guy fitting his description comes and goes from there."

"Anything else?"

"Not as far as that fucker is concerned. Mostly, I wanted to check to see how you were doing. In that meeting," he says thoughtfully as he scrubs his cheek with his palm, "you weren't yourself."

I frown and cross my arms over my chest. "How so?"

He shrugs. "I don't know. You were focused. Not just on her but everything around you."

Ever since Violet caught my eye, I seem to notice a lot of things. Mostly the things that directly affect her but she seems to touch everything around her, which means I notice those things as well.

"Violet makes me better," I tell him, confidence in my tone.

He smirks. "I can see that. I can see she's warmed up to you."

"She's mine," I tell him absently as if that is the reason why she is no longer frigid around me.

"Does she know that?" he probes, amusement in his voice.

"I told her a time or two."

He snorts and rubs at the back of his neck. "Of course you did. Does she know you're a fucking stalker?"

I flip him off and he laughs.

"Seriously. Does she know the depths of your obsession?"

"I told her I'd do anything for her," I grunt out. "Even kill that fuckface Vaughn."

His eyes widen in surprise. "And she didn't run for the hills?"

"Nope."

"Well, Jesus Christ, Hawk, I think you found yourself the perfect woman," he jokes.

"Goddamn right I did."

"Good for you," he says with a chuckle. "Don't fuck it up. Maybe lay off the stalker shit now that she's into you."

But there's so much more to learn about her…

"Hmph."

He snorts again. "Don't get arrested, psycho."

"I'll try not to, asshole."

His smirk is my parting gift as he leaves for the day. I thumb through the folder and read through Vaughn's rap sheet. He's a fucking stalker too. The guy has more restraining orders against him than I've ever seen one person have. This could work in my favor…

I shut the folder and hide it in my drawer. Once the drawer is locked, I grab my jacket and go look for my woman. When I find her leaned over the planter of violets I bought for her empty desk, inhaling their sweet scent, I can't help but smile at her.

She's the most beautiful woman I've ever seen.

"You ready?"

She swivels around and beams at me. "Let me run to the restroom, and then we can go."

I love how eager she is to want to spend more time with me. When she's gone, I sit down in her chair. Her phone buzzes.

Sean: How about lunch one day this week to discuss some business? Same place as Friday? I promise to be a perfect gentleman.

Rage bubbles in my chest. I'm dying to write him back and tell him he's a fucking idiot but the clack of her heels tells me she's on her way back. With a huff, I set the phone back down.

"Trying to steal my chair already?" she teases as she grabs her purse.

"The chair isn't the only thing around here I'm going to steal." When I smirk at her, she laughs but then her smile falls as she picks up her phone to read her text. With a frown, she taps out a response. I'm dying to know what she said to him but I know I can sneak a peek later when she's asleep.

"What are we doing?" she questions as we start out of the building.

I guide her to where my car is parked. "Well," I say as I open her door, "first we're going to go eat." She pulls her bottom lip between her teeth as she regards me. "And then I'm going to take you back to your place and fuck you." Her eyes widen, but I shut the door before trotting around to the other side.

"Gray," she hisses as soon as I sit inside and start the car. "What if I don't want to fuck?"

I flash her a panty-melting—*not that she's wearing any*—grin. "I'll convince you."

She's been locked away in her bathroom for a good forty minutes now. After we ate a nice steak dinner at one of my favorite restaurants, I brought her back to her place. And just like I'd arranged, her locks had been replaced. I'd asked the locksmith to leave me the extra key under her doormat. I swiped that when I'd heard the shower running.

While she takes forever in the bathroom, I use the time to rifle through the closet I'd been searching through last night. Coats hang from the racks and boxes line the shelves. I'd been in the process of checking the pockets when she woke up.

I locate a letter in one coat pocket addressed to "Momma." It isn't sealed but it is addressed already. With my phone, I snap a picture of it for later investigation. I open it and read it quickly when I hear the hair dryer going.

Momma,

I miss you. One day maybe things can be different. You know I love you. Everything just got so bad, and I needed to get away. You know this. Of course you know this. I've been telling you the same thing for years. I hope the money helps. It's all that I can afford to send, but I hope it's enough so you don't have to break your back every night at the diner.

Love you always.

She didn't sign the letter nor did she add a return address. The money she sends away—the reason she lives in this shithole—makes more sense now. I fold the letter back up and stuff it in the coat pocket. I'm just closing the closet door when her cell phone starts ringing from the bedroom. Figuring it's Sean, I stalk in there. The number is unknown.

I answer it but don't speak.

Someone breathes heavily on the other line and my hackles raise.

"Is that you, Letty Spaghetti?" a deep voice growls.

I can fucking growl too.

But I don't.

"I think you've reached the wrong number," I bite out, my rage barely controlled. But I'll be damned if I let on that this is her phone.

Click.

I quickly block the number and delete the trace of the call from her phone. I've just set it down when the bathroom door opens.

Violet steps out of the bathroom, a nervous look on her face. "Were you talking to someone?"

"Wrong number," I assure her. My eyes peruse her perfect body that's barely covered by her silky robe. Her nipples are hard beneath the fabric, and I can tell she's completely naked underneath. All the anger and fury from learning that fuckface has her number washes away as heat rushes to my cock. "Wow," I growl. "So much wow."

A smile tugs at the corner of her lips. "Oh, this old thing," she teases as she spins in a circle. My cock jolts when I see her delectable ass beneath the robe.

"Come here," I order.

She stiffens and shoots me an unsure look. "Gray…"

"I just want to kiss you." Not entirely a lie. I want to kiss every part of her. My words seem to calm her because she walks over to me and tilts her head up as if she's waiting for that promised kiss.

My palms grab her gorgeous ass, and I pull her against me so she can feel just how hard I am for her. A gasp of air escapes her.

"Anyone ever tell you you're the most beautiful woman on this fucking planet?"

She chuckles but I'm dead serious.

I squeeze her ass as I drop a kiss to her supple lips. Our kiss is sweet at first, but soon she's helping me peel off my suit jacket. Her palms roam up my chest and then she's working frantically at the knot of my tie. I tug at the strings on her robe and she wiggles out of it until she's completely naked before me. Grabbing hold of her shoulders, I push her away until she's at arm's length so that I can properly view her. Sure, I've seen her naked plenty of times over the last few days but never like this.

"You're so goddamned beautiful," I praise and then run my tongue along my bottom lip.

She chews on hers and stands there looking uncomfortable under my scrutinizing stare. I let my gaze drink up every beautiful curve on her perfect body while I rid myself of my tie and shirt. When my eyes dart up to hers, she's staring at my chest.

"You have tattoos," she whispers.

I frown. "I do."

"I like them." Her brown eyes are molten with lust. "I like them a lot."

Smirking, I look down at my colorful chest. Dad ingrained in me to be structured and focused, but Bull helped me rebel. He was there with me for every single tattoo inked on my chest and arms, in solidarity. I unbuckle my belt and lift an eyebrow at her. "You ready for this?"

She laughs. "It's a penis not an introduction to the president."

I let my slacks fall to the floor and step out of them. Her greedy eyes find my cock that is straining through my black boxers. "That's Mr. President to you."

"Hmmm," she says, amusement in her tone. "Let's see him."

I flash her a wicked grin as I lose the boxers. When I start stroking my impressive length, she lets out another one of those sexy, needy sounds I've grown to love.

"Crap," she breathes. "We're really doing this."

I lift a brow. "Unless you don't want to."

"Oh," she says with a wild look in her eyes, "I certainly *do* want to."

Releasing my cock, I step toward her and capture her face in my hands. I brush kisses along her soft lips and jaw until she's clawing at me. My cock is hot and throbbing and oh-so-fucking eager between us. When her hand reaches between us and grips my dick, I let out a guttural groan of pleasure.

She's my fantasy come to life.

A dream come true.

With each stroke of her hand, I feel closer to coming. So after another selfish moment of having her small hand wrapped around me, I pull away and regard her hungrily. "Get on the bed and show me your pussy."

Her eyes widen at my brazen words, but she sits down on the edge and scoots back. Once she lies back and her body is ripe for my visual tasting, I take hold of her knees and spread her apart. Her cunt glistens with her arousal, and I can't wait to have my nose buried in it. I want to suck her taste until she can't speak or think.

"Touch your nipples," I growl.

She lets out a whimper but obeys me. I crawl toward her and inhale her sweet scent. When I drag my tongue along her slit, she jolts on the bed.

"Grayyyy…"

I chuckle and press a kiss to her clit. "Mmmmm?"

"Oh, shit," she breathes. "That's too much."

I cock an eyebrow up and challenge her. "When I hum against your clit?"

"Yes." Her eyes are wild and frantic as she pinches her nipples.

"Good," I murmur before capturing her clit between my lips. I apply pressure with my lips and let out a growling sound that no doubt reverberates to her sensitive bundle of nerves because she cries out. Slowly, I push one finger into her soaked entrance. She's so fucking tight, and I can't wait to feel her perfect body gripping mine. We were made to be together. Everything about this feels right. She doesn't know it yet, but I'm going to make her my wife. My partner. The goddamned mother of my children.

Mine.

"More," she moans.

I urge another finger inside her and she starts to tremble. With firm circles, I begin pleasuring her clit that's hot beneath my tongue. My fingers slide easily in and out of her because she's so wet for me. When I start pushing a third finger inside, she loses control. An orgasm tears through her quickly and forcefully. Her tight channel grips my fingers as she goes wild on the bed. The moment she stops shuddering, I slide my fingers out and crawl over her. My cock slides against her drenched pussy lips, but I don't let it enter her.

"Gray," she begs, her eyes dark with lust and need. "Please."

I inch the tip of my cock in but don't let it go any farther. I want her juices soaking me from the tip to the base. Those other men Vaughn made her sleep with didn't deserve her perfection. She was always mine...I just hadn't found her yet.

"I want to fuck you bare," I tell her boldly, my eyes fixating on hers. "I want to feel every hot part of you wrapped around me. I want to drain my orgasm inside of you. I want to watch it pour from your sore pussy when we're finished."

She lets out a moan. "God, why does that sound so hot?"

"Because it is," I assure her and tease her some more by pulling the tip back out and letting it run along her clit before pushing it barely inside of her again.

"It's irresponsible."

It takes every ounce of self-control not to slam into her. "I'm going to fuck you bare," I growl again. "We both want it. All we're waiting on is for you to admit it."

Her body wiggles as if she's trying to get me to slide in all the way. When her heels dig into my ass to pull me closer, it takes everything in me to fight against her. I want to hear the damn words.

"I'm going to come inside you," I murmur and dip down to nip at her bottom lip. "So fucking deep, Violet."

"This is...oh, God..." Her body trembles with need.

"Beg for it, baby. I want to please you. All you have to do is ask for it."

My stubborn girl bites on her bottom lip. "I don't know who you've been with…and my past is…we hardly know each other…this isn't me…"

Our eyes lock as I inch deeper inside her. My cock is halfway in her tight cunt. I almost pass out from the pleasure. I reach between us and capture her clit between my thumb and finger, twisting it just enough to hug the line between pain and pleasure.

"Gray," she mewls, her fingernails clawing into my sides. She's losing control. This woman is usually wound up so tight, but right now she's unraveling fast and just for me.

"I'm going to take care of you," I assure her with a fierce growl. "*Let* me take care of you."

I slide the rest of the way in and my cock throbs almost painfully. I've never been inside a woman bare before. It's as if I can feel every part of her. Her eyes are wild and those pouty lips of hers are parted.

"Do you like this? Me inside of you like this?" I question, my nose dragging along hers.

"Y-Yes," she chokes out. "So much yes."

"You want me to fuck you so hard you scream?" I trail kisses to her ear and nip the flesh just below it. "Hmmm?"

"Yes," she whines. "Fuck me hard."

"I'm going to come inside you, Violet."

Her fingernails claw at me as she becomes positively manic. "Stop talking and fuck me. I want to feel all of you inside of me."

With a wicked grin, I slide out just so I can slam into her violently. The scream that escapes her is pure heaven.

Thrust after thrust, I drive into her. I don't neglect her needy clit either. I massage her in unison to the speed I'm pounding into her. Our mouths meet for an uncoordinated kiss that has our teeth knocking together. Neither one of us cares, though. We're too wrapped up in our moment.

I manage to pull a lovely scream from her as another orgasm crashes through her. The moment her pussy clenches, I lose control. My seed gushes out inside of her, marking her with me.

She's mine.

Fucking mine.

I slow down until I'm completely still inside of her. Her eyelids are heavy, and I love how red her mouth is from where my stubble scraped her. She's completely sated and at ease. The soft, easy look in her eyes is one I could get used to seeing every day.

"Come bathe with me," I murmur as I press kisses to her parted mouth. "I want to take you again in the shower."

She whimpers and the familiar tension that always seems to have its tentacles around her tightens its grip. "What we just did…Gray, I'm not on the—"

I silence her with a kiss. At first, she protests but then her mouth joins in. Our tongues aren't interested in what's right or wrong or fucking irresponsible. Our tongues just want to fuck each other.

My cock starts to harden again but I want to take her when her soapy, slippery tits are in my grip. So instead of fucking her once more, I slip out and revel in the way my cum runs down the crack of her ass, soaking the bed. I wonder if this is how Bull feels about Sadie. The overwhelming need to consume her in every way.

I saunter off toward the bathroom. She lets out a sharp breath, but I don't stick around to see why and turn on the hot spray of the shower. I climb inside, and seconds later, she joins me. I'm grinning at her but her brows are furrowed together in sadness.

"What's wrong?" I demand, concern dripping from my voice.

She turns me to face the wall. Then, her palms skate over my burn scars on my back. I tense up which makes her hesitate. "Does this hurt?"

"Not anymore."

Her palms continue to ghost over my mangled flesh. I know it's hideous and ruined. I'm hoping she's not turned off.

"What happened?" she whispers, her lips kissing the flesh. A shiver ripples its way straight to my dick, making it bounce.

"I was a sniper in the Marine Corp during the Gulf War. RPG nearly got me," I say with a sigh. "The explosion did a number on me."

Her arms wrap around me and her cheek rests against my mottled flesh. "I'm so sorry. That had to have been horrifying."

I shrug and cover her arms with my hands. "I don't re-member the explosion. All I remember is waking up in the hospital on my stomach and being in excruciating pain. It took many skin grafts and months of recovery. A very dark time in my life."

She sniffles. "I suppose we all have dark times…they're just different. No less terrifying."

I twist back around so I can hug her. Whatever that

fucker did to her must have been bad if she's comparing it to RPG explosions and third-degree burns. Under the hot spray of the shower, I hold her to me and stroke her hair.

"I want to take you to the resort in a couple of days. We'll miss a few days of work and stay through the weekend. When was the last time you got away?" I question.

"I've been on vacation the past six years since I've lived here," she says with a humorless laugh.

I grip her chin and tilt her head up. "Working for me was no vacation."

"But I was free of…" she trails off and her bottom lip quivers. "Him."

"Yes," I agree and press a kiss to the wobbling lip. "But when was the last time you splurged and spoiled yourself?"

"Never."

"Which is exactly why we're going on Wednesday."

She doesn't get to argue anymore because I grab her tiny ass and lift her. My mouth covers hers in a hot kiss as my dick slides into her.

I'm going to show her over and over what it means to be spoiled.

T-minus eleven days…

SEVENTEEN

Violet

I wince as I sit in my new comfy desk chair. The chair may be comfortable but it does nothing to ease the ache between my legs. It's all Gray's fault. Last night, he fucked me until I kicked him out. I needed sleep, and if he stayed in my bed, neither of us would get it.

God, did he ever fuck me, though.

Life after Vaughn has been cold and difficult. But last night, I was on fire. Everything was easy. For once in a really long time, I relaxed and enjoyed myself.

A little too much.

With a grunt of frustration, I dig around in my purse to locate the morning-after pill I bought on the way to work this morning. I'm praying to God he's clean because we had sex carelessly four times without a condom. I quickly down the pill with my water bottle and put my purse away.

Heat creeps up my neck as I steal a glance toward his office. The door is closed, and I can hear Jeff's deep voice booming on the other side. Whatever they're talking about doesn't seem like it's good.

Once my computer is finally powered up, I find I have two emails waiting for me. The first is from Clint and the second is from Gray. I ignore Mr. Fuck-A-Lot and open the important one. Clint's sent me a Word document, listing all of all my new duties. I already do everything on the list each day, aside from manage people. After I reply to him that I received it and save it for easy access, I open Gray's email.

Violet,

Last night was incredible. YOU are incredible. I want to take you to lunch.

Gray

I smile because he's pretty incredible too. After my ex, I should be hesitant to dive right into something with someone—my boss no less—so quickly, especially considering he's extremely attentive but I can't help myself. His magnetism draws me in.

Vaughn was the same way…

I squash the thought because I refuse to let my past dictate my future. Gray is generous and thoughtful and sweet. He's not psychotic. I've worked for him for six long years, and although he'd been nicknamed Mad Max for his eccentric ways, not one time had I thought he was an evil person.

He's just hyper-focused.

Obsessive about his company.

Driven to succeed.

But not a possessive lunatic.

I'm still trying to convince myself when Gray's office door creaks open, and Jeff steps out. His gaze darts over to mine. Guilt shines in his eyes. My heart rate speeds up, and I frown at him. He gives me a quick wave in greeting before stalking back to his office. I'm still staring at him when Gray comes sauntering out. He's scowling until he sees me. All irritation melts from his expression as his face lights up. And dammit, I feel my face lighting up too. I love how my presence seems to cheer him up.

"Good morning," I say with a smile.

He strolls over to my desk and sits on the edge. When he reaches out to toy with a strand of my hair, my eyes flutter closed and I exhale a tiny sigh. His fingertips brush along my jaw and down my throat. I pop my eyes open when he touches the string of pearls my mother gave to me as a high school graduation present.

"I like this necklace on you," he praises, his dark brows pulled together as he inspects my jewelry. This necklace was the only thing I was able to take with me when I ran away from Vaughn because I happened to be wearing it that day.

My heart is thundering because, God, he smells delicious and he's touching me intimately, despite our workplace setting. Warning bells are going off inside my head because all it takes is the wrong person seeing our exchange to give me hell. Unfortunately for me, I've never been one to heed warnings very well and tend to float off into the deep end without a raft.

Gray will save me.

Once, I thought Vaughn would too.

A rough thumb brushes against my bottom lip and my eyes dart to his. His icy blue eyes are narrowed as he scrutinizes me. Seconds pass by—*tick, tick, tick*—as I remain under his microscope. The thing with Gray is, it's almost as if he can see right into my head. As if he knows exactly what's running through my mind. I feel naked and exposed around him.

"Are you sore?" he questions, his voice husky. His eyes flicker with heat that burns its way straight to my core.

I jerk my gaze around the office but nobody is paying attention. "Yes," I admit with a whisper.

A smug grin tugs at his handsome mouth. "Good. I like the idea of you thinking about my big cock every time you sit down."

"Gray!" I hiss and once again do a visual sweep of the office for nosy co-workers.

He shrugs. "What? I'm just being honest. How busy are you right now?"

This feels like a trick question, and like the naïve girl I am, I follow him right into the proverbial white van where he promises candy and puppies. "Not very busy."

"Good," he says with a wolfish grin that has my panties becoming wet between my thighs. "I need your assistance in my office."

He stands and turns away to walk back to his room. My gaze roams his fit body that looks too perfect in a suit. It's a good thing I'm leaving this company soon because having to stare at him each day looking good enough to eat is quite distracting.

I'll be leaving soon.

Several days ago, I'd have been thrilled.

But that was all before Gray finally noticed me.

Guilt and indecision wars within me. He's already done so much for me. We've gone from co-workers to friends to lovers in a matter of days. Grayson Maxwell is so intense that I've easily been swept up into his vortex.

How will it feel when I finally crawl my way out?

Will I be the same?

Rising from my chair, I push away those thoughts for now as I stride into his office and close the door behind me.

"Lock it."

His rough command sends shivers through my body. I flip the lock and regard him with my hands on my hips.

"What do you need help with?" I question, my voice raw and shaky.

He sheds his jacket and hangs it on the back of his chair. The powder blue dress shirt he's wearing today molds perfectly against his skin. I can see his tattoos through the fabric and it sends another thrill shooting through me.

"Gray," I try again, my voice rising. "What do you need?"

He arches a brow at me and pins me with a smoldering glare. "You know what I need."

As I choke on my words, he unbuttons his shirt at his wrist and begins rolling up his sleeve. The veins in his forearm bulge and the muscles flex with his movement. I find myself staring at his wrist of all things with my mouth watering for a taste. He continues on with the other side. Then, he begins working at the knot on his navy-colored tie.

My body is about to combust. Between my thighs, my panties are drenched. Hardened nipples scratch against my bra. And an internal fire alights my flesh from the inside out. He sheds the tie and undoes the first two buttons before placing his hands on his hips to mimic my position.

"I need you to look over some contracts with me. I want some advice," he says as he strolls over to sit in his chair. I'm so dumbfounded by the quick turn of events that it takes me a second for my mind to catch up to his words.

"Contracts?" I murmur.

His dark brow arches up again, and he smiles crookedly at me. "Contracts." Then his gaze narrows as he roams my body. "You didn't think we were going to fuck in here, did you? With everyone listening?"

I swallow and shake my head before hurrying over to the seat across from his desk. Snagging the nearest folder on his desk, I snap it open and stare at the words on a page. My brain is running a hundred miles per hour. Nothing on the page makes sense.

He reaches across the desk and snags my wrist. I let out a yelp when he pulls my hand to his face. Then, in a shocking move, he sucks on my middle finger. I dart my gaze to his blazing one, my lips parted open in surprise. His tongue teases the underside of my finger like he's done on my clit which has a low moan escaping me.

"Baby," he growls and playfully bites my flesh before pulling away. "I most definitely want to fuck you. Right here on this desk. I want to make you scream. I want your pussy to drip all over these files and smear the ink. Violet, I want my cock buried so deep in your sore cunt that you beg me to stop." Another growl. "But that's the thing, beautiful, I wouldn't be able to stop. I'd fuck you all day over and over. You'd be weak from all the orgasms, and I'd be worthless to run this company. Together, we're explosive." He kisses the tip of my finger. "Which is why the fireworks have to stay outside of this building."

I swallow and nod. "You drive me crazy with the way you talk…"

"I know." He winks and flashes me a knowing grin before releasing me.

Now that I know I won't be getting spread out over the desk and feasted upon like a Thanksgiving dinner, I can focus. Focus. Focus.

Violet, focus.

"I had a pet bird once," he murmurs, his voice soft.

My fingers had been stroking circles on his bare chest. "Mmm?" I look up to find him staring up at my bedroom ceiling, lost in thought. After a productive day at work, he took me out for sake and sushi. Then, we ended up in my bed where he made me come so hard I nearly forgot my name.

But I didn't forget the condom.

I managed to throw one at him and even ignored his groans of complaint.

The sex was amazing.

This cuddling thing, though, is even better. I'd missed human connection. Simple kissing and touching.

"I'd been hunting quail with my dad. We killed a mother. She left behind a squawking baby bird. My father was pissed when I told him I was going to keep it as a pet," he tells me gruffly. "I hardly ever acted out against my father. But I wanted it, Violet. I needed it. Something about that bird spoke to me."

I smile because him caring for a little bird is sweet. "How old were you?"

"Nine." His hand covers mine on his chest and he rubs his thumb along my flesh. "I took it home. Named it Wail the Quail." We both laugh. "Wail was loud and needy. But I loved him. I'd marched my butt down to the library and checked out every book I could find on quails. I learned about their feeding, nesting, sleep habits. Everything there was to know about Wail, I made it my job to figure out."

"That's so sweet," I say, leaning forward to kiss his jaw.

He's quiet for a moment before speaking. "I loved that bird. Dad knew it." His voice grows cold, sending shards of ice poking at me. "One day, Mom cooked a nice dinner. As we were eating, Dad not-so-kindly pointed out that we were eating Wail's mother."

I tense and stare at him. His eyes are clenched shut and his nostrils flare with fury. I kiss him again in hopes to calm him, but it doesn't work. A ripple of rage quakes through him.

"When I stood from the table and told him I would not eat my pet's mother, he threatened to murder Wail if I didn't eat the meat. With tears in my eyes, I choked down that bird. Mom had mentally checked out, staring at her plate and not touching the meat she'd prepared." His voice cracks which causes tears to well in my eyes.

"I'm so sorry," I whisper.

He swallows. "When I finished, I went back to my room. I'd felt so guilty and wanted to apologize to my bird but…"

My heart pounds in my chest. "What?"

"He wasn't there," he chokes out. "Wail was gone."

A tear leaks out of my eye and I sit up. My palm strokes his stubbly cheek. "Where did he go?"

His eyes are hard when they meet mine. "My father said my bird stunk up our house. He killed my bird. Dad plucked the feathers and cleaned his carcass. Handed it to my mother and made her cook it up."

"No…"

"She didn't know," he murmurs. "Always doing what he asked of her. But I didn't eat Wail's mom. I ate Wail."

I press a kiss to his mouth. Soft kisses. Comforting kisses. Over and over again because I don't want him to think about his asshole father. He's still at first, but when I straddle him to kiss him harder, he parts his mouth to meet my tongue with his. His fingers spear into my hair to guide our kiss.

A moan escapes me when his hard cock rubs against my ass. When he reaches between us, I lift my body and let him guide himself into me again. My body aches from all the sex we've had, but this feels different. Not just fucking. Something else. I slide up and down on his thick length as my gaze meets his. Sadness lingers in his eyes, but the hunger he always seems to have for me slides into the forefront. His strong fingers find my hips. He grips them almost to the point of pain as he lifts his hips to drive into me.

"Gray," I moan as my head tilts back. One of his hands slips to my breast while the other begins massaging my clit. I ride him wildly until an orgasm is rippling through me, causing every muscle in me to spasm. I'm trying to find the sense to slide off of him before he comes, but then he's gripping my hips again. With hard, measured thrusts, he seeks out his own climax. And with a groan on his end, I feel his heat surge into me.

Fuck.

Why am I so careless with him?

He yanks me to him, and I fall hard against his chest. Our heartbeats are thundering against one another through our chests. His fingers tangle in my hair as he whispers sweet nothings against the shell of my ear through my messy hair.

You're mine.

I want you forever.

Let me keep you.

Mine.

Let me love you.

Forever.

The words are intense and spoken quickly, but I drink them up. I greedily take them all as though I have no self-control around men like him. They offer intensity and I devour it as if it nourishes me somehow. Vaughn fed me this same way. It's what I'm attracted to.

This attraction was, at one time, nearly fatal.

As my eyes drift close, my thoughts drift to the night I ran and never looked back.

"This way, Letty Spaghetti," Vaughn grumbles as he drags me by my wrist down the dilapidated hallway of the apartment building we came to.

I tug at the short hem of my dress but it's so tight it hardly moves. I settle for fingering my pearls that belonged to Momma in a nervous manner. Vaughn and I have been playing this game for months. The sane part of my brain that survives when the pills wear off tells me I'm a prostitute. This is not my boyfriend. He's my pimp. But prostitutes get paid, don't they? What does it make me if he forces me to have sex and I see nothing in return?

A slave.

It makes me his damn sex slave.

Anger begins to bubble up inside me. Earlier when he shoved the pill into my mouth, I tucked it into the side of my mouth between my teeth and cheek. He's so used to me swallowing without complaint that when he looked, he didn't really look. Just a simple glance. I managed to pull it out on the walk down to the car and tossed it into the bushes.

My brain is clear.

My heart is angry.

My soul is broken.

He stops in front of a door and knocks loudly. A large black man answers the door wearing a tight white wife beater, a beanie on his head, and a baggy pair of jeans that hang several inches off his hips showing his blue boxers.

"V, my man," he greets in a deep voice. "I got your money, dawg." He pulls a wad of bills rubber banded together and hands it to Vaughn.

Vaughn nods and fist bumps the guy. "I knew you were good for it, Fuzz."

The guy named Fuzz lets his gaze roam over to me. "Your girlfriend? Damn, she fine."

"Could be yours for the night if you got more cash," Vaughn tells him.

Fuzz's easygoing features harden as he steps aside to inspect me as I cower behind Vaughn. He lets out a whistle of appreciation. "Shit, V, she's got some fine-ass legs. Her cunt tight?"

I shudder at his crude words. Normally, I'm high off my ass by the time we get to these men he sells me to. Awareness prickles through me. I wish I were fucked up right now.

"The tightest," Vaughn brags, a lingering hint of possessiveness in his tone.

"How much?" Fuzz questions as he blatantly eye-fucks my tits.

"How much you got?"

Fuzz laughs. "You took all my money, man."

"You got any brown left?" Vaughn asks.

"I got a gram or two," Fuzz tells him, his gaze never leaving the way my dress hugs my tits.

"I need it."

I swallow and gape at him. Surely he's not selling my body for a couple of grams of crystal meth.

"Come in, man, shit's over there," Fuzz says and points to the couch.

Vaughn drags me into the dingy and trashed apartment by my wrist. Terror spikes through me. I don't like this guy Fuzz and the way he stares at me as if he wants to hurt me.

"You got twenty minutes with her," Vaughn tells him as he sits on the lumpy sofa and reaches for the tray of drugs. "No anal."

Fuzz lets out a whistle before grabbing me from behind. I scream when I'm lifted off the floor and carried into the bedroom. Vaughn's laugh sends ice shooting through my veins. This is an all-time low for him. So many times he's hurt me but this betrayal runs deep.

Once inside the bedroom that reeks of body odor, I'm shoved to the floor. Fuzz shuts the door behind him and starts ripping off his shirt. He's giant and solid muscle. It's the evil glint in his eyes that has me scrambling away. I'm halfway toward the window when he grabs me by my hair and hauls me over to the bed. The screams ripping from me are otherworldly as he shoves me over the edge of the stinky stained mattress. He rips my dress up over my hips exposing my bare ass to him.

"No anal," he mimics as he begins unbuckling his pants.

Tears stream down my cheeks and I once again try to claw my way away from him. He's strong as he presses the back of my head down against the mattress with his massive hand. I'm squirming but it doesn't stop him from pushing his fat erection into my dry pussy. I sob and claw my fingernails into the soiled mattress but to no avail. He drives into me brutally. His grunts and moans are like alcohol in a cut, stinging me from the outside in.

"This ass is so fucking hot," he tells me as he slams into me. "I'm going to hit it too."

I start screaming for Vaughn. Begging him to save me. Fuzz pulls out of my pussy and begins pushing the head of his cock against my asshole. Fire burns through me from the tiny intrusion. I'm fearful for when he manages to get all the way in.

"V-Vaughn, p-please," I sob.

Pain, excruciating and all-consuming, explodes within me when Fuzz pushes all the way into me. I black out but the fire won't let me go. It holds me just out of reach from passing out all the way. Some sick torturous game.

I will myself to think about anything other than the brutalization but I can't. All I can think about is Fuzz's giant cock in my ass while my boyfriend ignores my screams.

I start to truly black out when I hear a slam. Then a grunt. The pain seems to lessen the moment Fuzz pulls out.

Crack! Crack! Crack!

I manage to roll over to my side, wincing in pain. Vaughn has Fuzz by the throat as he slams his fist over and over again into the man's face.

"I. Said. No. Anal," Vaughn roars, gripping Fuzz by the throat and then slamming his head into the edge of a dresser.

Pop! Pop! Pop!

Sickening sounds of crunching bone and puncturing flesh cause me to vomit. Bile spews all over the mattress as tears blur the scene before me. Vaughn doesn't stop for what seems like forever.

He lets go of Fuzz who hits the floor with a thud. When Vaughn's eyes meet mine, they're dilated and wild from the drugs. He winks at me before stalking out of the room. I'm shaking so badly but I manage to sit up on my side. When I glance out of the room, I'm horrified to see Vaughn prepping another syringe. I drag my gaze to the floor. Fuzz, or what's left of him, faces the ceiling. His face is crushed in and he's not breathing or moving.

Vaughn killed him.

He's going to kill me one day soon too.

I know that to be true with every part of my being. And without the drugs confusing me, I'm able to take action. I ease myself off the bed and stand on wobbly legs. Everything hurts, especially my ass, but I manage to drag my dress back down to cover myself. Bright red blood runs down my thigh past my knee.

Oh, God.

I sway at the sight of the blood but dart my eyes over to the window. With newfound urgency, I make my way over to the window and begin fiddling with the lock. I flip it open and wrench the window up. It takes some work, but I manage to get it up high enough to squeeze through. The fire escape provides me with the out I need. With each passing second, I find more clarity.

I must get away.

And I need to make sure he never finds me again.

Abandoning my heels so I can run faster, I scale down the fire escape ladder as quickly as I can. When I reach the bottom, I hop down the rest of the way right into a puddle. The alley of the apartment building is empty, but at the end of one side is a busy street. I take off, sprinting toward the cars that keep passing by.

"Hey, baby, stay awhile," some guy smoking hollers at me.

I ignore him and run faster right out into the middle of traffic. A car slams on its brakes. I lock eyes with a woman around my mom's age as the front of her car bumps my hip. She has a teenage girl in the passenger side with her, who wears a similar stunned reaction.

"Please," I beg through my tears. "I need help."

She's still gaping at me when I round the side of the car. Other vehicles swerve around her car, that's stopped in the middle of the street, and honk. I beat on her window as terror threatens to consume me. A quick look over my shoulder tells me he isn't after me yet.

"Please," I plead again, "I've just been raped."

This seems to jolt her into action. With a shaking hand, she hits the unlock button on her car. I scramble into the backseat and find myself staring at a wide-eyed toddler in a car seat.

"Wh-Where do you want me to go?" the woman asks.

"Anywhere away from here," I cry out. "Just hurry."

She peels out and hauls off down the road. The baby in the back starts to cry. When I look at the girl in the front seat, her flesh is pale as she stares out the windshield. She grips her mother's hand to the point her knuckles turn white.

"Are you okay?" the woman asks, her panicked eyes meeting mine in the mirror.

I swallow and nod. Relief floods through me as realization sets in. I've escaped. I've finally slipped from Vaughn's death grip.

"I am now."

"Baby," a deep voice coos, dragging me from my nightmarish past. "It's me, Gray."

I chance a peek and am thankful to see his concerned blue eyes darting all over me. My face is cradled in his strong hands as he regards me.

"Talk to me, Violet," he murmurs, worry in his tone. "You scared the shit out of me."

With hot tears welling in my eyes, I blurt out the memory of the night I escaped. Detail by horrifying detail. I don't stop until I finish. The room grows silent for a few moments before I chance a look at him.

Gray's features are positively manic with hate and fury. He's clenching his jaw so hard it's a wonder it doesn't break in two. But the way he drags his thumb across my bottom lip is gentle and reverent.

"I'm going to obliterate his goddamned skull into a thousand pieces," he seethes. "That is my vow to you."

Again with these intense proclamations—proclamations that should scare me but instead warm me to my very soul. I want him to hurt Vaughn. I want Vaughn eliminated from this earth so he doesn't hurt other women.

"I'm fucked up," I tell him, my voice wobbly. "You're the first person I ever told that story to. My therapist knows the gist and the women's shelters I bounced around to in the beginning had an idea. But nobody knows, in detail, what happened." I bite on my bottom lip and frown. "Maybe I should have spared you the graphic details."

His grip is firm on my jaw and he shakes his head. "I need to know every single detail about every single thing that ever happened to you. I want to steal those horrific memories and wear them like the burn scars on my back so you don't have to fucking carry them around anymore. Please," he pleads, his lips pressing to mine. "Give them all to me. Let me take them and replace them with something good. We can be good together. Don't you feel that, Violet?"

I nod and smile because I can feel it.

His presence overwhelms me with safety and warmth.

A giant security blanket.

I've been shivering with the chill of my past for far too long. It's long past time I relied on someone else to help carry that burden for me.

He starts kissing me feverishly once again until his phone rings. A growl escapes him. "That's Gwen's ring tone."

I miss his body pressed against mine the moment he pulls away. His body is all lean defined muscles hiding beneath tattooed and scarred flesh. He's beautiful—like God created a special masterpiece and named it Gray. But Gray is far from boring, he's colorful and bright and charming.

"Fuuuuck," he hisses into the phone. "I'll be right there."

"What is it?" I demand when he tosses the phone onto the bed and begins rapidly throwing clothes on.

Sadness flashes in his eyes. "Mom. She fell. The paramedics won't come into the house anymore so if she gets hurt or falls, Gwen or I have to help her." He runs his fingers through his hair. "I'll be back when I can."

I jolt from the bed and hurry to my dresser to hunt for some panties. "I'm coming with you."

He stalks over to me and hugs me from behind. His slacks are back on but he's still bare chested. The warmth radiating from him calls to me. Sings to quiet parts deep within me.

"Baby," he coos against my hair. "She's worse than Gwen. You need to stay."

I twist in his grip to face him. My palms find his stubbly cheeks and I shake my head at him. "Not a chance. I was being inconsiderate of your family's illness before. But now…" I trail off and stand on my toes to kiss his lips. "I want to help. You've listened to me unload my past on you. This is the least I can do."

Emotion shines in his eyes. "Really?"

"Really," I assure him with a smile. "Let's go help your mom."

EIGHTEEN

Grayson

I'm still seething with rage as we drive to Mom's. The things that Vaughn did to her…sick. The things I'm going to do to him…sicker. From the passenger seat, Violet nervously chews on her nail. She's similar to me in the way that she is neat and orderly. Because of her past, she's been driven to keep her life organized just so. I hate having to take her to Mom's but she seems so willing to help.

It fucking moves me.

I knew Friday when I locked eyes with her that I'd sentenced us to death. After a lifetime of love of course. But she'd be mine until the end. A crooked piece inside of me seemed to straighten the moment she became the main fixture in my life.

I'm trying desperately not to move too fast. The last thing I want to do is scare her away. But keeping my shiny little Violet on her pedestal in front of me is where she belongs. I want to cherish her forever.

I reach over and grab her thigh through her jeans. Her palm covers the back of my hand, giving it a comforting squeeze. This woman is the filling for the void that's sat inside my chest for as long as I can remember. My life feels complete now. I'm going to work myself so far into her heart, she'll never want me to leave.

As we drive, I can't help but feel disappointed about earlier when she wanted to use a condom. Doesn't she know I want to put my seed inside of her? That I want her pregnant with my child? I'd suggest we marry tomorrow if I didn't think she'd send me packing. Violet is like an abused puppy. It will take time to gain her trust. I want to cuddle the fuck out of her and put a collar around her throat that says she belongs to me.

"What are you thinking about?" she questions, her thumb stroking across the back of my hand.

How crazy you make me.

How my heart beats only for you.

How my brain won't let your face leave its presence.

How I'm going to blurt out that I love you long before the socially acceptable time because the internal raging fires that burn for you are out of fucking control.

"How beautiful you are," I tell her with a smile.

She laughs. "Somehow I feel there's more, but I'll let it slide since you're so sweet."

She has no idea just how much more…

"We're here," I tell her, my smile fading as anxiety sets in as I park next to my sister's Camaro.

"This is a nice home," she murmurs.

It's more than nice on the outside. My childhood home sits at the end of the street in an expensive neighborhood. The homes in the area sell in the millions.

The neatly manicured lawn and fresh paint job hide the

horrific secrets that lie inside. The chaos and disorder. The absolute madness. The hired lawn people on call help keep up pretenses.

"Do you want to sit in the car?" I question.

She's already climbing out. "No. I can handle this. Your mom needs you."

I scrub my face with my palm and inhale a fortifying breath. This is going to be difficult. Last time I came by was when one of Mom's shelves fell on her. My skin still crawls from having to pull all that shit off of her.

I hop out of the car and stalk across the lawn to the front door. Behind me, Violet is quiet but I know she has my back. I'm embarrassed, but she's already seen Gwen and she's been warned.

"Breathe through your mouth," I mutter as I push through the unlocked door.

One of the only few clean rooms in this house is the foyer but I can tell that will soon change. Her mess is starting to spill out of doorways into the space. Soon, there will be no hiding this from people. I cringe to think about that day when a postman or nosy neighbor spreads the news about what lies in this house.

A scent that's part feces and part rotting garbage immediately suffocate me. Despite breathing through my mouth, I can't help but choke on the disgusting smell. Violet doesn't let on her disgust because she's quiet.

"Gwen?" I call out.

"In the basement," she hollers back from within the house.

"Fuck," I hiss under my breath. "The basement is the worst."

I stalk down the hallway until I reach the dining room that leads to the kitchen where the basement door is. As soon as the dining room comes into view, I shudder. There is a small walking path but garbage and shopping bags and boxes are stacked waist high. You can't see the dining room table—the same table my father made me eat Wail at. The entire room is a sea of junk and trash.

"This way," I utter, grabbing Violet's hand. I guide her behind me so she doesn't fall.

"Oh," she chokes out upon reaching the kitchen. More of the same in here. Trash and a pile of stinking dishes are bulging from the sink. There is a small walkway to the refrigerator and one more to the basement door that's been wrenched open. I grab the handle and pull it open more so I can squeeze through. Light illuminates the stairwell but there is so much crap piled up on the stairs that it's no wonder she fell. At the bottom of the stairwell, Gwen sits in a pile of garbage with Mom's head in her lap.

"Mom," I call out. "You okay?"

She waves a hand at me dismissively. "Of course, sweetheart. Just being clumsy again. I told your sister not to call you and that when I catch my breath I'll get back up."

"Nonsense," I grumble. "I'll carry you out of there."

"Do you need help?" Violet questions, her breath merely a whisper.

I look over my shoulder and shake my head. "Just hold the door open when I make it back up here." Once she nods in confirmation, I squeeze through the door and begin my descent.

"Shield her from anything that falls," I instruct Gwen.

My sister scrambles into a standing position and moves

in front of our mother. "Okay. Ready."

I'm larger than both of them so when I begin climbing down, boxes and bags and garbage start crashing down to the bottom. I nearly knock over a stack of magazines but right the wiggling tower before it topples over.

The smell gets worse the farther down I go. Stinks of raw sewage. Fuck. I don't know what to do when it comes to Mom and Gwen. Once, I tried to get people out here to clean up and they were both so distraught, I pulled the plug immediately. But the thought of Mom getting sick from leaky pipes creating mold or something worries me.

When I reach the bottom, Gwen hugs me tight. "Thanks for coming, big brother."

I kiss the top of her head and grunt. "You just use me for my muscles," I tease.

Mom laughs. "Oh stop, you two. How's work been, honey?"

"Good," I tell her as I slide my arms beneath my mom's slight frame. "Just closed on a property recently. I'm going to go out of town to see it for a few days."

"How wonderful," she says beaming at me. "You look so handsome. Just like your father." Her smile fades and her eyes grow distant. "How is he, anyway?"

I'm not going down that rabbit hole.

Not now. Not ever.

"He's fine. He told me to tell you hello," I lie.

Her blue eyes flicker with light. "Oh, how I miss him. Tell him I'll come visit him for lunch in the city next week."

I nod and smile back at her. We both lie to each other. She's never leaving this house except on a gurney. He never asks about her.

I trip over something and crash toward the wall. My shoulder hits the drywall, but it's better than her head. With more exertion and grunting, I manage to climb the mountain of trash until I reach the top. The door gets wrenched open, and I step into the narrow pathway.

"You need to lie down. Where are you sleeping these days?" I question. The bedroom upstairs has long been filled and abandoned.

"Laundry room beside the front bathroom," she tells me.

I wince. "Laundry room it is." I twist my body to face Violet. "Mom, this is Violet. My girlfriend."

"Oh…" Mom chokes out, embarrassment causing her to tense up. "Oh…"

"Violet?" Gwen squeaks out in surprise when she emerges from the basement stairwell. "What are you doing here?" The terror in her voice makes my heart rate quicken.

"We were together when you called," I tell Gwen gently. "She wanted to help."

Gwen's features harden and she shoves past me disappearing out of the kitchen. I shoot Violet an apologetic look.

"Excuse my manners," Mom says to Violet. "And Gwen's. We're just not used to visitors. Had I known you were coming, I'd have straightened up a bit."

"Violet doesn't care about a little clutter," I assure Mom. "Do you, baby?"

Violet shakes her head. "Nope. Your home is lovely. Were those begonias I saw by the front porch?"

Mom nods and beams at her. "Enrique planted those. I'm quite fond of them."

"They're beautiful," Violet murmurs.

I flash her a look of gratitude before wading my way through the hoard of junk toward the laundry room. Once inside, I'm irritated to find that my mom folded up a bunch of blankets to make a makeshift bed on top of the side-by-side washer and dryer. Even the laundry room is filled with junk. I've long gotten over the fact that Mom doesn't wash laundry or dishes or anything. I pay the city to take the trash two times a week but my gut tells me Mom never has anything to put out at the curb.

Violet pushes past me into the laundry room and smoothes out the blankets and situates the pillows. I set Mom down on her bed and Violet proceeds to cover her up. Mom, no longer embarrassed, stares at Violet as if she's the most beautiful thing she's ever seen.

I glance over at my woman.

She's sure as fuck the most beautiful thing I've ever seen.

"I'm going to go check on Gwen. Can you stay and make sure she's okay?" I ask Violet.

When she smiles and nods, I lean forward and kiss her forehead. "Thank you, baby."

I can hear Mom chattering to her as I exit the laundry room. The mere idea of climbing the stairs has me shuddering, but I know Gwen is upstairs in my old room. It's the only place in the house they won't fill up with junk for some reason. Whenever I tell Mom she should sleep in there, she just shakes me off and says she's saving the room in case I ever need to come back.

It takes several minutes and a couple of dry heaving moments until I pass by one of the bathrooms but I eventually make it to my bedroom. Once I push inside, I take a deep breath. Everything is just as I left it. Dad, that asshole, had been right. I needed to get away. I'd let Mom nurse me back to health after my extensive burns, but the moment I was healed, I left.

Gwen lies on the bed with her back to me. With a sigh, I crawl in beside her and hug her. "Don't be mad, sis."

She sniffles. "She'll think we're disgusting. How could you bring her here?"

Guilt shoots through me. "Violet's different. She's going to be a part of this family one day. I don't want to start something with secrets. Everything is out in the open."

She rolls onto her back and regards me with a tear-stained face that reminds me of when she was younger. "Does she know what's in the chest?"

I frown. "There's just stuff in there."

"What kind of stuff?"

"Nothing important," I huff.

Her nostrils flare. "She must not be that important then."

When Gwen gets upset, she goes on the offensive and says things that are meant to sting. Luckily, I've played these games a thousand times with her.

"Are you okay?" I ask, changing the subject.

"Mom just scared me," she admits with a choked sob. "When she called me, she was disoriented." A tear leaks out of her eye. "She's been falling a lot lately but mostly she seems to be forgetting things." Another tear races out. "People."

"What do you mean?" I demand, worry creeping its way through me.

"She hasn't recognized me a couple of times."

I frown and look past her out the dark window. "Gwen…"

"I know."

"I'll call tomorrow."

She sniffles. "I'm not like her."

Oh, baby sister, but you're exactly the same.

"I know." Lies.

"I'm just messy. Artists are messy," she assures me. "I can clean it all up whenever I want."

I smile. "Of course you can."

Her eyes fall closed. "Maybe I should see Dr. Ward again."

Hope blossoms in my chest. "She was one of the few people you liked."

"But she made me angry," she whispers, her eyes flying open.

I smirk at her. "I make you angry all the time and you don't fire me."

"I wish I could sometimes," she teases, amusement flickering in her eyes.

"I'll call Dr. Ward and set it up." I lean forward and kiss her forehead. "Thank you."

She nods and sniffles again. "I can't face Violet right now, though."

"It's okay," I assure her. "Can you look after Mom tonight for me? I'd like to go home and finish what I started with my girlfriend." I waggle my eyebrows to tease her.

A groan escapes her. "Gross. And girlfriend?" Her eyebrow lifts playfully. "That was awfully quick."

I shrug as I climb back off the bad. "Since when do I

ever take my time with anything?"

"Since never."

"Damn straight."

"Are you sure?" I ask as I wrap one of my thick plush towels around Violet's perfect body.

She laughs. "I'm here, aren't I?"

"I think I like you here at my place," I tell her with a grin. "My bed is bigger anyway. More room to fuck you on."

"Honestly, Gray!" she squeaks. "You're always so crude."

"You like it," I argue as I saunter my naked ass out of the bathroom and into the bedroom. I'm just pulling back the covers when I notice her stop in front of the chest.

"What's in there?"

All happiness and playfulness fade away. "Nothing important."

Her eyes narrow at me. "I care about unimportant things too."

"It doesn't matter," I tell her, scowling. "Trust me. It doesn't matter."

Hurt flashes in her eyes. As much as I want to open up to her, I don't want to about this. At least not this early on.

"Open it," she whispers.

"No."

Fire flashes in her eyes as she kneels and starts fiddling with the lock.

"Stop," I growl. If she tries too hard, she'll figure out the combination. It's the same as her debit card PIN number. I know this because I made them the same.

She starts turning the dial, ignoring me.

"Goddammit, Violet," I snap. "It's none of your fucking business."

My words cause her back to stiffen. The towel loosens and slides down her back to her hips. Her smooth flesh calls to me but it reddens quickly with her anger. She jerks her gaze over her shoulder.

"I want to go home."

My heart sinks and I fall to my knees behind her. "No," I tell her as I hug her middle and pull her bare back against my clean chest. "Stay."

"I'll stay if you tell me what's inside."

I growl when she tosses away the towel and rubs her naked ass against my hardening cock. "No."

"Please," she begs, her voice breathless.

"Nothing inside that chest matters," I reply as my hands roam her silky body. "All that matters to me anymore is you."

To prove my point, I guide my dick inside her. She grips the chest and lets out a needy moan. I tangle my fingers in her wet hair, pulling her head back, as I drive hard into her.

"Gray," she hisses.

My balls slap against her pussy with every thrust. She's tight and clean and fucking mine. As I fuck her, I stick my thumb into my mouth to wet it. When I push it against her tight asshole, she lets out a whimper.

"Touch your clit," I order, my voice low and husky.

She obeys but her ass clenches. "It's going to hurt."

"What happened was a long time ago," I assure her, my tone gentle. "I'm going to make you feel good."

Trust—such a beautiful little bird—gets released from her cage. She relaxes and allows me access. As promised,

I ease my thumb inside her tight channel. My thrusting slows until I've got my thumb all the way inside her.

"You okay, little quitter?"

"Yes…"

"Yes but?"

"I'm still scared."

I begin slowly sliding my thumb in and out of her in unison with my cock that's inside her cunt. Soon, she's rocking against me, very much into our little ass play.

"When it comes to me, you have nothing to fear. Ever," I vow. "Every single thought. Every goddamned action revolves around you. I don't think you understand how much you've embedded yourself inside me."

She moans in response. "Gray…"

"Nobody else will ever have you because you're mine," I bite out as impending pleasure begins to settle in my balls. "Say it, baby. Tell me who you belong to."

"You," she whispers without hesitation.

Pride surges through me. I'm not the most normal guy on the block. I'm obsessive to a fault and possessive as fuck. I don't quite understand her quickness to give in to me but I feed off it.

"I'm going to protect you, and when you let me, I'm going to love you. I'm going to stamp myself all over your heart and your pussy. You're going to wear my ring and take my last name. Why, Violet?"

She cries out when I slap her ass. "Because I'm yours."

"Fucking right you are. And I'm going to come inside your pretty little cunt. No more goddamned condoms." I growl. "Why, Violet?" When she doesn't answer, I slap her ass again.

"Because I'm yours."

"Good girl," I praise. "No more morning-after pills."

She shudders as an orgasm ripples through her. Her body seems to choke the hell out of my cock. I'm grunting, my thrusts ragged and uneven, as I desperately try not to come too soon. "How did you know—" she starts.

"No more morning-after pills," I hiss, interrupting her. "Why, Violet?"

"B-Because I'm yours," she murmurs, her entire body still quivering.

"If you get knocked up, it's going to be okay. Why, Violet?"

When she doesn't respond, I reach around and swat her hand away so I can massage her clit. She starts shuddering wildly from the overdose of pleasure.

"Why, Violet?"

"Because I'm yours."

Her words send me over the edge, and I come with a feral growl. This seems to set her off again because she screams my name as her body seizes wildly with pleasure. I slide my thumb out of her ass and admire how her hole clenches back tight. One day I'll show her how good it will feel to have all of me there. My cock throbs out the rest of my release. As soon as I've given her all I have, I slide out and watch with fucking glee as my white seed runs back out of her glistening red cunt. It drips on the floor, pooling between her knees.

"Jesus fucking Christ, you're hot," I tell her, pride rippling from my voice.

"When you talk dirty, you're pretty hot too," she admits, peeking at me over her shoulder. Her eyes are hooded and her cheeks are rosy from exertion. I pin her with a serious stare.

"I meant every word, baby."

Her plump lips part open. She starts to say something but then closes her mouth. "I'm tired."

I snag her towel and clean her up. When I scoop her into my arms, she regards me with a soft look that makes me want to climb inside her head.

"This is happening," I tell her, my forehead resting against hers. "*We* are happening. I want this." Her eyes remain slightly guarded, but I see the flicker of hope.

She wants this too.

NINETEEN

Violet

"I can't believe how beautiful it is here," I murmur as I sip my wine. I'm still in my swimsuit from earlier, but my feet are propped up on the balcony edge as I stare out into the ocean without a care in the world. This was supposed to be work, but for the past four days, we've done nothing but play.

"It sure is," Gray replies, his voice husky.

When I turn to look at him, I find him staring. My body begins to heat from the inside out. We've been seeing each other in some capacity for a little over a week now. He's such a whirlwind that I lose all sense of time and reality. It feels like much longer.

"I always dreamed of having a place like this. A place to take my family one day. A place where the mother was involved and the father wasn't a giant asshole. A place where the kids would look forward to visiting every summer." He threads his fingers behind his head as he stares off into the ocean. His dark hair is messy and flutters in the wind. I find myself fixated on the way his biceps bulge from that position. "Now I own such a place."

"That you do," I tell him, a hint of dreaminess in my voice.

He turns his heated, intense gaze on me. "All I need is the family."

Once again, my throat and cheeks heat. When he says these powerful things to me, I just fall deeper in a hole that he's dug for me. I just hope he doesn't bury me one day.

"One day maybe you will," I offer and gulp down the rest of my wine.

"Come here."

He pats his thigh and flashes me a grin that looks entirely too good on him. Despite being much older than me, he remains fit and has a young, vulnerable edge about him that I find myself drawn to. His intensity, though, is that of an ancient god. Unwavering and dominant.

I stand from the lounge chair and then straddle his lap. He's only wearing a pair of swim trunks so the moment I sit on him, his hard length presses against the place I want him most.

"I want to make this our thing," he says, as he reaches behind me to tug at the string of my bikini top. The material slinks away from my breasts. "This"—he motions at the resort and to the beach—"should be our thing."

His words.

His implications.

They're all too much.

Desperately, I cling to them. For so long, I've craved just what he's offering. But it doesn't seem real. A fairy-tale. A dream that he's woven for me while he fucks me beyond sanity. What happens when it all goes up in a poof of smoke? Where does that leave me?

"You do realize you only figured out I exist a week ago. Now you're ready to impregnate me and run off into the sunset. You don't live in the real world." This is why they call him Mad Max. "We're just having fun."

His blue eyes darken to a shade of navy as he tugs the upper string behind my neck. My top falls between us baring me to him. "I live in the world *I* create," he tells me, his words fiery with need. "And in *my* world, it's you and me."

I bite on my bottom lip and regard the handsome man. Was this how it was with Vaughn in the beginning? I don't remember him being this dedicated or consumed. Intense and possessive, yes. But never…sweet and passionate. Gray is just…different.

"We're moving way too fast," I try, though the fight is gone the moment he tugs my bikini bottoms to the side and slides the tip of his finger along my clit.

He leans forward to capture my breast between his teeth. His eyes lift to find mine. They're blazing with emotions I want to peel back and discover. Truth is, I love the way he looks at me as though I'm the only thing in his life that matters. With his tongue darting across my flesh and his teeth biting into me, I'm overcome with need. He's never looked hotter than he does in this moment, with his messy hair and wild eyes. His finger expertly strokes me to the point I'm practically dripping with desire.

"Oh, God…" I whimper.

He suckles away the pain from his bite and then breathes against me. "Tell me what I need to hear."

I grip his hair and tilt my head back. The balcony is private considering it's the penthouse suite, so I throw caution to the wind and let myself free.

"I'm yours," I tell him as I rock against his finger that massages me only from the outside despite my need to have him on the inside.

"Tell me this is more than fun," he growls, nipping at my skin. "Tell me this is our world and you want it just as much as I do."

When he talks to me like this, I lose all sense of right and wrong. There is no reality with him.

"Yes," I assure him, my body quivering with pleasure. "Our world."

His finger speeds up its motion until I lose it. The world darkens around me as an explosive orgasm surges through me, obliterating every nerve ending in my body. I'm still shuddering when he pulls his hand from my bottoms to tug his cock from his trunks. Once it's out and standing upright between us, he lifts my hips and once again pushes my bikini bottoms to the side. This time, he impales me with his cock. His strong hands on my hips control our rhythm. All I can do is latch my lips to his and enjoy the ride.

Our kiss is all consuming and powerful.

We kiss as though the other holds the key to our future and happiness.

I'd be a liar if I said I didn't want what Gray is offering. I'm dying to let him suck me into his storm and never let go. When he owns me from the inside, the answer is always yes.

"That's it, baby," he groans against my mouth. "Take this thick cock because it belongs to you."

Damn him and his crazy dirty talk that drives me wild.

Like the good girl I am, I ride him as if I own him. I use

his cock to pull out the pleasure I crave and need. Arching my back, I position myself so he hits me against my G-spot. Zings of bliss pulsate through me.

"Beg me to come inside you, Violet. Fucking beg me to put a baby inside you," he snarls, his teeth nipping at my breasts. "Beg me."

His words are insane. A game of pretend. Apparently, I like these games.

"Yes," I plead. "I want it. I want all of it."

"You're going to carry my kid in your sexy little stomach, aren't you?" he demands.

"Mmmhmmm."

"Say the words, Violet."

"I want your baby."

He nips at me again. "We're going to be a family. Promise me."

"Yes," I whine as my body tightens with another impending orgasm. "I promise."

The moment my climax shudders through me, he loses control. His bite on my breast feels as though he broke the skin, but I don't even care because his heat surges inside of me carrying with it all of his promises.

I'm so fucked in the head by this man.

He's going to tear my world apart. Deep down, I know this. I can feel it down to my toes.

And yet…

"Don't break me," I beg, my lips finding the shell of his ear. "Please don't break me."

He hugs me tight and growls his fierce proclamation that I want to believe so badly. "I won't break you. Fucking never."

"In two months, I have to go to Hong Kong for business," Gray says, his finger tracing softly up and down my bare stomach in the dark.

"I'm jealous," I tease and smile.

"I want you to come with me," he tells me with a chuckle. "You're the VP, after all."

I stiffen. "I won't be working for you then. I only have one week left."

His hand stops moving and I'm glad I can't see his expression. "But I thought…"

"That just because we're seeing each other right now that I'd give up my prior commitments?"

He pulls away and flips on the lamp. When he turns back, his nostrils flare with anger. "I promoted you. I assumed you were staying."

The money is way better than what Sean is offering.

And I'd be doing what I know.

But I'd be spending every waking moment with Gray's undivided attention on me. What happens when this blazing flame of his flickers out? Will I be cast aside and forgotten again? If so, and I chose to stay at Maxwell, I'd have passed up an opportunity for a career change.

"Gray," I start but am interrupted when he jerks out of the bed.

"I need to make a phone call," he growls before slamming the bedroom door.

I sit up and bring the sheet up over my bare breast. He did not take that well at all. Butterflies take flight in my belly as my nerves threaten to consume me. I snag my phone from the end table and text Sean.

Me: Everything still a go?

Despite it being close to midnight, he responds.

Sean: I thought you'd changed your mind. You know, after all that happened. Then you never responded. Is everything okay?

My mind has been distracted the past week, but I didn't think I'd ignored any of his messages.

Me: Everything is fine. Looking forward to starting up soon.

He responds back immediately.

Sean: Oh good! I'm counting down. If you want to drop by one day on your lunch, I'll show you where your office will be. We can have lunch in my office.

Me: I'll let you know a day I'm free. Talk soon.

I try not to watch the clock but seconds turn into minutes and then minutes turn into hours. Gray hasn't returned. I'm just drifting off when I hear the lamp being turned off and the bed sinking down with his weight. He curls his massive body around mine and hugs me to him. I feel like we've just had our first fight. It's not hard to see his point. He's promoted me and fired several employees because of how they treated me. We're sleeping together and spend every waking moment with one another. I can see how he'd assume I was staying.

But…

I can't risk everything on a week's worth of his attention.

"I'm sorry," he murmurs against my ear, his thumb running circles around my belly button.

When I pretend to be asleep, he relaxes and kisses me softly on my head. Tears well in my eyes because Vaughn was never affectionate like this. It makes me feel guilty for even comparing him to my psycho ex.

His breathing evens out. As warm as he feels curled up against me, I think we need space. I'm losing sight of myself by getting swept up in him. I can't go through what I went through with Vaughn again. I'm not mentally capable.

Tomorrow I'm going to try and untangle myself from Grayson Maxwell.

Until then, I'll stay warm in his arms for one more night.

"Congratulations," a lady named Deb chirps when she passes by my desk. "What an achievement."

I smile until she walks off. What the hell is everyone congratulating me for? She's at least the fifth person to do so today. I thought my promotion was old news. My eyes skip over to Gray's door, but it's closed. After the weirdness of Saturday at the resort, he brought me home Sunday where he dropped me off. I didn't invite him inside to stay. The drive home was polite but mostly quiet. I could practically see the gears turning in his head, but he was careful not to say anything to spook me further.

And, boy, am I spooked.

I've made one horrible decision after the other since I put my notice in.

My phone buzzes and I'm surprised to see it's Gwen.

Gwen: Hey girl! We should do lunch one day. I wanted to apologize in person for how I behaved last week.

When I think of Gwen and Gray's mom's house, I shudder. She was a nice woman but she was definitely a little spacey. I was glad when Gray told me he'd arranged for her to go to an assisted living home. It was Gwen who went with her and got it all set up, but he's the one who found the top of the line facility and shelled out the money for it. Once she's settled, he said he's going to pay some people to come in and go through the house. He'd confided in me that he hoped he could get Gwen to clean up her mess too but he was only dealing with one problem at a time.

Me: It was fine. You were stressed. Lunch sounds great.

"Congratulations, Letty," another person chirps as they pass by my desk. "Front page. Unbelievable."

This grabs my attention. "Excuse me? What are you talking about?"

The guy slaps the *New York Times* down on my desk. On the front page is my face. I blink once in shock. Then, I blink once more as horror sets in. My age. My location. My entire damn name. All splashed across the front page. The article goes on to not only talk about my promotion for one of the biggest acquisition firms in the country but also talks about my overcoming sexual harassment and breaking through the glass ceiling. But it's what's at the end of the article that has my blood running cold.

Maxwell Subsidiaries bought Slante Mortgages.

One simple sentence, stuck in at the end.

But it has me seeing red. So much so, that it overshadows for the moment that my anonymity is gone. I snatch the paper up and stalk over to Gray's door. When I charge inside and slam the door behind me, I find him sitting at his desk with his fingers steepled as if he was waiting for me. Even Jeff wears an expectant look.

"How could you?" I seethe, my tone low and deadly.

His gaze is sharp as he skims over my blouse and skirt before roaming back up to my eyes. "How could I what?"

I slam the newspaper down on his desk. "Do you know what you've done?" My voice is shrill.

"That was me, actually," Jeff pipes up. "I contacted my buddy at *The Times* and told him the story."

"You don't know what you've done," I tell him, a slight quiver in my voice. When I think of Vaughn seeing the paper and knowing where I am, my knees buckle and I crash up against the desk. Jeff tries to right me but Gray has already come around the desk. I'm dragged into his powerful grip.

His scent.

His touch.

His overpowering presence.

I fall victim to his gentle touch for a moment and let him protect me from the repercussions. But just for a moment. Then, the fury sets in.

"You didn't want me to leave so you bought Slante Mortgages?" I screech.

He rubs my back. "There's more to the story that you don't know."

"So. Tell. Me." I lift my chin and glare at him.

His jaw ticks and he nods at Jeff who slips out of the office without another word. Then, his features soften as he regards me. I try to wriggle away but his grip tightens.

"Sean has a bad history," he grits out, anger morphing his features.

"A bad history for what?!"

"For fucking his employees." His words are snarled out, jealousy clinging to each one.

I scoff. "*You* fuck your employees."

This earns me a growl. "No, I just fuck *you*."

Embarrassment causes my neck to heat. This poor guy just lost his company because my new boyfriend is jealous and doesn't want me to quit? Unbelievable.

"That was his company," I mutter, disgust seeping in my tone. "You just made a few phone calls and bought his company out from under him?"

"I hardly call twenty million a bad deal. I doubled his asking price." His voice is smug and it irritates me.

"When?" I hiss. "When did you do this? After our fight on Saturday?"

His features harden. "He was pleased with my offer. After I dropped you off, I met with him and our lawyers. Everything went smoothly. This morning, the wire transfer went through. He's staying on to manage, though. But…"

He doesn't have to say it.

I know.

"But the caveat was he couldn't have me."

He has the sense to look shameful. "Violet."

"No," I murmur. "All of that is horrible, and I'm furious with you. But splashing my face and name all over the front page of the country's biggest paper when you know I'm hiding from my psychotic and abusive ex? That's unforgivable." This time when I push away, he releases me. He looks wounded.

"You don't understand—"

"Apparently not." I choke back tears. "I'm taking the

day off. I'm not feeling well."

He sees through my lie but gives me a clipped nod. "Let me drive you home at least."

I shake my head and hold my hands up. "You've done enough."

TWENTY

Grayson

I hate having to bite my tongue but I can't tell her the truth. I can't let her know that I had Jeff run that article so that Vaughn would come out of his hiding place. Dusty is still trying to find the slippery motherfucker. Using Violet as bait seemed like the quickest way to draw him out.

I've been unable to work all day. Not without Violet nearby. Instead, I've sat in my car across the street from her building watching for creepy assholes that might be casing the place. When it's well past midnight, I climb out of my car and stretch my legs. I haven't eaten or moved in hours.

Once I'm on her floor and my forehead is pressed against her door, I listen. The apartment is quiet. She's probably sleeping but I need to talk to her.

Me: I'm sorry.

She responds immediately which makes my heart rate quicken.

Violet: Me too.
Me: Can I see you?
Violet: I'm a mess.

Me: What if I told you I was waiting at your front door?

Violet: I've been watching you from the window all day. I'll let you in.

I straighten my body and slide my phone into my pocket. A few minutes later, I hear the bolt locks disengaging. The moment she opens the door, I can't wait any longer. I tug her into my arms where she belongs and kiss the top of her head.

"I'm sorry."

She sniffles but her grip on me is tight. "I'm sorry too."

I pull away to lock the doors before scooping her slight frame into my arms. She rests her head against my shoulder as I carry her through the dark apartment to her bedroom. I kick off my shoes and set her down on the bed.

The lamp beside her bed casts shadows on her face, highlighting the dark circles under her eyes. Her face is puffy and red from crying. I reach forward and swipe a shiny brown strand of hair away from her face. Kneeling in front of her, I hug her waist and rest my cheek against her thigh. Her fingers stroke my hair. Touching her soothes my heart. I hope I fix her the way she fixes me.

"I don't know what to do," she murmurs, her voice wobbly. "He's going to come for me."

I kiss the inside of her thigh. "I'm going to keep you safe, like I promised."

When I lift up to look at her, tears race down her pretty swollen cheeks. I don't like seeing her cry. I want to put smiles on her face. And once that fucker is dead, she'll never have to fear for her life again.

I sit up on my knees and tug at her T-shirt. She lifts her

arms, allowing me to shed her of the garment.

"Lie back, baby," I instruct as I begin peeling off my clothes.

She scoots back and then shimmies out of her panties. I shed the rest of my clothes before killing the light. Once darkness shrouds us, I claim my woman. The moment our bare skin touches, the usual connection we share seems to flare to life with a jolt. Our mouths meet for a desperate kiss. She wraps her smooth legs around me, and in the next instant, I'm buried deep inside her. Instead of moving, I simply cradle her cheek with one hand and kiss her until she's breathless.

I trail kisses along her cheek to her ear where I whisper to her all the things I need for her to hear.

I'm obsessed with you.

I can't live without you.

I'd die without you.

My words turn her on because she wiggles and moans and begs for more. Slowly, I rock against her. Her body is tight and accepting. Warm. Mine. I continue murmuring the words she clearly needs to hear too.

You're mine.

I'll do whatever it takes to keep you.

Whatever it takes.

Mine.

She whimpers in pleasure. My thrusting has quickened. I'm so overcome with my need for her that my movements are uncoordinated and ragged.

I can't spend another day like the past two days away from you.

I need to see you and be with you.

You're mine, goddammit.

"Yours," she agrees, her voice catching as her orgasm nears.

You've consumed me.

You own me.

I'm nothing without you.

I love you.

She comes with a screech and her body jerks from beneath me. I'm so lost in our lovemaking that I come like a fucking virgin teenager. Quick and explosive. I mark my woman from the inside out.

Her fingers thread into my hair and she sighs. "You're so intense. I don't know what to think."

I rub my lips along the shell of her ear. "You don't *think*. You *feel*. I don't care about rules or norms. All I know is I've been completely spellbound by you since the moment you slapped your notice on my desk."

"I'm still upset with you," she admits, her voice shaking. "I feel so out of control around you."

I lift up and brush my lips across hers. "So take back control."

"How?"

Cradling her face, I nuzzle my nose against hers. "We'll set some ground rules. What makes you feel like you have no control?"

She lets out a ragged sigh. "We should use condoms. I can't think about having a baby right now. My life is too messy."

It pains me to do so but I agree. "Done. What else?"

"You can't just blast through my life and make financial or career decisions for me behind my back," she murmurs.

"Buying Slante and stealing that opportunity for me, no matter what your intentions were, was wrong. I don't trust easily, and doing stuff like that will make me not trust you."

My heart squeezes. "I want you to trust me."

"I want to trust you too."

I kiss her nose. My cock that had softened inside her is already hardening again. I wonder if she wants me to pull out and wrap my dick up. "What else?"

"I need some space," she whispers but then moans when I rock against her.

"How much space?"

"Tonight, I need to sleep by myself. I need space to think and sort out everything that's happened mentally. It's too hard when you're curled around me and in me."

I thrust again and nip at her bottom lip. "Where are your condoms?"

Her lips curve into a smile against mine. "I need to buy some more."

"Should I stop?" I murmur as I slide slowly inside of her in a teasing manner. "I don't want to break rule number one five minutes into this."

"Don't stop, Gray."

She made good on rule number three. After we made love and talked late into the night, she kicked me out. Sweetly of course, but she forced me out the door.

Luckily, for me, I have a key.

And once I'm sure she's most likely fallen asleep, I slip back inside.

I open the curtain in her room so that I can see her

properly. She looks positively angelic sleeping soundly and curled up on the bed. Her arm is wrapped around the pillow I'd been lying on.

I'm completely consumed by her.

I've allowed certain things in my life to take control.

Violet controls my every thought and action. Everything I do now is under consideration of how it will impact her. The newspaper article wasn't an accident. Nothing, when it comes to her, is an accident.

I wasn't lying when I told her I want my last name to erase hers.

I want my carefully chosen and rare—*like her*—diamond weighing her tiny hand down.

Despite the new condom rule, I'm going to wear her down until she lets me put baby after baby inside her body.

She's mine.

We're supposed to be together.

That motherfucker Sean Slante would have treated her no better than the pricks I fired from my own company. At first, when I called him Sunday, he'd been resistant. But when I dangled an ungodly sum in front of him, he was giddy as fuck to sell. She's excellent at her job—at *my* company. At a company that will one day be hers too when she bears the Maxwell name.

I lean forward on the bed and brush her hair away from her eyes as she sleeps. She's adorable as hell and I'm proud she's mine. I just have to eliminate all of the shit that stands between us.

Sean Slante is gone.

Vaughn Brecks is next.

I should be sleeping but I'm wired up in her presence.

She's just as invigorating as the coffee she used to bring me. I'm proud to say I now make it myself. After she showed me how, of course. Violet makes me a better person. Even Bull has noticed that.

I peel back the covers and frown to see she put on a T-shirt after I left. With careful movements, I remove that and her panties. When she fully gives in to our relationship, I'll insist she sleeps naked every night. The time we spent at the resort, she had no problem sleeping with our bare bodies pressed together. It was perfection.

Once I deposit her clothes into the hamper, I rummage around in her closet a little and inspect her jewelry. I take a mental inventory so I know what to buy her. This costume shit is getting thrown out and I'll replace it all with high-quality pieces that belong draped across her. Once I've cataloged everything she owns jewelry-wise, I check the sizes of her shoes and clothes. When I move her into my home soon, I'm going to shower her with gifts, including a new wardrobe.

I come across the box tucked away and pull out the picture of her mother. Upon Dusty's researching, he located her mother and was able to dig into her finances for me. She does, in fact, receive the money Violet sends her. The woman no longer works at the diner, which is because Dusty said she was sick. Mountains of hospital bills bulge from her mailbox each day. I had him send me the totals and creditors so that I could pay them off immediately.

Violet's family is my family.

Her burdens are my burdens.

One day I'm going to eliminate her ex so that I may reunite her with her mother. That is the ultimate gift I vow to give her. I want Violet to be happy. I will make her happy.

I tuck everything away in the closet and saunter back out. She still sleeps soundly. Her full tits are gorgeous in the moonlight. My cock rouses in my pants. Quickly, I remove all my clothes and shoes before kicking them under the bed. Then, I slide in next to her.

God, she's beautiful.

I press kisses down her throat to her breasts. My tongue slides across one of her nipples, causing it to harden. I'm addicted to touching and kissing her. I'll never get my fill. I brush kisses along her abdomen. I'm dying to spread her apart and eat her until sun up but I refrain. Instead, I press a soft kiss to her clit before sliding back up the bed. Kneeling beside her, I fist my cock. I'd prefer to be inside her again but this will have to do. I stifle my groans as I worship her with my eyes. With each jerk, I imagine I'm inside her tight cunt that only belongs to me. I imagine coming in her so many times I eventually knock her up. I imagine her lying in my bed back home with her stomach swollen with our child and her wedding ring shimmering in the sunlight through the window.

So beautiful.

With a moan that I barely contain, I come hard. My hot semen splashes across her perfect tits, marking her as mine. I should clean away the cum that runs down her flesh but I can't. I can't swipe away my mark.

She belongs to me.

And I'm hers.

A sigh escapes her and I freeze. I can't let her wake up to me jizzing all over her while she sleeps. That would probably seem fucking creepy. Carefully, I slide off the bed, my dick dripping along the way and then kneel on the floor. Then, I slide underneath the bed. The nasty carpet scratches at my back and irritates my scarred flesh. I much rather be in bed with her. But love makes you do crazy things.

I maneuver until I locate my pants. Once I pull out my phone, I check my emails and do more research. As I hunt for more clues on Vaughn, I can't help but think about how my life has improved since Violet came into focus.

I cleaned out the trash at my company and promoted someone worthy.

I've made that someone my friend and will ultimately make her my wife.

Her presence kick-started something with my mother and sister. My mother willingly went to the home, knowing she needed the help. So many years she clung to the fact that Dad would come back. Dad is never coming back. I know this for a fact. And Gwen? She was just embarrassed enough to want to do something about her problem. I know she doesn't want to end up like our mother. The fact that she wants to see Dr. Ward is such a huge feat.

Violet and I have tapped into something that most people never have.

Love. A future. Happiness.

It's ours for the taking.

And we're going to motherfucking take it.

I set my phone down and grip my cock. I'm always hard around Violet. Her scent climbs its way inside of me, clawing away at my senses. It's as though she flows through my veins just as naturally as my blood does. And like my blood, she floods straight to my cock every time.

With her sweet smell overpowering me and knowing

she sleeps soundly above me, I fist my dick, reveling in the pleasure. I'm overcome with the need to spurt my release all over the fucking place. Part of me craves to slide back out from under the bed—to push her knees apart and ease my cock inside her tight body. The thought of being inside her bare again has me losing control. I can't hold in the groan as I shoot my load up my belly. I'm still flying high with my heart hammering in my chest when my blood runs ice cold.

"Who's there?"

Fuck.

TWENTY-ONE

Violet

I blink away my sleepiness and strain my ears. I heard something. A voice. It was loud enough that it woke me up. If my heart weren't thundering in my chest, I'd be able to hear better.

"Who's there?" I call out again as I ease my gun out from between the mattress and box spring. I scoot back against the headboard and squint in the darkness. My gaze travels over to the window.

Someone opened the curtain.

I'm not going crazy.

Before going to bed, I remember shutting it. I felt exposed, as if Vaughn were watching from across the street. I'd felt the need to hide from him if he was.

Cold awareness trickles through me.

I'm naked.

I'm fucking naked.

Terror climbs its way up my throat along with a scream that I barely stifle. Someone undressed me. Those other times, even though I convinced myself otherwise, weren't me. A reality that I'd chosen to ignore because I couldn't mentally deal with it being truth. I'd been too terrified to admit it so I pushed it into the back of my mind.

I swallow as I reach for the lamp. My skin on my chest is tight. As though something sticky has dried on my flesh. A tear races down my cheek and drips off my jaw. I flip on the lamp and my thoughts are confirmed when I look down at my bare breasts.

Cum.

I have someone's cum dried up on my breasts.

Vaughn is toying with me.

"V-Vaughn?" I whimper.

Discreetly, I reach for my phone and quickly dial Gray. Please answer. Please fucking answer.

Buzzzzz.

Buzzzzz.

Buzzzzz.

I'm frozen when I realize the sounds are coming from under my bed. It's as though I'm the star of a horror movie. Tearfully, I swipe my tears away when he doesn't answer. I drop my phone onto the bed and lean over the edge to look. The tip of a black dress shoe peeks out.

No.

No.

Fucking no!

I leap from the bed as far as I can and train the barrel of the gun at the shadow between the floor and the bedframe.

"Get out," I hiss. "Get out!"

A grunt—a familiar grunt—resounds from underneath the bed. Terror causes my entire body to shake. I'm naked and scared to fucking death but I don't dare take my gun from the monster under the bed.

"GET OUT!"

A man's hand slides out from the shadows, strong and powerful. I nearly shoot it on the spot. Now my phone is trapped on the other side of this hand. Stupid! More tears streak out, but I hastily blink them away so I can focus. Slowly, a man slides his very naked body out from beneath my bed. His toned and tattooed chest shimmers with what looks like his spent orgasm. Disgust rises in my throat. The moment I actually see who's emerging from my bed, I am overcome with betrayal.

"How could you?" I hiss, the gun in my hand wobbling wildly. "You fucking sicko!"

"Violet," he murmurs as he slowly slides the rest of the way out and stands up. His impressive cock hangs limp and dripping between his powerful thighs. Hours ago, this man was inside me. Owning and loving my body. I trusted him.

"It was you. All of this was you," I sob.

"Put the gun down, baby," he whispers.

"I AM NOT YOUR BABY!"

He winces at my tone and starts for me. "Listen to me."

"Stay back or I'll shoot your cock off," I threaten through my tears. As if it reacts to being spoken to, his dick hardens and bobs.

"I love you," he tells me as if this solves fucking everything.

"You're a stalker!" I screech. My heart is confused because the look of crushing devastation on his face weighs heavily on me. But my mind is telling me to unload the entire magazine into his psychotic chest.

"Violet." His blue eyes are tender as he regards me. "I

can't stay away from you. I'm addicted to you."

"This is insanity, Gray. This is illegal!"

He runs his fingers through his hair and his jaw clench-es. I hate how brutally handsome he is. I hate everything about him. This is worse than Vaughn somehow. Vaughn destroyed me straight to my face. Gray has done it behind my back.

A crippling sob ripples through me blurring the world around me. It's a terrible mistake because I lose sight of him. By the time my eyes clear, he's on me. His strength overpowers mine, and together we struggle with the weap-on. He manages to tackle me to the floor. When my head hits the floor with a thud, the room spins. The gun is torn from my grip.

"Listen to me," he urges, his voice soft but command-ing. I scream and struggle, but he pins my wrists above my head. My entire body convulses in fear. His body is heavy against mine, his erection thick and hard between us. Terror bubbles up inside of me, and I'm transported to so many nights with Vaughn. But instead of hurting me, he kisses my neck. Over and over again. It's almost worse than Vaughn's abuse because I like Gray's kisses. Each one is like a painful stabbing reminder of what we could have had.

"I hate you," I sob. "I hate you."

He works his body between my parted thighs. His breath is hot against the shell of my ear. "Liar."

His single word makes my heart clench. "You ruined everything."

A whimper escapes me when his cock rubs against my clit. He suckles the flesh just below my ear. Despite my fears and being unable to move my hands, my body betrays me.

I'm wet and desperate for his touch.

This is his storm.

I was never meant to escape it.

I'm his to obliterate and destroy.

He's doing it gently with kisses and love.

"I hate you," I try again, but my body is wiggling with need. "The moment I escape, I'll run far away from you."

He lifts and regards me with a fierce glare as he tortures me with teasing thrusts against my clit. "I'll follow you to the ends of the earth, Violet. Don't you see? I've committed my heart to you and nothing, fucking nothing, will stand in my way."

Why do I attract psychos?

Furthermore, why do I love them back?

"Please…" I don't even know what I'm begging for at this point. In the shadows of my mind, I know. My sanity refuses to admit it. "Please…"

"Please stay?" he questions, his cock sliding away from my clit and toward my opening. He doesn't enter me, just rubs against me.

"I hate you."

"I love you."

His teasing and proclamations of love have me so confused. My heart is thundering right out of my chest. It wants to run away with him and never look back. My mind is at war, though. I can't wrap my head around what he's done. It's twisted. Fucking insane.

"Let me make love to you," he breathes against my lips. I've lost feeling in my hands where he grips me tight. The thought of him pushing inside me has a low moan rumbling in my throat. Everything throbs for him despite the anger exploding through me. "Say the words and you're mine again. It's been all about you from the moment I laid eyes on you. I can't get you out of my head. The only thing that'll stop me from loving you—from fucking consuming you—is a bullet to my skull. Is that what you want?"

I whimper and hiss out, "Yes."

"Liar," he growls, his cock barely pressing into me. "You want my cock to stretch you open. You hate that you can't hate me. You hate that you want me to fuck you. You love that I'm obsessed with you. You want my children and my last name. Fucking admit it, Violet."

"I can't," I choke out. "I can't admit it."

"You're beautiful even when you're in denial."

I shiver and plead once more. "Please."

"This?" he questions. The tip of his cock slides further into me.

I can't breathe. He's too much. He's overwhelming. "Y-Yes."

A scream rips from me because before I've barely spit out the word, he drives into me with enough force to rip me in two. Gray is an F-5 tornado destroying me with every touch. And yet I can't step out of his path. I allow him to consume me.

"I love you," he tells me over and over again as if it's a prayer.

All I can do is ride out the storm. My orgasm teases and taunts me. Reminds me that if I give in, he'll give me everything.

He's not like Vaughn, he's worse. My ruthless attempts to convince myself aren't working because, deep down, I know. He's not worse. He doesn't hurt me.

Gray just clouds around me in his intoxicating haze until I'm drunk off his heady scent and whispered vows. I'm so lost in him that I don't realize he's released my hands until my fingers claw at his hair. This time, when his lips brush against mine, he follows it with a demanding kiss. So much emotion and power comes with the kiss that I fall victim to it. I want his overpowering attention and affection. I want his gentle love but rough lovemaking. I want him to stalk me to the ends of the earth.

This means I'm sick too.

"Come for me, baby," he breathes against my mouth as his fingers slip between our slick-from-sweat bodies. The moment he touches my clit, I lose all sense of time and reason. My world tilts off its axis as pleasure crashes through me. I come so hard, my bones feel as though they're rattling inside me. "Oh, fuck," he groans as his release spills from him. "My God you're perfect."

I close my eyes as his seed pours into me and my body goes limp. I'm exhausted from the tears and the emotions that were exploding through me. The adrenaline that was spiking through me has slowly drained away from me like his cum that leaks from my body.

"Let me take care of you," he coos as he slides out of me.

I no longer have any fight left in me. He's a stalker. The man has crept into my home, jacked off all over me, probably touched me while I slept, gone through my things, and lied to me.

And yet I still somehow feel safe with him.

It makes absolutely no sense.

"I don't know what to think," I murmur as he carries me to bed.

He kisses my forehead. "I know. So don't think. Just let me take care of you, like I always will."

I curl up into a ball once he sets me on the bed. He leaves and several moments later he comes back. Dutifully, he shoves the gun back under the mattress and plugs my phone back in. Then, he uses a wet cloth to clean my stomach and between my legs. Once the light is turned off, he slides into the bed behind me. I shiver until he envelops me with his warmth. My skyrocketing heart slows to a crawl, as my eyelids grow heavy.

I'm tired, and truth be told, I like him wrapped around me.

I know what's right and wrong, yet here I am, choosing wrong because it feels right.

"I love you, Violet," he murmurs against my hair.

I shiver again. "I love you too." Because it's true. Fucked up, but so very true.

TWENTY-TWO

Grayson

"This is fucked up," Bull growls into the phone.

I pinch the bridge of my nose and nod. "I know, but it's reality."

"How is she this morning?"

I glance up at the bathroom. The door is closed as she dries her hair.

"Contemplative but responsive."

He grunts. "What does that even mean?"

"It means she's quieter than usual but she didn't put up an argument when I went down on her this morning in the shower."

A long, disappointed sigh escapes him. "Where do you guys go from here? I hate to sound like an asshole, but why is she still with you?"

Her phone buzzes on the table. Ignoring him for a moment, I let out a deep breath I'd been holding the moment I see it's Gwen.

Gwen: Can we do lunch today?

My heart swells.

"Hello?" Bull questions.

"Sorry," I grunt. "I'll see you in the meeting this morning. We'll talk after." I abruptly hang up, my focus on something new.

Me: It's Gray. Violet's drying her hair. I'm sure she'd love to go to breakfast instead. I have a meeting with a London client at 9. Can you pick her up at the office?

Gwen: Of course.

The dryer stops, and a second later, the bathroom door opens. Violet is absolutely stunning today. Her silky brown hair has been blown straight and I love how strands of gold glimmer in the sunlight shining in from the window. A towel remains wrapped around her body that bears red marks—marks I made from sucking on her all night and into the morning.

"Who are you texting?" she questions.

"Gwen. She wants you to have breakfast with her." I search her gaze. After all that went down last night, I feel that she's fragile. I need to put her back together if she starts to break again.

She takes her phone and reads through the texts. "Okay."

I'd only made it to putting my slacks back on but am still without a shirt. Her eyes roam my chest before she turns her back to me. I grab her hips and pull her into my lap. My arms snake around her middle.

"You feeling okay?" I question as I press kisses along the back of her shoulder.

"Surprisingly, yes," she says with a sigh, relaxing against me. "I should be a lot of things but not content." Her shoulders sag. "I shouldn't be happy."

I tug her towel loose and then urge her to straddle me so I can see her face. My fingers ghost up her ribs on both sides as I look at her, my stare fierce. "You should be so fucking happy, baby," I argue, pressing kisses to the hollow of her throat as I squeeze her bare ass.

Her palms find my cheeks and she frowns. "This isn't normal, Gray. Nothing about this is normal. We're sick."

I slide my hand up to cup the back of her neck and draw her closer. We kiss softly. Our kisses are gentle and filled with promises. I pull slightly away and rest my forehead against hers. "We don't have to follow the rules. We just have to be together."

She seems to soften and relax. "You make it sound easy."

I grin at her, which makes her eyes twinkle in return. "It's that easy. You let me take care of you like I want. After everything you've been through, you deserve it. I sure as hell don't deserve you but I'm going to have you anyway."

Her thumb brushes along my jaw. "Are you always this intense?"

"Only when it comes to you," I say with a smirk.

She smiles but then it falls away. "What you did was not okay."

Shame fills my chest, and I nod. "I know. I'd do it a thousand times over, though. I don't think you understand the level of my need for you."

"I believe I get it now," she says in a wry tone. "After Vaughn, this took me by surprise. Had I not gone through such a toxic relationship with him, I'd never be able to accept this."

I study her features. Her lips are pressed together in a firm line and her brows are pinched together.

"I won't hurt you like he did," I promise. "You have to realize that."

She smiles. "I do know that. But…" Her smile falls again. "What happens when the intensity fades? Six months down the road? Six years down the road? What happens then, Gray?"

I kiss her mouth. "It won't happen. If anything, each second that passes, I become worse. My brain is scrambled with you. I can't think straight. I can't work. I can't sleep. Not when I'm worrying about you. When you're sleeping in my arms or by my side, my life seems to level out. The way I hyper focus on shit seems to fade away. Yes, I'm completely focused on you but I also somehow see the world around me for the first time. You make me better."

Her cheeks redden slightly. "I want you to be better."

"I *am* better with you."

We're quiet for a moment, simply content to hold each other.

"What do you want to do? I know mortgages wasn't it." I look up at her with a brow lifted in question.

She lets out a small chuckle. "Actually, I'm doing it. I love the stuff I do at Maxwell. Especially now that my job doesn't revolve around making coffee. I love analyzing every aspect of the properties and businesses you want to acquire. It's like a puzzle I have to put together to make sure it's a good fit for the company."

I beam at her. "You're nearly as good as me at it," I tease. "What do you like to do for fun? You know…when I'm not embedding myself in every second of your life?"

She grows thoughtful and looks past me at the window. "I love watching those shows on HGTV. You know…the ones where they flip old homes and spaces. I've never had a home of my own to do that sort of thing with. I love the idea of taking something old and ruined and then turning it modern and beautiful."

"I'll buy you a house to fix up," I tell her, my tone fierce. I'll buy her a thousand houses.

She smirks and darts her eyes back to me. "You're literally insane. You know that, right?"

"There are worse things I could be than your stalker."

Her eyes close as she shakes her head. "I'm still trying to wrap my head around this. If I had any friends, they'd be telling me to run for the hills."

"I'd just follow you there."

"Crazy. You're crazy."

I laugh. "I know."

Bull is mid-sentence explaining about a new client when my phone buzzes in my pocket. Violet is off at brunch with Gwen so I've actually been able to focus on work for a change. Assuming it's her texting, I pull out my phone to make sure everything is okay.

Dusty: Found the slippery fuck.

I flash Bull a look that has him going silent. With one nod, he knows what to do. He rises from his chair and stalks out of my office.

Me: Here or there?

Dusty: There. You're not gonna like this.

I scratch at the stubble growing in along my jaw. With Violet, I never seem to have any time or means to shave. Once I have her at my house indefinitely, I can settle back into a normal routine—one that doesn't require me spending the night under her bed.

Me: Spill.

Dusty: I saw him and two men go into her mother's house. Then, the target left alone. I'm in pursuit now. He's headed that way.

My heart rate spikes. I knew I'd draw the little cocksucker out.

Me: Eyes on him. Give me the location of her mother's house. I need pictures. Send one of your guys to get me the layout. I need to know everything down to the motherfucking weather.

Dusty: On it, Hawk.

It's hard to remain calm, but I have to. Vaughn has been slippery thus far, but I won't let him get away from me. He thinks he can use her mother to find her now that he knows where she lives and works. I'll be damned if he ever harms her again.

I quickly shoot off a text to her. There isn't any time for me to intervene. All I can do is follow the plan.

Focus.

Adjust.

Hoping she'll see my text before it's too late, I fire off a message.

Me: Be brave for me. I'm going to get you your life back but I need you to be brave. I love you.

When she doesn't respond, I worry it's too late. I bolt from my office just as Bull is striding my way. Together, we haul ass out of there.

We have a plan.

Focus.

TWENTY-THREE

Violet

I stare down at my phone in confusion.

Be brave?

Gray's cryptic words send alarm shooting through me. With him, I forget to always be aware of my surroundings. I've felt protected from Vaughn, even if Gray was stalking me like a creep.

A sexy creep.

Oh my God, I have issues.

"So, anyway, Dr. Ward thinks I should take on the task with a friend or family member. Gray has always offered to help when I was ready, but I'd kind of like it to be you," Gwen says as she pokes at her eggs. "I mean, if you want to."

I look up at her and smile. "I'd love to help you. You know that."

"I know you think I'm disgusting," she murmurs, tears shining in her eyes. "It just got out of hand."

I reach across the table and grab her hand. "Together we can work through it. I love to clean and organize things. When I had a peek, I saw some useful salvageable things.

I bet you'd be able to donate a lot of stuff to those in need."

Her lips quirk up on one side. "I think I'd like that. Dr. Ward says I need to connect with people, not things. She thinks I should ask some local churches to see if they would help us clear out the trash."

"I think that's a great idea," I tell her gently. "And just think, once you get your rooms cleared out, maybe you could help your mom with her house."

Gwen sniffles and pulls her hand away from mine to swipe away a tear. "Gray said once the house gets cleaned back out, we can bring Mom back home. That we can hire a nurse to look after her. And with him being serious with you…" she trails off. "I thought I could move back in to take care of her."

"I think she'd like that," I assure her. "Then maybe we could fix it up. Redecorate and make it look nice."

She nods. "Do you think Dad would come back home then?" Her eyes soften and she regards me with such an innocent look it makes my heart hurt. All I can think about is the way he forced Gray to eat his pet. The anger swells up inside me but I don't let her see. Apparently she was too young to know what an asshole her father was to her brother.

"Maybe," I say to placate her.

She starts babbling on about one of the paintings she's working on. I nod and engage but my gaze keeps darting out the window.

Be brave.

Everything Gray does and says has a reason. Everything he does revolves around me.

Gwen continues to ramble. My eyes keep roaming the

street outside when they land on something that makes my blood run cold. Across the street, a man leans against a sleek vehicle. He's wearing a baseball cap and his head is lowered, hiding his face, but something in his stance is familiar. His body is larger and more filled out—as if he's spent six years straight working out.

I know exactly how he found me too.

The newspaper article. My promotion was splashed all over one of the biggest newspapers in the country. Plain as day, he was told where I worked. All it would take is one phone call. I'd let the receptionist know earlier this morning that I was having brunch with Gwen at the best waffle house in the city. Our receptionist babbles a lot and probably mentioned this. So many careless moments led to this.

When he lifts his head and I lock eyes with familiar evil ones I know, I realize I have to get the hell out of here. Away from Gwen. Vaughn would destroy her like he once destroyed me.

"Gwen, sweetie," I say, jerking my eyes back to hers. "I need to leave. You have to stay here for me. Okay?"

Her nose scrunches in confusion. "Why? What's wrong? You're white as a ghost."

"Tell Gray I need him."

"Violet," she whines. "You're scaring me."

My eyes dart out the window and I see Vaughn stalking across the street with a purposeful look in his eyes. "Just promise you'll call him right after I leave and make him find me." I shove my phone down into my bra and shakily hand her my purse. "Keep this for me, please."

I don't wait for an answer. I bolt out of the restaurant, shoving past people along the way. The moment I step outside and the warm breeze whips around me, I'm chilled by a voice.

"Letty Spaghetti," he chides. "You know I hate Hide and Seek."

Terror claws its way up my throat, but I don't fight him when he grips my elbow. Willingly, I walk with him across the street. He opens up the passenger door and closes it behind me once I'm seated. My gaze flits across the street and I'm thankful to see Gwen staying on her side of the road with her phone pressed against her ear. Vaughn slides into the driver's seat and wastes no time peeling out into the busy traffic.

The silence is deafening.

I'm too afraid to look at him or speak to him. When I finally chance a peek, he's gripping the steering wheel so tightly that his knuckles are white. His jaw is hard and his thick neck muscles keep ticking.

This is bad.

This is so bad.

I suck in a frantic breath but will myself to calm down. I need to think and plan. He doesn't know I have my phone yet, so if my stalker boyfriend is tracking me—which I have no doubt he is—then maybe he'll find me.

"I've looked for you for a long time," he tells me, his voice every bit as cold as I remember. "Your style has changed since I saw you last." His gaze roams up my bare legs as he takes in my sleek pencil skirt and bright pink cashmere button-down blouse. "You look like a damn naughty librarian."

I look down into my lap but don't speak. I'm too afraid of setting him off. He's calm right now but I know his monster will rear its ugly head sooner than I'd like.

"You know," he grits out. "I was so fucking pissed when I found out you bailed on me that night. I mean, I get it. I shouldn't have lent you to that asshole. But, angel," he says as his strong hand rests on my thigh. "I killed him for you. You should have seen me as a hero."

My body begins to tremble and as a physiological response to this monster, my leg begins to go numb where he touches me. At one time, I was able to numb everything. Even my mind.

"You were always quiet, Letty Spaghetti, but never this quiet. What's got a grip on your throat?" he growls. "I know it sure as hell ain't me. But it will be soon."

My phone buzzes against my breast, and I pray he doesn't hear it. Of course my prayers fall on deaf ears because he most definitely hears. With a rough yank, he grabs the material of my shirt and pulls it until the buttons ping off. Then, he snags my phone from my bra. I'm not at all surprised when he tosses it out of the window.

"Your tits look just as nice as I remember," he praises as he cups my breast over my bra. "I bet your pussy is every bit as perfect too."

I close my eyes and try to block out his touches. He squeezes my breast so hard that I yelp, popping my eyes back open.

"Your mom says hi," he tells me with a harsh laugh as he tugs the front of my bra down. His fingers dive beneath the fabric where he pinches my nipple.

"Leave my mom out of this," I hiss, tears welling in my eyes.

He snorts. "She speaks! She fucking speaks!"

"Please, Vaughn."

He yanks at my bra until I'm halfway over the console and nearly into his lap as he continues to drive. "I love it when you beg."

I try to wriggle away from him, but he twists his wrist and my bra tightens around me, causing my ribs to scream in pain. Just when I don't think I can take much more of it, the clasp in the back breaks and frees me.

"Sit down and enjoy the ride," he grumbles before shoving me back over into my seat. My bra hangs loose around my breasts. "Give me your shirt and bra."

Remembering all too well what it means for me to ignore or fight off Vaughn, I immediately jolt into action. Maybe if someone sees me half naked on the highway, they'll call the cops. One can hope. With shaking hands, I slowly remove my shirt and broken bra. Once he has these in his grip, he tosses them out the window as well.

"What are those?" he bellows, his fiery gaze on my bare tits.

I drop my eyes down to all the hickeys Gray marked me with. The warm memory surges through me causing my nipples to harden in response. After all the hell we went through last night, we still ended up all but fused together.

Gray might be a creepy-ass stalker but I feel safe with him. He doesn't hurt me. If anything, he loves me when he shouldn't. I'd been hurt and horrified but I couldn't push him away. My mind and heart were at odds but my heart won. I'm obsessed with him too. He fills voids in me that I didn't know were empty. Gray breathes himself into every pore. He takes up space in every part of my being.

"You still whoring it out?" he demands and hits his fist

on the steering wheel.

I don't want to set him off by telling him my boyfriend gave them to me. But I can't help but jab at him. "I learned from the best."

His hand flies across the car so fast, I don't even see it coming. Hard knuckles crack across my cheekbone, causing millions of stars to explode in front of me. My head lolls to the side as I fight for consciousness after the blow to the face.

"I see you've turned into a little bitch while you were hiding too," he snarls. "Time to knock you down a few pegs."

Something sharp jabs into my leg jolting me awake. I stare down in horror at the syringe sticking out of my thigh.

"What did you just do?" I choke out.

He shrugs but his body relaxes. "I've gotten a lot better at keeping my girls compliant, that's for damn sure. Sleep, Letty. You'll see Mommy soon."

Darkness clouds around me as a million thoughts swim in my head. He said *girls*. As in more than me. I always knew deep down it wasn't going to just be me.

And then I think of my mother.

I'm going to get to see her.

I come to as I'm carried into my old childhood home. Even though I'm groggy and confused, the familiar smells of home permeate my senses and warm my heart. My God, I've missed this house and my mother. Tears roll out on their own accord. I drag my heavy lids up so I can stare at Vaughn. He's no longer wearing the ball cap and longish blond hair hangs in his eyes. At one time, I thought he was so handsome.

Now, I'm scared shitless of him.

"W-Where's my mom?" I croak out.

He smiles at me. I hate his wolfish grins. They're meant to intimidate me and they always work. "She's sleeping in her room. You'll see her later when she wakes up. For now, we have some catching up to do."

A sob is lodged in my throat. Each of my limbs feels as though they're weightless. Whatever he gave me makes it so that I can't feel much. In a way, that's a blessing. When he hurts me, I won't feel it.

When we reach my old bedroom, I start to cry harder. Momma left everything just as it was when I ran off with Vaughn. My heart shatters into a million pieces. I should have never gone anywhere with him. I walked right into a nightmare.

He lies me down on the bed and then looms over me. I attempt to move my arms and legs, but they feel like they're not attached to my body. So when he unzips the side of my skirt and starts yanking it down, I can't do anything but stare at him. He pulls it away, along with my panties. My shoes have long since disappeared. I'm naked and at his mercy. Just like all those years ago.

Gray, I'm trying so hard to be brave…

Another tear sneaks out when he palms my thigh. His fingers walk up my flesh slowly until he reaches my sex. He slaps it hard and thankfully I don't feel it. "This isn't yours to just give away, Letty Spaghetti."

"I d-didn't g-give it away," I whisper.

"So you traded it for something?" he questions, a blond

brow raised in question.

"I'm n-n-not for sale or for b-barter."

He laughs. The dark, sinister sound of it creeps its way through me and settles in my bones. "It belongs to me. I can do whatever the fuck I want with it. If I want to trade it or your goddamned ass for some meth, I'll fucking do it. Understand me?"

When he peels off his shirt, I close my eyes so I don't have to see my name tattooed on his chest. I don't want to see any part of him. My thoughts drift to Gray. I'd been so crushed finding him under my bed. Everything we'd created together in such a short time felt like it was a fraud. I had every intention of shoving him out of my life for good.

But he consumed me.

Plowed right through my heart like he always seems to do.

Made love to me on the floor of my bedroom and had me forgiving him so easily.

Looking back, I was too harsh on him. Gray is nothing like Vaughn. Crazy, yes. Overwhelming, definitely. Obsessed, you bet.

But evil?

Never.

Strong fingers bite into my jaw and I jerk my eyes open. Vaughn is naked and his cock is hard with a rubber wrapped around it bobbing between us. Thank God I won't feel this.

"You're going to come back home to me, Letty," he tells me as he releases my jaw to grab hold of his cock.

I glare at him. "No."

Fury flares in his eyes. "You remember the first time you told me no?"

And just like that, I'm launched into a past that is worse than the present.

"I'm not ready," I tell my new boyfriend. Momma always lectures me on how guys only want sex. That you're supposed to not give it to them because they'll just leave you once they get what they want. I like Vaughn. I don't want him to leave me.

"Please," he begs, his teeth nibbling at my lower lip. He finger fucks me inside my panties under my dress. It feels good—too good.

"I like what we're doing," I moan. "Just this."

He trails kisses down to my throat. When he bites down on my flesh, I cry out. "I want more. Pull my cock out."

His words warm me. I reach over and desperately tug at his jeans. Once his impressive cock is freed, I stroke it like I've done many times.

"Come sit on it," he murmurs, his finger sliding harshly in and out of me.

"Vaughn," I whimper. "No sex."

He yanks his finger from me. "Why the fuck not?"

"Because. I'm not ready."

"Well, I'm beyond ready," he grits out, his hand striking at me like a snake. I'm shocked when he grips my throat. His grip is so tight that I abandon touching him to try and claw at his wrist so he'll stop choking me. I'm stunned at his aggressive behavior. He's always been so good to me.

His grip tightens as he pushes me down on his sofa. All of my focus is on the fact that he's cutting off my air supply. I slap at his face to get him to stop. Blackness eats at the edge of my vision. My world tilts and spins.

And then explosive pain.

I black out completely as my mind shuts down.

He's inside me.

That's my only thought as I begin to lose consciousness.

I'm roused by a slap to the face. He's no longer choking me but he's very much fucking me. The pain is intense but I don't know what to do. I'm at his mercy. This man—whom I was falling fast and hard for—is raping me.

He starts kissing me but I'm limp. I can't participate. I've crawled so deep inside myself that I'm just a shell. That is until he reaches between us. His finger starts massaging my clit in a way that has confusing thoughts rippling through me. Zings of pleasure dart through me despite my tears that won't stop rolling out. What were tiny zaps soon turn into full-on ripples of bliss.

I'm enjoying this.

It feels good.

A self-loathing begins to fester inside me.

Who enjoys being raped?

This time, when he kisses me, I find myself kissing him back. I'm losing myself inside of him. This world of his. His darkness.

"There she is," he purrs. "So beautiful. You belong to me now, babe."

His words seem to tip me over the edge. I'm spiraling out of control. The pleasure he's giving me outweighs the bad, and I greedily accept it. I moan and beg like a whore.

No more begging him not to.

All that comes out of my mouth is, "Don't stop."

Don't stop.

Tears of shame leak from my eyes as I selfishly latch onto my orgasm. I ride the waves of pleasure with his name a scream on my lips. And before I'm even off my high, he slides out and comes all over my belly.

"I knew you'd love it," he says in a playful tone that used to be sexy. Now it makes my blood run cold.

"Y-You shouldn't have done that," I murmur. "That was rape."

He strokes my hair from my sweaty forehead and frowns. "When you come like that and beg for it, it's not rape. Sorry to burst your bubble, sweetheart."

Confusion washes over me.

I did like it toward the end.

I orgasmed.

"Oh."

"Time to take you home," he snaps. "I won't be accused of being a fucking rapist."

Tears well in my eyes, and I shake my head. Maybe I am being crazy. "I want to stay with you," I tell him boldly despite the quiver in my voice.

His jaws clench. "Don't ever fucking tell me no again."

I'm jerked from my memory when I hear a pop.

Vaughn, who still looms over me, ready to take what he thinks belongs to him, widens his eyes in confusion. The moment we hear another pop, he's leaping off the bed and jerking on clothes.

"What have you done?" he snarls. His glare is vicious enough that I almost feel bruised by it.

Be brave, Violet.

Be brave.

TWENTY-FOUR

Hawk

Eyes on target.

Always.

I don't have to watch my back because Bull has it.

Always.

Sniper and spotter.

Two best friends since the seventh grade.

"Both of his men are down. You still got eyes on your girl?" Bull questions as he smacks his gum.

I don't answer but I do have eyes on her. My eyes never leave her if I can help it. The target, who was positioned to rape my woman, jerks off the bed. He quickly yanks on his pants and is pointing to her in accusation.

Smack. Smack. Smack.

A cool breeze skitters across the back of my neck. Sweat is trickling down the side of my temple but I don't dare move. Instead, I'm calculating the wind not just up here from my position on the top of a hill across the road but also where my target is at. The wind picks up and thunder rumbles in the distance.

Click.

I make an adjustment to the windage turret.

"Elevation?" Bull questions as if I'd forget. I never forget.

I double-check the elevation turret, but it's where it needs to be. Bull doesn't require an answer. He knows how we work. When I'm in position, I don't speak. I don't move. I hardly fucking breathe. Any movement could affect my shot. I absolutely cannot afford to miss. I will *not* miss.

Smack. Smack. Smack.

The target keeps moving. I keep adjusting.

Click. Click. Click.

Adjust.

My sights have moved slightly to accommodate my target. A target that is almost clear.

Focus.

Smack. Smack. Smack.

"Stay still motherfuck—" Bull starts.

When my sweet naked girl lifts her chin and says something to him that makes him tremble with rage, I take my shot.

Despite the suppressor on my rifle, the crack echoes off the homes around me the moment I pull the trigger.

"We have to go," Bull growls.

I blink once and watch the target fall face down onto the bed. He's unmoving, a deadly head wound causing blood to rush from his skull.

Target eliminated.

TWENTY-FIVE

Violet

"What have you done?" Vaughn accuses again.

He's in a furious rage that would have once scared me, but I'm not afraid anymore. Gray asked me to be brave. Gray knew this would happen.

"The answer was always no," I hiss at him. "You were never allowed to take from me. And now you'll pay."

Another pop.

My eyes close for just a moment, and then Vaughn's attacking me. I screech and wriggle but halt my movements the moment hot blood gushes over my bare chest. When I reopen my eyes, I'm both horrified and elated in one single breath.

He's dead.

Vaughn Brecks, the monster from both my nightmares and reality, is nothing more than a blown out skull sitting on an unmoving body. It baffles me how one moment the room is rippling with evil and the next moment it's completely snuffed out.

He's heavy, but I manage to push him off me.

My mother cries out in a raspy voice from down the hallway. On shaky legs, as blood drips down my naked body, I make my way to her room. Sadness washes over me the moment I see her frail form curled up in the bed. When she sees me, she reaches out to me as if she's trying to hold onto a dream that's quickly slipping through her fingertips.

"Momma," I sob as I wobble over to her. I crawl into bed next to her as we frantically hug one another.

"Y-You're really here," she cries. "He told me you were coming, but that I wouldn't live long enough to see you. Oh, baby girl."

"H-He said he would kill you. That's w-why I l-l-left all those y-years ago," I stutter out through my tears.

"Shh, honey. Shh. You're here now. That's all that matters," she coos.

I'm still hugging her when two strong arms grab at me from behind. I start screaming like a wild banshee but then fall limp when I smell him.

Gray.

He came for me.

He killed the monster just like he promised.

"I'm here, Violet," he murmurs, his lips pressing kisses all over me. He covers me with a blanket and hugs me tight. "I'm always here."

"I-I was b-brave," I chatter out.

"I know you were. I never had a doubt."

The past week has been a whirlwind. Cops. FBI. Dealing with my mother moving to the city. I've been walking around in a fog. If it weren't for Gray, I'd have let all the stress swallow me up.

But Gray is more than the storm.

He's also the calm within it.

With the patience of a saint and the smooth tongue of a sinner, he's woven a tale they believe. His private investigator Dusty had all sorts of information on Vaughn. After Gray shot the men, Bull took the gun and casings with him. There wasn't any evidence for the police to find. Not that they were truly worried about Vaughn and his goons. Once they discovered it was someone on the FBI's wanted list, their efforts switched from wanting to find the killer to finding the missing women that were believed to be hidden away by Vaughn somewhere. I was able to tell them what I knew about his old stomping grounds and past residences. And with the intel they had from Dusty, they were able to piece together some locations. The same day Vaughn was murdered, the FBI found the warehouse where seventeen girls and women between the ages of fifteen and thirty were found. Most were drugged out of their mind. Many were raped beyond reason. All were rescued and returned to their families.

"Happy anniversary," Gray murmurs, his palm cupping my breast as he begins kissing my neck. "You still leaving, little quitter?"

I roll onto my back on his bed and regard his handsome face. Once Vaughn was truly gone, I shed about ten pounds worth of stress. My life began to drip with color again. My favorite is *gray*.

"I guess my two weeks' notice is up, huh?"

He slides his erection against my thigh. "You could always ask for an extension."

I start giggling so loud that I have to cover my mouth so nobody hears. My mother has come to stay with Gray and me at his house. Gwen has been so good to both of us. I've missed Momma so much and getting to see her every day has been the icing on the cake.

"I'm happy," I blurt out, hot tears quickly filling my eyes. "I'm happy because of you."

A growl rumbles low in his throat and he attacks my mouth. Our kisses are needy and fervent. It doesn't take much shifting before he's driving deep inside me. He devours my lips to stifle my moans, so we don't wake up the whole house.

As he fucks me, he lifts up to regard me. His icy blue eyes are sharp and focused on me. It's my favorite thing about him. The way he watches me like a hawk. As if I'm the only thing he sees.

But he's not like Vaughn.

Gray is good to me.

He loves me.

And I love him too.

Six months later…

"Here?" Gwen asks, her nose scrunched in question.

I frown and shake my head. "Over just a bit." My back aches from all the work we've been doing. My sister-in-law made good on her vow to deal with her hoarding problems. With intense therapy and help from not only Gray and I, but my mother as well, she's been able to clear out all her rooms. The church near her mom's house has been helping us with the donations. It's been a lot of work, but I'm happy to see Gwen working through her issues.

"You think he'll notice?" she questions once the picture is hung.

I laugh. "He notices everything."

We both admire the painting she's been working on for weeks. It matches the décor of the room perfectly.

"I love it," I tell her with a sigh. "What's next on our list?"

She shakes her head. "Not so fast, missy. You need to rest. I promised Gray I wouldn't work you to death. You know how he worries."

"He worries way too much," I say with a faux pout. Truth is, though, his worrying makes me feel safe. If it weren't for him obsessing over my well-being, we wouldn't be here today. I'd probably be drugged out of my mind in some warehouse once again under Vaughn's thumb.

"I have two to worry about now," a deep voice rumbles from behind me just as his strong arms wrap around my middle. I lean back against his solid chest. He palms my swollen stomach and kisses the side of my neck.

"How'd painting go?" I question.

"Bull can't paint for shit," he gripes. Our son rolls in my belly. "Oops, I think I woke little man up."

I laugh and Gwen lets out a huff. "Umm, hello? Notice anything?"

"What? Did you cut your hair?" Gray teases her. I know he sees the painting on the wall but he likes to razz her.

"You're an ass," she gripes and points in exaggeration to the hawk painting.

"Looks good," he tells her in an absent tone. "I'll come

inspect it more later once I've seen to it that my wife is taken care of."

Gwen pretends to gag. "Gross. Go away. Bye."

I'm scooped into Gray's strong arms and finally get a good look at his face. White paint speckles cover his forehead and cheeks. There are even flecks all in his hair. He looks downright adorable.

"You're a mess," I tease as he carries me to our bedroom.

He smirks and kicks the door shut. "And you're beautiful."

When he sets me on the bed, he doesn't waste any time stripping me out of my clothes. Once I'm naked, he steps back and lets out a groan.

"Goddamn you're hot when your belly is rounded with my kid," he observes, flashing me a smoldering grin.

I lie back so he can enjoy the view. He was right about everything. Being his wife fills one of those holes I had deep inside me. Carrying his child fills another hole. This life he forged for us is one I don't ever want to lose.

"So beautiful," he praises as he kneels on the floor and starts kissing my thighs. Gray is so thorough. He hardly misses a day where he isn't worshipping every part of my body. His breath tickles along my flesh as he makes his way to the part of me that throbs for him. Once he reaches his destination, he kisses my clit. Softly at first. Then, he begins sucking and tonguing me until I'm writhing in pleasure.

I barely have time to recover before he's pulling my hips to the end of the bed. He enters me gently at first but then thrusts into me raggedly as if he'll die if he doesn't get enough of me.

Don't worry, honey, I'll give you everything.

It isn't until he comes with a loud groan and falls on his side beside me that my gaze falls on the chest across the room. My question is always the same. His answer is always the same.

"What's in the chest?"

His palm finds my cheek and he turns my head to look at him. His mouth hovers over mine. "It doesn't matter."

And honestly, it doesn't matter.

What matters is the man who's now kissing me and the boy rolling around in my belly.

What matters is us. They are what I notice.

Everything else is out of focus.

EPILOGUE

Grayson
Fifteen years later…

Thomas is different than most kids his age. Brooding and introspective. He harbors dark thoughts but never acts on them. I don't miss the storm that brews in his icy blue eyes that match mine exactly. A storm he needs to gain control of.

His three younger sisters are all loud, playful, and funny.

It's as if he stands out like a sore thumb in his own family with his frowns and sulking.

I know it bothers Violet, but she doesn't understand him. I'm the only one who gets what goes on in that mind of his. And it's long past time for me to help him gain control.

"Daddy! Daddy!" my youngest daughter Emily screeches as she comes barreling down the hallway. I scoop up my four-year-old and squeeze her tight.

"Where's your brother?" I question with a smile.

Her lip pouts out. "Hiding in his room. He told me to go away."

I kiss her forehead. "Thomas is getting to be a big boy now. He likes to do grown up things. Why don't you go play with your sisters? Later we'll walk down to the creek behind the house."

"Yay!" she squeals. "I want to catch a lightning bug."

I set her to her feet and ruffle her hair. "Maybe Thomas can help you catch one."

Her nose scrunches as if she doesn't believe me. Then she changes subjects on a dime like she's notorious for doing. "When can we go to the beach again? I want to build a sand castle."

The kids love the resort. We spend at least three weeks there during the summer. It's a place where my family can laugh and play without a worry in the world. The mother is involved and the father is kind. It's what I always wanted.

"We'll go soon," I promise.

She bounds off through the house to look for her sisters. I turn and stride in the opposite direction toward Thomas's room. When I twist the knob and walk in, a familiar pang settles in my chest. His room is immaculate. It reminds me so much of mine growing up. He sits in his desk chair hunched over looking in a shoebox in his lap.

"What're you doing, kiddo?"

He looks up from the box and shrugs. "I found this."

I stride over to him and drop to one knee to look in the box. When I see an old squirrel skull, I smile at him. "Did you find it in the woods?"

"Yeah. Can I keep it?"

"Of course." I meet his sharp stare. "How do you think he died?"

Something flickers in his eyes. Curiosity. The fact that

anything flickers in him surprises me. He walks around so emotionless all the time. "I don't know. Got eaten by a puma maybe?"

I smirk. "Maybe he ate a bad nut or starved to death."

"What if a dog bit his tail off and he bled to death?" he asks as he picks up the tiny skull.

He hands it to me and I turn it over in my palm. "You know, Thomas, you're a lot like me."

His shoulders stiffen. "I guess."

"I get obsessed with things. People. Stuff. Ideas. Does that ever happen to you?"

Our eyes meet, and for a moment, he looks so vulnerable and lost. It crushes me.

"Maybe sometimes."

"It can be kind of scary. Thinking about something to the point of exhaustion, huh?" I ask.

He nods and takes the skull from my palm before sticking it back in the box. "Yeah."

"I want to tell you a story."

For the next thirty minutes, my son morphs from a brooding boy to someone who once again has light in his eyes. The secret obsessions he'd been harboring were set free. It sure makes a difference when you have someone to share them with. I always had Bull. Now I have Violet. And Thomas has me.

"I hate him," he growls, his voice surprisingly deep. Another few years and my boy will be grown up. He'll turn into a man before my very eyes.

"I hate him too."

My father was an awful man. After spending all that time in the hospital and once I was nursed back to health by my loving mother, I went to see him in the city. I followed and watched him. My father became my obsession.

He was a monster.

Not just toward me, but toward everyone.

A liar. A cheat. A thief.

I'd uncovered how he embezzled from his company. How he slept with anything that was female. And his computer that was littered with sick shit that no eyes should ever have to see.

I didn't like watching him through the window but I did.

I hated the way he touched himself while looking at pictures of my sister.

So I took care of the problem.

I set my sights on him.

"Want to see?" I ask Thomas.

He nods eagerly. Together we go to my room and stand in front of the chest. I tell him the combination. Once he pulls the lock free, he lifts the lid with a creak.

"This must be Wail," he points to a plastic zippered bag full of my pet's bones.

"That's him."

His fingers run across the plastic and he smiles sadly at me. "I'm sorry, Dad."

"It's okay."

He refuses to touch the other. Curled into a fetal position is a full skeleton in pristine condition. Aside from the gaping hole missing from the skull. A human skull. *My father.*

"How'd you do it?"

I kneel beside him and run my finger along the jagged

hole. "I shot him at his favorite hunting site on some land upstate he owned."

I eliminated my target.

"He deserved it," he assures me, clutching my shoulder. For once in what feels like years, I'm connecting with my son again. It's like he's found a way out of his darkness and discovered me.

We're the same.

We're special.

"I'll never tell a soul," he vows, his gaze serious. He knows how important it is to keep the secret from his grandma, his aunt Gwen, and his mother. "But, Dad?"

"Yeah, buddy?"

He beams at me—a smile that reminds me exactly of Violet. "Will you teach me how to shoot?"

I grin back as I close the chest. "You want to be a sniper one day?"

"Maybe," he says as he hooks the lock into place and snaps it closed. "But mostly, I just want to be like you."

The End

PLAYLIST

Listen on Spotify.

"Obsession (Cover)" by Golden State

"Violet" by Hole

"The Devil Within" by Digital Daggers

"Bad Intentions" by Digital Daggers

"The Monster" by Eminem

"I Will Possess Your Heart" by Death Cab for Cutie

"Six Underground" by Sneaker Pimps

"Stand By Me" by Ki:Theory

"Sweet Dreams (Are Made of This)" by Marilyn Manson

"Tainted Love" by Marilyn Manson

"The Red" by Chevelle

"Even Though Our Love is Doomed" by Garbage

"(Don't Fear) The Reaper" by Blue Oyster Cult

"Every Breath You Take" by The Police

"Afraid" by The Neighbourhood

"Black Sun" by Death Cab for Cutie

"Pony" by Genuwine

"What's Up?" by 4 Non Blondes

"S&M" by Rihanna

"Demons" by Imagine Dragons

"Motel" by Meg Myers

"Oh My" by Big Wreck

"Madness" by Muse

"Supermassive Black Hole" by Muse

"Psycho" by Muse

"Wild Horses" by Bishop Briggs

"Stressed Out" by Twenty One Pilots

"Way Down We Go" by Kaleo

"Uninvited" by Alanis Morissette

"River" by Bishop Briggs

"Are You Alone Now?" by Dead Sea Empire

"I Put A Spell On You" by Annie Lennox

"Life Like Mine" by Welles

"Deficiency" by Bad Pony

"Bringing Me Down (feat. Ruelle)" by Ki:Theory

BOOKS BY
k webster

The Breaking the Rules Series:
Broken (Book 1)
Wrong (Book 2)
Scarred (Book 3)
Mistake (Book 4)
Crushed (Book 5 – a novella)

The Vegas Aces Series:
Rock Country (Book 1)
Rock Heart (Book 2)
Rock Bottom (Book 3)

The Becoming Her Series:
Becoming Lady Thomas (Book 1)
Becoming Countess Dumont (Book 2)
Becoming Mrs. Benedict (Book 3)

War & Peace Series:
This is War, Baby (Book 1)
This is Love, Baby (Book 2)
This Isn't Over, Baby (Book 3)
This Isn't You, Baby (Book 4)
This is Me, Baby (Book 5)
This Isn't Fair, Baby (Book 6)
This is the End, Baby (Book 7 – a novella)

2 Lovers Series:
Text 2 Lovers (Book 1)
Hate 2 Lovers (Book 2)

Alpha & Omega Duet:
Alpha & Omega (Book 1)
Omega & Love (Book 2)

Pretty Stolen Dolls Duet:
Pretty Stolen Dolls (Book 1)
Pretty Lost Dolls (Book 2)

Taboo Treats:
Bad Bad Bad

Standalone Novels:

Apartment 2B

Love and Law

Moth to a Flame

Erased

The Road Back to Us

Surviving Harley

Give Me Yesterday

Running Free

Dirty Ugly Toy

Zeke's Eden

Sweet Jayne

Untimely You

Mad Sea

Whispers and the Roars

Schooled by a Senior

B-Sides and Rarities

Blue Hill Blood by Elizabeth Gray

Notice

ACKNOWLEDGEMENTS

Thank you to my husband…I'll always be your number one stalker!

A huge thank you to my Krazy for K Webster's Books reader group. You all are insanely supportive and I can't thank you enough.

A gigantic thank you to my betas who read this story. Elizabeth Clinton, Ella Stewart, Shannon Miller, Amy Bosica, Brooklyn Miller, Robin Martin, Amy Simms, Jessica Viteri, Amanda Söderlund, and Jessica Hollyfield, you all helped make this story even better. Your feedback and early reading is important to this entire process and I can't thank you enough.

Also, a big thank you to Vanessa Renee Place for proofreading this story!! Love you!

A big thank you to my author friends who have given me your friendship and your support. You have no idea how much that means to me.

Thank you to all of my blogger friends both big and small that go above and beyond to always share my stuff. You all rock! #AllBlogsMatter

I am totally thankful for my author group, the COPA gals, for being there when I need to take a load off and whine. Y'all rock!

Ellie at Love N Books, thank you for editing my crazy Gray! You were a pleasure to work with.

Vanessa with Prema Editing, thanks so much for being my second round of eyes. You're amazing.

Thank you Stacey Blake for being a super star as always when formatting my books and in general. I love you! I love you! I love you!

A big thanks to my PR gal, Nicole Blanchard. You are fabulous at what you do and keep me on track!

Lastly but certainly not least of all, thank you to all of the wonderful readers out there that are willing to hear my story and enjoy my characters like I do. It means the world to me!

ABOUT THE AUTHOR

K Webster is the author of dozens of romance books in many different genres including contemporary romance, historical romance, paranormal romance, dark romance, romantic suspense, and erotic romance. When not spending time with her hilarious and handsome husband and two adorable children, she's active on social media connecting with her readers.

Her other passions besides writing include reading and graphic design. K can always be found in front of her computer chasing her next idea and taking action. She looks forward to the day when she will see one of her titles on the big screen.

Join K Webster's newsletter to receive a couple of updates a month on new releases and exclusive content. To join, all you need to do is go here.
www.authorkwebster.us10.list-manage.com/subscribe?u=36473e274a1bf9597b508ea72&id=96366bb08e

Facebook: www.facebook.com/authorkwebster

Blog: authorkwebster.wordpress.com

Twitter: @KristiWebster

Email: kristi@authorkwebster.com

Goodreads:
www.goodreads.com/user/show/10439773-k-webster

Instagram: instagram.com/kristiwebster

CPSIA information can be obtained
at www.ICGtesting.com
Printed in the USA
FSHW022256250721
83538FS